The Tuesday/Thursday games were playground games, played under playground rules. Playground moves. Hard basketball. *Mean* basketball.

As the other team brought the ball down I saw an odd sight. Five of the Cobae had stood up and were walking out onto the court. The scientists had risen out of their chairs.

"Do you want to join the game?" I asked.

"Yes," said one Coba.

"What we goin' to do with these blue bastards?" whispered Foster.

"Play them loose," I said. "Maybe they just want to try it for a while. Don't hit any of them."

The final score was...

Berkley books by George Alec Effinger

IDLE PLEASURES
THE WOLVES OF MEMORY

IDLE PLEASURES

GEORGE ALEC EFFINGER

BERKLEY BOOKS, NEW YORK

IDLE PLEASURES

A Berkley Book / published by arrangement with
the author

PRINTING HISTORY
Berkley edition / January 1983

ISBN: 0-425-05744-5

This book is for:

the Bedford Bearcats
the Yale Bulldogs
the Cleveland Indians
the New York Knicks
Rocky Colavito, Jimmy Piersall, and Harvey Haddix
Brian Dowling
Abebe Bikila and Jesse Owens
Mendy Rudolph, Richie Powers, and
Butch van Breda Kolff
Jimmy Dudley and Roger Angell
Ludmilla Turischeva and Nelli Kim
and the Ballets Trockadero do Monte Carlo

Contents

Naked to the Invisible Eye   1
From Downtown at the Buzzer   31
The Exempt   53
25 Crunch Split Right on Two   73
The Pinch Hitters   97
Breakaway   111
The Horse with One Leg   137
Heartstop   149

Writing a good science fiction story is not a simple matter. Neither is writing a solid piece of sports fiction. Combining the two genres in one story is so formidable a challenge that unless one is truly in love with both forms, the finished product stands a good chance of cheating the reader: either the story will be a pure sports story with artificially applied science fiction gimmickry, or the story will be science fiction all the way through and the sports aspect is neither essential nor relevant. The sports setting must be integral; the story should not be able to function without it. The same must be true of the science fiction—otherwise the author is not playing fair.

Introducing science fiction into a sports milieu means taking one of two possible routes. The first is to change the game in an exotic way, according to some internal logic. The second method means changing the player himself. In Naked to the Invisible Eye I chose the latter. In his ineffable wisdom, Yogi Berra once said, "You can't think and hit at the same time." Ask any of the people in this story and they'll tell you that the

1

exact opposite is the truth: You can't not think and hit at the same time.

This story is first in this book because of all games, baseball was and is my first love.

Naked to the Invisible Eye

THERE WERE FEWER than a thousand spectators in the little
ballpark, their chatter nearly inaudible compared to the heart-
ening roar of the major league crowds. The fans sat uneasily,
as if they had wandered into the wake of a legendary hero. No
longer was baseball the national pastime. Even the big league
teams, roving from franchise to franchise in search of yesterday's loyal bleacher fanatics, resorted to promotional gimmicks
to stave off bankruptcy. Here the Bears were in third place,
with an unlikely shot at second. The Tigers had clinched the
pennant early, now leading the second-place Kings by nine
games and the Bears by an even more discouraging number.
There was no real tension in this game—oh, with a bad slump
the Bears might fall down among the cellar teams, but so what?
For all intents and purposes, the season had ended a month
ago.

There was no real tension, no pennant race any longer, just
an inexpensive evening out for the South Carolina fans. The
sweat on the batter's hands was the fault of his own nervous
reaction; the knots in his stomach were shared by no one. He

went to the on-deck circle for the pine-tar rag while he waited for the new pitcher to toss his warm-ups.

The Bear shortstop was batting eighth, reflecting his lame .219 average. Like a great smoothed rock this fact sat in the torrent of his thinking, submerged at times but often breaking through the racing surface. With his unsteady fielding it looked as if he would be out of a job the next spring. To the players and to the spectators the game was insignificant; to him it was the first of his last few chances. With two runs in already in the eighth, one out and a man on first, he went to the plate.

He looked out toward the kid on the mound before settling himself in the batter's box. The pitcher's name was Rudy Ramirez, he was only nineteen and from somewhere in Venezuela. That was all anyone knew about him; this was his first appearance in a professional ball game. The Bear shortstop took a deep breath and stepped in.

This kid Ramirez looked pretty fast during his warm-ups, he thought. The shortshop damned the fate that made him the focus of attention against a complete unknown. The waters surged; his thoughts shuffled and died.

The Venezuelan kid looked in for his sign. The shortstop looked down to the third base coach, who flashed the *take* signal; that was all right with him. *I'm only batting two-nineteen, I want to see this kid throw one before . . .*

Ramirez went into his stretch, glanced at the runner on first . . .

With that kid Barger coming off the disabled list I might not be able to . . .

Ramirez' right leg kicked, his left arm flung back . . .

The shortstop's shrieking flood of thought stilled, his mind was as quiet as the surface of a pond stagnating. The umpire called the pitch a ball.

Along the coaching lines at third Sorenson was relaying the *hit-and-run* sign from the dugout. *All right,* thought the shortstop, *just make contact, get a good ground ball, maybe a hit, move the man into scoring position . . .*

Ramirez nodded to his catcher, stretched, checked the runner . . .

My luck, I'll hit an easy double-play ball to the right side . . .

. . . kicked, snapped, pitched . . .

The shortstop's mind was silent, ice-cold, dead, watching the runner vainly flying toward second, the catcher's throw beating him there by fifteen feet. Two out. One ball and one strike.

Sorenson called time. He met the shortstop halfway down the line.

"You damn brainless idiot!" said the coach. "You saw the sign, you *acknowledged* the sign, you stood there with your thumb in your ear looking at a perfect strike! You got an awful short memory?"

"Look, I don't know—"

"I'll tell you what I *do* know," said Sorenson. "I'll bet that'll cost you twenty dollars. Maybe your spot in the lineup."

The shortstop walked to the on-deck circle, wiped his bat again with the pine tar. His head was filled with anger and frustration. Back in the batter's box he stared toward the pitcher in desperation.

On the rubber Ramirez worked out of a full windup with the bases empty. His high kick hid his delivery until the last moment. The ball floated toward the plate, a fat balloon belt-high, a curve that didn't break . . .

The hitter's mind was like a desert, his mind was like an empty glass, a blank sheet of paper, his mind was totally at rest . . .

The ball nicked the outside corner for a called strike two. The Tiger catcher chuckled. "Them people in the seats have to pay to get in," he said. "They're doin' more'n you!"

"Shut up." The Bear shortstop choked up another couple of inches on the handle. *He'll feed me another curve, and then the fast ball . . .*

Ramirez took the sign and went into his motion.

Lousy kid. I'm gonna rap it one down his lousy Cuban throat . . .

The wrist flicked, the ball spun, broke . . .

The shortstop watched, unawed, very still, like a hollow thing, as the curve broke sharply, down the heart of the plate, strike three, side retired.

The Tigers managed to score an insurance run in the top half of the ninth, and Rudy Ramirez went back to the mound with a 5–3 lead to protect. The first batter that he was scheduled to face was the Bear pitcher, who was replaced in the order by pinch hitter Frank Asterino.

A sense of determination, confidence made Asterino's mind

orderly. It was a brightly lit mind, with none of the shifting doubts of the other. Rudy felt the will, he weighed the desire, he discovered the man's dedication and respected it. He stood off the rubber, rubbing the shine from the new ball. He reached for the rosin bag, then dropped it. He peered in at Johnston, his catcher. The sign: the fast ball.

Asterino guarded the plate closely. Johnston's mitt was targeted on the inside—start off with the high hard one, loosen the batter up. Rudy rocked back, kicked that leg high, and threw. The ball did not go for the catcher's mark, sailing out just a little. A not overpowering pitch right down the pipe—a perfect gopher ball.

Rudy thought as the ball left his hand. He found Asterino's will, and he held it gently back. *Be still. Do not move; yes, be still,* and Asterino watched the strike intently as it passed.

Asterino watched two more, both curves that hung tantalizing but untouched. Ramirez grasped the batter's desire with his own, and blotted up all the fierce resolution there was in him. Asterino returned to the bench, disappointed but unbewildered, amid the boos of the fans. He had struck out but, after all, that was not so unusual.

The top of the batting order was up, and Rudy touched the minds of the first and second hitters. He hid their judgment behind the glare of his own will, and they struck out; the first batter needed five pitches and the second four. They observed balls with as much passive interest as strikes, and their bats never left their shoulders. No runs, no hits, no errors, nothing across for the Bears in the ninth. The ball game was over; Rudy earned a save for striking out the four batters he faced in his first pro assignment.

Afterward, local reporters were met by the angry manager of the Bears. When asked for his impression of the young Tiger relief pitcher, he said, "I didn't think he looked that sharp. I mean, Queen Elizabeth would look good pitching to the bunch of zombies I've got on this team. How you supposed to win?" In the visitors' clubhouse the Tiger manager was in a more expansive mood.

"Where did Ramirez come from?" asked one reporter.

"I don't really know," he said. "Charlie Cardona checks out Detroit's prospects down there. All I know is the telegram said that he was signed, and then here he is. Charlie's dug up some good kids for us."

"Did he impress you tonight?"

Marenholtz settled his wire-rim glasses on his long nose and nodded. "He looked real cool for his first game. I'm going to start him in the series with the Reds this weekend. We'll have a better idea then, of course, but I have a feeling he won't be playing Class B baseball very long."

After the game with the Bears, the Tigers showered quickly and boarded their bus. They had a game the next night against the Selene Comets. It was a home game for the Tigers, and they were all glad to be returning to Cordele, but the bus ride from the Bears' stadium would be four or five hours. They would get in just before dawn, sleep until noon, have time for a couple of unpleasant hamburgers, and get out to the park in time for practice

The Tigers won that game, and the game the next night also. The Comets left town and were replaced by the Rockhill Reds, in for a Saturday afternoon game and a Sunday double-header. This late in the summer the pitching staffs were nearly exhausted. Manager Marenholtz of the Tigers kept his promise to the newspapermen; after the Saturday loss to the Reds he went to Chico Guerra, his first-string catcher, and told him to get Rudy Ramirez ready for the second game the next day.

Ramirez was eager, of course, and confident. Marenholtz was sitting in his office when Rudy came into the locker room before the Sunday doubleheader, a full half hour before practice began. Marenholtz smiled, remembering his own first game. He had been an outfielder; in the seventh inning he had run into the left field wall chasing a long fly. He dropped the ball, cracked his head, and spent the next three weeks listening to the games on the radio. Marenholtz wished Ramirez better luck.

The Tigers' second-string catcher, Maurie Johnston, played the first game, and Guerra sat next to Ramirez in the dugout, pointing out the strengths and weaknesses of the opposing bat-ters. Ramirez said little, just nodding and smiling. Marenholtz walked by them near the end of the first game. "Chico," he said, "ask him if he's nervous."

The catcher translated the question into Spanish. Ramirez grinned and answered. "He say no," said Guerra. "He jus' wan' show you what he can do."

The manager grunted a reply and went back to his seat,

thinking about cocky rookies. The Tigers lost the first game, making two in a row dropped to the last-place Reds. The fans didn't seem to mind; there were only twenty games left until the end of the season, and there was no way possible for the Tigers to fall from first place short of losing all of them. It was obvious that Marenholtz was trying out new kids, resting his regulars for the Hanson Cup playoffs. The fans would let him get away with a lot, as long as he won the cup.

Between games there was a high school band marching in the outfield, and the local Kiwanis club presented a plaque to the Tigers' center fielder, who was leading the league with forty-two home runs. Ramirez loosened up his arm during all this; he stood along the right field foul line and tossed some easy pitches to Guerra. After a while the managers brought out their lineup cards to the umpires and the grounds crew finished grooming the infield. Ramirez and Guerra took their positions on the field, and the rest of the team joined them, to the cheers of the Tigers' fans.

Skip Stackpole, the Reds' shortstop and leadoff batter, was settling himself in the batter's box. Rudy bent over and stared toward Guerra for the sign. An inside curve. Rudy nodded.

As he started into his windup he explored Stackpole's mind. It was a relaxed mind, concentrating only because Stackpole enjoyed playing baseball; for him, and for the last-place Reds, the game was without urgency. Rudy would have little difficulty.

Wait, thought Rudy, forcing his will directly into Stackpole's intellect. *Not this one. Wait.* And Stackpole waited. The ball broke sharply, over the heart of the plate, for the first strike. There was a ripple of applause from the Tiger fans.

Guerra wanted a fast ball. Rudy nodded, kicked high, and threw. *Quiet,* he thought, *do not move.* Right down the pipe, strike two.

This much ahead of the hitter, Guerra should have called for a couple of pitches on the outside, to tease the batter into swinging at a bad pitch. But the catcher thought that Stackpole was off balance. The Reds had never seen Ramirez pitch before. Guerra called for another fast ball. Rudy nodded and went into his windup. He kept Stackpole from swinging. The Reds' first hitter was called out on strikes; the Tiger fans cheered loudly as Guerra stood and threw the ball down to third base. Ramirez could hear his infielders chattering and encouraging him in a language that he didn't understand. He got the ball back and looked at the Reds' second man.

The new batter would be more of a challenge. He was hitting .312, battling with two others for the last place in the league's top ten. He was more determined than anyone Ramirez had yet faced. When Rudy pitched the ball, he needed more mental effort to keep the man from swinging at it. The pitch was too high. Ramirez leaned forward; Guerra wanted a low curve. The pitch broke just above the hitter's knees, over the outside corner of the plate. One ball, one strike. The next pitch was a fast ball, high and inside. Ball two. Another fast ball, over the plate. *Wait,* thought Rudy, *wait.* The batter waited, and the count was two and two. Rudy tried another curve, and forced the batter to watch it helplessly. Strike three, two out.

Ramirez felt good now. The stadium full of noisy people didn't make him nervous. The experienced athletes on the other team posed no threat at all. Rudy knew that he could win today; he knew that there wasn't a batter in the world that could beat him. The third hitter was no problem for Rudy's unusual talent. He struck out on four pitches. Rudy received a loud cheer from the fans as he walked back to the dugout. He smiled and waved, and took a seat next to the water cooler with Guerra.

The Tigers scored no runs in their part of the first inning, and Rudy went back to the mound and threw his allotment of warm-ups. He stood rubbing up the ball while the Reds' cleanup hitter settled himself at the plate. Rudy disposed of the Reds' best power hitter with three pitches, insolently tossing three fast balls straight down the heart of the plate. Rudy got the other two outs just as quickly. The fans gave him another cheer as he walked from the mound.

The Tigers got a hit but no runs in the second, and Ramirez struck out the side again in the top of the third. In the bottom of the third Doug Davies, the Tiger second baseman, led off with a sharp single down the left field line. Rudy was scheduled to bat next; he took off his jacket and chose a light bat. He had never faced an opposing pitcher under game conditions before. He had never even taken batting practice in the time he had been with the Tigers. He walked to the plate and took his place awkwardly.

He swung at two and watched two before he connected. He hit the ball weakly, on the handle of the bat, and it dribbled slowly down the first base line. He passed it on his way to first base, and he saw the Reds' pitcher running over to field it. Rudy knew that he'd be an easy out. *Wait,* he thought at the pitcher, *stop. Don't throw it.* The pitcher held the ball, staring ahead dazedly. It looked to the fans as if the pitcher couldn't decide whether to throw to first or try for the lead runner going into second. Both runners were safe before Rudy released him.

Rudy took a short lead toward second base. He watched the coaches for signs. On the next pitch Davies broke for third. Rudy ran for second base. The Reds' catcher got the pitch and jumped up. *Quiet,* thought Rudy. *Be still.* The catcher watched both Davies and Rudy slide in safely.

Eventually the Tigers' leadoff man struck out. The next batter popped up in the infield. The third batter in the lineup, Chico Guerra, hit a long fly to right field, an easy enough chance for the fielder. But Rudy found the man's judgment and blocked it with his will. *Not yet,* he thought, *wait.* The outfielder hesitated, seeming as if he had lost the ball in the setting sun. By the time he ran after it, it was too late. The ball fell in and rolled to the wall. Two runs scored and Guerra huffed into third base. "Now we win!" yelled Rudy in Spanish. Guerra grinned and yelled back.

The inning ended with the Tigers ahead, three to nothing. Rudy was joking with Guerra as he walked back on the field. His manner was easy and supremely confident. He directed loud comments to the umpire and the opposing batters, but his Spanish went uninterpreted by his catcher. The top of the Reds' batting order was up again in the fourth inning, and Rudy treated them with total disregard, shaking off all of Guerra's signs except for the fast ball, straight down the middle. Stackpole, the leadoff batter, struck out again on four pitches. The second batter needed only three, and the third hitter used four. No one yet had swung at a pitch. Perhaps the fans were beginning to notice, because the cheering was more subdued as the Tigers came back to the bench. The Reds' manager was standing up in the dugout, angrily condemning his players, who went out to their positions with perplexed expressions.

The game proceeded, with the fans growing quieter and quieter in the stands, the Reds' manager getting louder in his damnations, the Tiger players becoming increasingly uneasy about the Reds' lack of interest. Rudy didn't care; he kept pitching them in to Guerra, and the Rockhill batters kept walking back to their dugout, shrugging their shoulders and saying nothing. Not a single Rockhill Red had reached first base. The ninth inning began in total silence. Rudy faced three pinch hitters and, of course, struck them out in order. He had not only pitched a no-hit game, not only pitched a *perfect* game, but he had struck out twenty-seven consecutive batters. Not once during the entire game did a Rockhill player even swing at one of his pitches.

A perfect game is one of the rarest of baseball phenomena. Perhaps only the unassisted triple play occurs less frequently. There should have been a massive crowd pouring out to congratulate Rudy. Players and fans should have mobbed him, carried him off the field, into the clubhouse. Beer should have been spilled over his head. Pictures should have been taken with Fred Marenholtz' arm around Rudy's neck. Instead, the infielders ran off the field as quickly as they could. They patted Rudy's back as they passed him on the way to the dugout. The fans got up and went home, not even applauding the Tiger victory. Marenholtz was waiting in the dugout. "Take a shower and see me in my office," he said, indicating both Guerra and Ramirez. Then the manager shook his head and went down the tunnel to the dressing room.

Marenholtz was a tall, thin man with sharp, birdlike features. He was sitting at his desk, smoking a cigar. He smoked cigars only when he was very angry, very worried, or very happy. Tonight, while he waited for Guerra and the new kid, he was very worried. Baseball, aged and crippled, didn't need this kind of notoriety.

There were half a dozen local newsmen trying to force their way into the dressing room. He had given orders that there would be no interviews until he had a chance to talk to Ramirez himself. He had phone calls from sportswriters, scouts, fans, gamblers, politicians, and relatives. There was a stack of congratulatory telegrams. There was a very worried telegram from the team's general manager, and a very worried telegram from the front office of the Tigers' major league affiliate.

There was a soft knock on the door. "Guerra?" Marenholtz called out.

"*Si.*"

"Come on in, but don't let anybody else in with you except Ramirez."

Guerra opened the door and the two men entered. Behind them was a noisy, confused crowd of Tiger players. Marenholtz sighed; he would have to find out what happened, and then deal with his team. Then he had to come up with an explanation for the public.

Ramirez was grinning, evidently not sharing Marenholtz' and Guerra's apprehension. He said something to Guerra. The catcher frowned and translated for Marenholtz. "He say, don' he do a good job?"

"That's what *I* want to know!" said Marenholtz. "What *did* he do? You know, it looks a little strange that not a single guy on that team took swing number one."

Guerra looked very uncomfortable. *"Si,* maybe he just *good."*

Marenholtz grunted. "Chico, did he look *that* good?"

Guerra shook his head. Ramirez was still smiling. Marenholtz stood up and paced behind his desk. "I don't *mind* him pitching a perfect game," he said. "It's a memorable achievement. But I think his effort would be better appreciated if one of those batters had tried *hitting.* At least *one.* I want you to tell me why they didn't. If you can't, I want you to ask *him."*

Guerra shrugged and turned to Ramirez. They conversed for a few seconds, and then the catcher spoke to Marenholtz. "He say he don' wan' them to."

Marenholtz slammed his fist on his desk. "That's going to make a great headline in *The Sporting News.* Look, if somehow he paid off the Reds to throw the game, even *they* wouldn't be so stupid as to do it that way." He paused, catching his breath, trying to control his exasperation. "All right, I'll give him a chance. Maybe he *is* the greatest pitcher the world has ever known. Though I doubt it." He reached for his phone and dialed a number. "Hello, Thompson? Look, I need a favor from you. Have you turned off the field lights yet? Okay, leave 'em on for a while, all right? I don't care. I'll talk to Mr. Kaemmer in the morning. And hang around for another half hour, okay? Well, screw the union. We're having a little crisis here. Yeah, Ramirez. Understand? Thanks, Jack." Marenholtz hung up and nodded to Guerra. "You and your battery mate here are going to get some extra practice. Tell him I want to hit some off him, right now. Don't bother getting dressed again. Just put on your mask and get out on the field." Guerra nodded unhappily and led Rudy away.

The stadium was deserted. Marenholtz walked through the dugout and onto the field. He felt strangely alone, cold and worried; the lights made odd, vague shadows that had never bothered him before. He went to the batter's box. The white lines had been all but erased during the course of the game. He leaned on the bat that he had brought with him and waited for the two men.

Guerra came out first, wearing his chest protector and carrying his mask and mitt. Behind him walked Ramirez silently, without his usual grin. He was dressed in street clothes, with his baseball spikes instead of dress shoes. Rudy took his place on the mound. He tossed a ball from his hand to his glove. Guerra positioned himself and Marenholtz waved to Rudy. No one had said a word.

Rudy wound up and pitched, a medium fast ball down the middle. Marenholtz swung and hit a low line drive down the right field line that bounced once and went into the stands. Rudy threw another and Marenholtz hit it far into right center field. The next three pitches he sent to distant, shadowed parts of the ball park. Marenholtz stepped back for a moment. "He was throwing harder during the game, wasn't he?" he asked.

"I think so," said Guerra.

"Tell him to pitch me as hard as he did then. And throw some good curves, too." Guerra translated, and Ramirez nodded. He leaned back and pitched. Marenholtz swung, connected, and watched the ball sail in a huge arc, to land in the seats three hundred and fifty feet away in right field.

Rudy turned to watch the ball. He said nothing. Marenholtz tossed him another from a box on the ground. "I want a curve now," he said.

The pitch came, breaking lazily on the outside part of the plate. Marenholtz timed it well and sent it on a clothesline into center field, not two feet over Ramirez' head. "All right," said the manager, "tell him to come here." Guerra waved, and Rudy trotted to join them. "One thing," said Marenholtz sourly. "I want him to explain why the Reds didn't hit him like that."

"I wanna know, too," said Guerra. He spoke with Ramirez, at last turning back to Marenholtz with a bewildered expression. "He say he don' wan' *them* to hit. He say you wan' hit, he *let* you hit."

"Oh, hell," said Marenholtz. "I'm not stupid."

Rudy looked confused. He said something to Guerra. "He say he don' know why you wan' hit *now*, but he do what you say."

The manager turned away in anger. He spat toward the dugout, thinking. He turned back to Guerra. "We got a couple of balls left," he said. "I want him to pitch me just like he did to the Reds, understand? I don't want him to *let* me hit. Have him try to weave his magic spell on me, too."

Rudy took a ball and went back to the mound. Marenholtz stood up to the plate, waving the bat over his shoulder in a slow circle. Ramirez wound up, kicked, and threw. His fastest pitch, cutting the heart of the plate.

Quiet, thought Rudy, working to restrain his manager's furious mind. *Easy, now. Don't swing. Quiet.*

Marenholtz' mind was suddenly peaceful, composed, thoughtless. The pitch cracked into Guerra's mitt. The manager hadn't swung at it.

Rudy threw ten more pitches, and Marenholtz didn't offer at any of them. Finally he raised his hand. Rudy left the mound again. Marenholtz stood waiting, shaking his head. "Why didn't I swing? Those pitches weren't any harder than the others," Guerra asked Rudy.

"He jus' say he don' wan' you to swing. In his head he tell you. Then you don' swing. He say it's easy."

"I don't believe it," said the manager nervously. "Yeah, okay, he can do it. He *did* do it. I don't like it." Guerra shook his head. The three stood on the empty field for several seconds in uneasy silence. "Can he do that with anybody?" asked Marenholtz.

"He say, *si.*"

"Can he do it any time? *Every* time?"

"He say, *si.*"

"We're in trouble, Chico." Guerra looked into Marenholtz' frightened face and nodded slowly. "I don't mean just us. I mean *baseball.* This kid can throw a perfect game, every time. What do you think'll happen if he makes it to the majors? The game'll be dead. Poor kid. He scares me. Those people in the stands aren't going to like it any better."

"What you gonna do, Mr. Marenhol'?" asked Guerra.

"I don't know, Chico. It's going to be hard keeping a bunch of perfect games secret. Especially when none of the hitters ever takes the bat off his shoulder."

• • •

The following Thursday the Tigers had a night game at home against the Kings. Rudy came prepared to be the starting pitcher, after three days' rest. But when Marenholtz announced the starting lineup, he had the Tigers' long relief man on the mound. Rudy was disappointed, and complained to Guerra. The catcher told him that Marenholtz was probably saving him for the next night, when the Kings' ace left-hander was scheduled to pitch.

On Friday Ramirez was passed over again. He sat in the dugout, sweating in his warm-up jacket, irritated at the manager. Guerra told him to have patience. Rudy couldn't understand why Marenholtz wouldn't pitch him, after the great game Ramirez had thrown in his first start. Guerra just shrugged and told Rudy to study the hitters.

Rudy didn't play Saturday, or in either of the Sunday doubleheader's games. He didn't know that the newspapermen were as mystified as he. Marenholtz made up excuses, saying that Rudy had pulled a back muscle in practice. The manager refused to make any comments about Ramirez' strange perfect game, and as the days passed the clamor died down.

The next week Rudy spent on the bench, becoming angrier and more frustrated. He confronted Marenholtz several times, with Guerra as unwilling interpreter, and each time the manager just said that he didn't feel that Ramirez was "ready." The season was coming to its close, with only six games left, and Rudy was determined to play. As the games came and went, however, it became obvious that he wasn't going to get the chance.

On the day of the last game, Marenholtz announced that Irv Tappan, his number two right-hander, would start. Rudy stormed into the clubhouse in a rage. He went to his locker and started to change clothes. Marenholtz signaled to Guerra, and they followed Ramirez.

"All right, Ramirez, what're you doing?" asked the manager.

"He say he goin' home," said Guerra, translating Rudy's shouted reply.

"If he leaves before the game is over, he's liable to be fined. Does he know that?"

"He say he don' care."

"Tell him he's acting like a kid," said Marenholtz, feeling relieved inside.

"He say go to hell."

Marenholtz took a deep breath. "Okay, Chico. Tell him we've enjoyed knowing him, and respect his talent, and would like to invite him to try out for the team again next spring."

"He say go to hell."

"He's going home?" asked Marenholtz.

"He say you 'mericanos jealous, and waste his time. He say he can do other things."

"Well, tell him we're sorry, and wish him luck."

"He say go to hell. He say you don' know your *ano* from a hole in the groun'."

Marenholtz smiled coldly. "Chico, I want you to do me a favor. Do yourself a favor, too; there's enough here for the two of us. You let him finish clearing out of here, and you go with him. I don't know where he's going this time of day. Probably back to the hotel where he stays. Keep with him. Talk to him. Don't let him get away, don't let him get drunk, don't let him talk to anybody else, okay?"

Guerra looked puzzled, but nodded. Ramirez was turning to leave the clubhouse. Marenholtz grabbed Guerra's arm and pushed him toward the furious boy. "Go on," said the manager, "keep him in sight. I'll call the hotel in about three or four hours. We got a good thing here, Chico, my boy." The catcher frowned and hurried after Rudy. Marenholtz sighed; he walked across the dressing room, stopping by his office. He opened the door and stared into the darkened room for a few seconds. He wanted desperately to sit at his desk and write the letters and make the phone calls, but he still had a game to play. The job seemed so empty to him now. He *knew* this would be the last regular game he'd see in the minor leagues. Next spring he and Ramirez would be shocking them all at the Florida training camps. Next summer he and Ramirez would own the world of major league baseball.

First, though, there was still the game with the Bears. Marenholtz closed the door to the office and locked it. Then he went up the tunnel to the field. All that he could think of was going back to the Big Time.

After the game, Fred Marenholtz hurried to his office. The other players grabbed at him, swatting at his back to congrat-

ulate him on the end of the season. The Tigers were celebrating
in the clubhouse. Cans of beer were popping open, and sand-
wiches had been supplied by the front office. The manager
ignored them all. He locked the door to the office behind him.
He called Ramirez' hotel and asked for his room.

Guerra answered, and reported that Ramirez was there, taking a nap. The catcher was instructed to tell Rudy that together
they were all going to win their way to the major leagues.
Guerra was doubtful, but Marenholtz wouldn't listen to the
catcher's puzzled questions. The manager hung up. He pulled
out a battered address book from his desk drawer, and found
the telephone number of an old friend, a contract lawyer in St.
Louis. He called the number, tapping a pencil nervously on
the desk top while the phone rang.

"Hello, Marty?" he said when the call was finally answered.

"Yes. Who's this calling, please?"

"Hi. You won't remember me, but this is Fred Marenholtz."

"Freddie! How are you? Lord, it's been fifteen years. Are
you in town?"

Marenholtz smiled. Things were going to be all right. They
chatted for a few minutes, and then Marenholtz told his old
friend that he was calling on business.

"Sure, Freddie," said the lawyer. "For Frantic Fred Marenholtz, anything. Is it legal?" Marenholtz laughed.

The photographs on the office wall looked painfully old to
Marenholtz. They were of an era too long dead, filled with
people who themselves had long since passed away. Baseball
itself had withered, had lost the lifeblood of interest that had
infused the millions of fans each spring. It had been too many
years since Fred Marenholtz had claimed his share of glory.
He had never been treated to his part of the financial rewards
of baseball, and after his brief major league career he felt it
was time to make his bid.

Marenholtz instructed the lawyer in detail. Old contracts
were to be broken, new ones drawn up. The lawyer wrote
himself in for five percent as payment. The manager hung up
the phone again. He slammed his desk drawer closed in sheer
exuberance. Then he got up and left his office. He had to thank
his players for their cooperation during the past season.

"Tell him he's not going to get anything but investigated if
he doesn't put in with us." It was late now, past midnight.

Ramirez' tiny hotel room was stifling. Rudy rested on the bed. Guerra sat in a chair by the single window. Marenholtz paced around, his coat thrown on the bed, his shirt soaked with perspiration.

"He say he don' like the way you run the club. He don' think you run him better," said Guerra wearily.

"All right. Explain to him that we're not going to cost him anything. The only way *we* can make any money is by making sure *he* does okay. We'll take a percentage of what he makes. That's his insurance."

"He wan' know why you wan' him now, you wouldn't play him before."

"Because he's a damn fool, is why! Doesn't he know what would happen if he pitched his kind of game, week after week?"

"He think he make a lot of money."

Marenholtz stopped pacing and stared. "Stupid Spanish bastard!" he said. Guerra, from a farming village in Panama, glared resentfully. "I'm sorry, Chico. Explain it to him." The catcher went to the edge of the bed and sat down. He talked with Rudy for a long while, then turned back to the manager.

"Okay, Mr. Marenhol'. He didn't think anybody noticed that."

"Fine," said Marenholtz, taking Guerra's vacated chair. "Now let's talk. Chico, what were you planning to do this winter?"

Guerra looked puzzled again. "I don't know. Go home."

Marenholtz smiled briefly and shook his head. "No. You're coming with me. We're taking young Mr. Ramirez here and turn him into a pitcher. If not that, at least into an educated thrower. We got a job, my friend."

They had six months, and they could have used more. They worked hard, giving Rudy little time to relax. He spent weeks just throwing baseballs through a circle of wire on a stand. Guerra and Marenholtz helped him learn the most efficient way to pitch, so that he wouldn't tire after half a game; he studied tapes of his motions, to see where they might be improved, to fool the hitters and conserve his own energy. Guerra coached him on all the fundamentals: fielding his position, developing a deceptive throw to first base, making certain that his windup was the same for every different pitch.

After a couple of months Ramirez' control was sharp enough to put a ball into Guerra's mitt wherever the catcher might ask.

Marenholtz watched with growing excitement—they were going to bring it off. Rudy was as good as any mediocre pitcher in the majors. Marenholtz was teaching him to save his special talent for the tight situations, the emergencies where less attention would be focused on the pitcher. Rudy was made to realize that he had eight skilled teammates behind him; if he threw the ball where the catcher wanted it, the danger of long hits was minimized. A succession of pop-ups and weak grounders would look infinitely better than twenty-seven passive strikeouts.

Before the spring training session began, Rudy had developed a much better curve that he could throw with reasonable control, a passable change-up, a poor slider, and a slightly off-speed fast ball. He relied on Guerra and Marenholtz for instructions, and they schooled him in all the possible situations until he was sick of the whole scheme.

"Freddie Marenholtz! Damn, you look like you could still get out there and play nine hard ones yourself. Got that phenom of yours?"

"Yeah, you want him to get dressed?" Marenholtz stood by a batting cage in the training camp of the Nashville Cats, a team welcomed into the American League during the expansion draft three years previously. The Florida sun was already fierce enough in March to make Marenholtz uncomfortable, and he shielded his eyes with one hand as he talked to Jim Billy Westfahl, the Cats' manager.

"All right," said Westfahl. "You said you brought this kid Ramirez and a catcher, right? What's his name?"

"Guerra. Only guy Ramirez ever pitched to."

"Yeah, well, you know we got two good catchers in Porto benez and Staefler. If Guerra's going to stick, he's going to have to beat them out."

Marenholtz frowned. Guerra was *not* going to beat them out of their jobs. But he had to keep the man around, both because he could soothe Ramirez' irrational temper and because Guerra presented a danger to the plan. But the aging catcher might have to get used to watching the games from the boxes. He collected three and a half percent of Rudy's income, and Marenholtz couldn't see that Guerra had reason to complain.

Rudy came out of the locker room and walked to the batting

cage. Guerra followed, looking uneasy among the major league talents on the field. Ramirez turned to Westfahl and said something in Spanish. Guerra translated. "He say he wan' show you what he can do."

"Okay. I'm game. *Somebody's* going to have to replace McAnion. It may as well be your kid. Let's see what he looks like."

Rudy pitched to Guerra, and Westfahl made a few noncommital remarks. Later in the day Rudy faced some of the Cats' regulars, and the B squad of rookies. He held some of them back, pitched to some of them, and looked no less sharp than any of the other regular pitchers after a winter's inactivity. In the next two weeks Marenholtz and Guerra guided Rudy carefully, letting him use his invisible talent sparingly, without attracting undue notice, and Ramirez seemed sure to go north with the team when the season began. Guerra didn't have the same luck. A week before spring training came to an end he was optioned to the Cats' AA farm club. Guerra pretended to be upset, and refused to report.

By this time Marenholtz had promoted a large amount of money. The newly appointed president of *RR Star Enterprises* had spent the spring signing contracts while his protégé worked to impress the public. Permissions and royalty fees were deposited from trading card companies, clothing manufacturers, fruit juice advertisements, sporting goods dealers, and grooming product endorsements—Rudy was hired to look into a camera and say, "I like it. It makes my hair neat without looking greasy." He was finally coached to say, "I like it," and the rest of the line was given to a sexy female model.

The regular season began at home for the Cats. Rudy Ramirez was scheduled to pitch the third game. Rudy felt little excitement before his game; what he did was in no way different in kind or quantity from his nervousness before his first appearance with the Cordele Tigers. The slightly hostile major league crowd didn't awe him: he was prepared to awe the four thousand spectators who had come to watch the unknown rookie.

Fred Marenholtz had briefed Rudy thoroughly; before the game they had decided that an impressive but nonetheless credible effort would be a four- or five-hit shutout. For an added touch of realism, Rudy might get tired in the eighth inning, and leave for a relief pitcher. Marenholtz and Guerra sat in field boxes along the first base side, near the dugout. Ramirez could hear their shouts from the mound. He waved to them as he took his place before the "National Anthem" was sung.

Rudy's pitches were not particularly overpowering. His fast ball was eminently hitable; only the experience of the Cats' catcher prevented pitches from sailing time after time over the short left field fence. Ramirez' weeks of practice saved him: his pitches crossed the plate just above the batters' knees, or handcuffed them close around the fists, or nicked the outside edge of the plate. Rudy's curve was just good enough to keep the hitters guessing. The first batter hit a sharp ground ball to short, fielded easily for the first out. The second batter lofted a fly to right field for the second out. Rudy threw three pitches to the third batter, and then threw his first mistake, a fast ball belt high, down the middle. Rudy knew what would happen— a healthy swing, and then a quick one-run lead for the White Sox. Urgently, desperately he sought the batter's will and grasped it in time. The man stood stupidly, staring at the most perfect pitch he would see in a long while. It went by for a called strike three, and Rudy had his first official major league strikeout.

Marenholtz stood and applauded when Rudy trotted back to the dugout. Guerra shouted something in Spanish. Ramirez' teammates slapped his back, and he smiled and nodded and took his place on the bench. He allowed a double down the line in the second inning, set the White Sox down in order in the third and fourth, gave up a single and a walk in the fifth, a single in the sixth, no hits in the seventh and eighth, and two singles to the first two batters in the ninth. Rudy had pitched wisely, combining his inferior skill with judicious use of his mental talent. Sometimes he held back a batter for just a fraction of a second, so that the hitter would swing late. Other times he would prevent a batter from running for an instant, to insure his being thrown out at first. He caused the opposition's defense to commit errors so that the Cats could score the runs to guarantee victory.

The manager of the Cats came out to the mound to talk with Ramirez in the ninth. Carmen Velillo, the Cats' third baseman, joined the conference to translate for Rudy. Ramirez insisted that he was strong enough to finish, but the manager brought in a relief pitcher. Rudy received a loud cheer from the fans as he went off the field. He didn't watch the rest of the game, but went straight to the showers. The Cats' new man put down the rally, and Ramirez had a shutout victory. After Rudy and Velillo had answered the endless questions of the newsmen, Marenholtz and Guerra met him for a celebration.

Marenholtz held interviews with reporters from national magazines or local weeklies. Coverage of Ramirez' remarkable successes grew more detailed; as the season progressed Rudy saw his picture on the front of such varied periodicals as *Sports Illustrated* and *People Magazine*. By June Rudy had won eleven games and lost none. His picture appeared on the cover of *Time* after he won his fifteenth in a row. An article in the New York *Post* announced that he was the greatest natural talent since Grover Cleveland Alexander. He appeared briefly on late-night television programs. He was hired to attend shopping center openings in the Nashville area. He loved winning ball games, and Marenholtz, too, gloried in returning a success to the major leagues that had treated him so shabbily in his youth.

The evening before Ramirez was to start his sixteenth ball game, he was having dinner with Marenholtz and Guerra. The older man was talking about his own short playing career, and how baseball had deteriorated since then. Guerra nodded and said little. Ramirez stared quietly at his plate, toying with his food and not eating. Suddenly he spoke up, interrupting Marenholtz' flow of memories. He spoke in rapid Spanish; Marenholtz gaped in surprise. "What's he saying?" he asked.

Guerra coughed nervously. "He wan' know why he need us," he said. "He say he do pretty good by himself."

Marenholtz put his cigar down and stared angrily at Ramirez. "I was wondering how long it would take him to think he could cut us out. You can tell him that if it hadn't been for us he'd either be in trouble or in Venezuela. You can tell him that if it hadn't been for us he wouldn't have that solid bank account and his poor gray mama wouldn't have the only color television in her banana wonderland. And if that doesn't work, tell him maybe he *doesn't* need us, but he signed the contracts."

Guerra said a few words, and Rudy answered. "What's he say now?" asked Marenholtz.

"Nothing," said Guerra, staring down at his own plate. "He jus' say he thank you, but he wan' do it by himself."

"Oh, hell. Tell him to forget that and pitch a good game tomorrow. I'll do the worrying. That's what I'm for."

"He say he do that. He say he pitch you a good game."

"Well, thank you, Tom, and good afternoon, baseball fans everywhere. In just a few moments we'll bring you live coverage of the third contest of this weekend series, a game between the Nashville Cats, leaders in the American League Midlands Division, and the Denver Athletics. It looks to be a pitchers' duel today, with young Rudy Ramirez, Nashville's astonishing rookie, going against the A's veteran right-hander, Morgan Stepitz."

"Right, Chuck, and I think a lot of the spectators in the park today have come to see if Ramirez can keep his amazing streak alive. He's won fifteen now and he hasn't been beaten so far in his entire professional career. Each game must be more of an ordeal than the last for the youngster. The strain will be starting to take its toll."

"Nevertheless, Tom, I have to admit that it's been a very long time since I've seen anyone with the poise of that young man. The interesting thing is that he hasn't let his success make him overconfident, which is possibly the greatest danger to him now. I'm sure that defeat, when it comes, will be a hard blow, but I'm just as certain that Rudy Ramirez will recover and go on to have a truly remarkable season."

"A lot of fans have written in to ask what the record is for most consecutive games won. Well, Ramirez has quite a start on that, but he has a little way to go. The major league record is nineteen, set in 1912 by Rube Marquard. But even if Ramirez doesn't go on to break that one, he's still got the makings of a spectacular year. He's leading both leagues with an earned run average of 1.54, and it looks like he has an excellent shot at thirty wins—"

"All right, let's go down to the field, where it's time for the singing of 'The Star-Spangled Banner.'"

After the spectators cheered and settled back into their seats, after the Cats' catcher whipped the ball down to second base, and after the infielders tossed it around and, finally, back to the pitcher, Rudy looked around the stadium. The Nashville park was new, built five years ago in hopes of attracting a major league franchise. It was huge, well-designed, and generally filled with noisy fans. The sudden success of the usually hapless Cats was easily traced: Rudy Ramirez. He was to pitch again today, and his enthusiastic rooters crowded the spacious park. Bedsheet banners hung over railings, wishing him luck and proclaiming Ramirez to be the best-loved individual on the continent. Rudy, still innocent of English, did not know what they said.

He could see Marenholtz and Guerra sitting behind the dugout. They saw him glance in their direction and stood, waving their arms. Rudy touched the visor of his cap in salute. Then he turned to face the first of the Athletics' hitters.

"Okay, the first batter for the A's is the second baseman, number twelve, Jerry Kleiner. Kleiner's batting .262 this season. He's a switch-hitter, and he's batting right-handed against the southpaw, Ramirez.

"Ramirez takes his sign from Staefler, winds, and delivers. Kleiner takes the pitch for a called strike one. Ramirez has faced the A's only once before this season, shutting them out on four hits.

"Kleiner steps out to glance down at the third base coach for the signal. He steps back in. Ramirez goes into his motion. Kleiner lets it go by again. No balls and two strikes."

"Ramirez is really piping them in today, Tom."

"That's right, Chuck. I noticed during his warm-ups that his fast ball seemed to be moving exceptionally well. Today it will tend to tail in toward a right-handed hitter. Here comes the pitch—strike three! Kleiner goes down looking."

"Before the game we talked with Cats' catcher Bo Staefler, who told us that Ramirez' slider is improving as the season gets older. You know that can only be bad news for the hitters in the American League. It may be a while before they can solve his style."

"Stepping in now is the A's right fielder, number twenty-four, Ricky Gonzalvo. Gonzalvo's having trouble with his old knee injury this year, and his average is down to .244. He crowds the plate a little on Ramirez. The first pitch is inside, knocking Gonzalvo down. Ball one.

"Ramirez gets the ball back, leans forward for his sign. And the pitch—in there for a called strike. The count is even at one and one."

"He seems to have excellent control today, wouldn't you say, Tom?"

"Exactly. Manager Jim Westfahl of the Cats suggested last week that the pinpoint accuracy of his control is sometimes enough to intimidate a batter into becoming an easy out."

"There must be *some* explanation, even if it's magic."

"Ramirez deals another breaking pitch, in there for a called strike two. I wouldn't say it's all magic, Chuck. It looked to me as though Gonzalvo was crossed up on that one, probably expecting the fast ball again."

"Staefler gives him the sign. Ramirez nods, and throws. Fast ball, caught Gonzalvo napping. Called strike three. Two away now in the top of the first.

"Batting in the number three position is the big first baseman, Howie Bass. Bass' brother, Eddie, who plays for the Orioles, has the only home run hit off Ramirez this season. Here comes Ramirez' pitch—Bass takes it for strike one."

"It seems to me that the batters are starting out behind Ramirez, a little overcautious. That's the effect that a winning streak like his can have. Ramirez has the benefit of a psychological edge working for him, as well as his great pitching."

"Right, Tom. That pitch while you were talking was a called strike two, a good slider that seemed to have Bass completely baffled."

"Staefler gives the sign, but Ramirez shakes his head. Ramirez shakes off another sign. Now he nods, goes into his windup, and throws. A fast ball, straight down the middle, strike three. Bass turns to argue with the umpire, but that'll do him no good. Three up and three down for the A's, no runs, no hits, nothing across."

The Cats' fans jumped to their feet, but Fred Marenholtz listened angrily to their applause. He caught Rudy's eye just as the pitcher was about to enter the dugout. Before Marenholtz could say anything, Rudy grinned and disappeared inside. Marenholtz was worried that the sophisticated major league audience would be even less likely to accept the spectacle of batter after batter going down without swinging at Ramirez' pitches. The older man turned to Guerra. "What's he trying to do?" he asked.

Guerra shook his head. "I don' know. Maybe he wan' strike out some."

"Maybe," said Marenholtz dubiously, "but I didn't think he'd be that dumb."

The Cats got a runner to second base in their part of the first inning, but he died there when the cleanup hitter sent a line drive over the head of the A's first baseman, who leaped high to save the run. Rudy walked out to the mound confidently, and threw his warm-ups.

"All right," said Marenholtz, "let's see him stop that nonsense now. This game's being televised all over the country." He watched Ramirez go into his motion. The first pitch was a curve that apparently didn't break; a slow pitch coming toward the plate as fat as a basketball. The A's batter watched it for a called strike. Marenholtz swore softly.

Rudy threw two more pitches, each of them over the plate for strikes. The hitter never moved his bat. Marenholtz' face was turning red with controlled fury. Rudy struck out the next batter on three pitches. Guerra coughed nervously and said something in Spanish. Already the fans around them were remarking on how strange it was to see the A's being called out on strikes without making an effort to guard the plate. The A's sixth batter took his place in the batter's box, and three pitches later he, too, walked back to the bench, a bewildered expression on his face.

Marenholtz stood and hollered to Ramirez. "What the hell you doing?" he said, forgetting that the pitcher couldn't understand him. Rudy walked nonchalantly to the dugout, taking no notice of Marenholtz.

Guerra rose and edged past Marenholtz to the aisle. "You going for a couple of beers?" asked Marenholtz.

"No," said Guerra. "I think I jus' *goin'*."

"Well, Tom, it's the top of the third, score tied at nothing to nothing. I want to say that we're getting that pitchers' battle we promised. We're witnessing one heck of a good ballgame so far. The Cats have had only one hit, and rookie Rudy Ramirez hasn't let an Athletic reach first base."

"There's an old baseball superstition about jinxing a pitcher in a situation like this, but I might mention that Ramirez has struck out the first six men to face him. The record for consecutive strikeouts is eleven, held by Cannon Shen of the old Cleveland Indians. If I remember correctly, that mark was set the last year the Indians played in Cleveland, before their move to New Orleans."

"This sort of game isn't a new thing for Ramirez, either, Tom. His bio in the Cats' pressbook mentions that in his one start in the minor leagues, he threw a perfect game and set a Triangle League record for most strikeouts in a nine-inning game."

"Okay, Chuck. Ramirez has finished his warm-ups here in the top of the third. He'll face the bottom of the A's order. Batting in the seventh position is the catcher, number sixteen, Tolly Knecht. Knecht's been in a long slump, but he's always been something of a spoiler. He'd love to break out of it with a hit against Ramirez here. Here's the pitch—Knecht was taking all the way, a called strike one."

"Maybe the folks at home would like to see Ramirez' form here on the slow-motion replay. You can see how the extra-high kick tends to hide the ball from the batter until the very last moment. He's getting the full force of his body behind the pitch, throwing from the shoulder with a last powerful snap of the wrist. He ends up here perfectly balanced, ready for any kind of defensive move. From the plate the white ball must be disguised by the uniform, appearing suddenly out of nowhere. A marvelous athlete and a terrific competitor."

"Thanks, Chuck. That last pitch was a good breaking ball; Knecht watched it for strike two. I think one of the reasons the hitters seem to be so confused is the excellent arsenal of pitches that Ramirez has. He throws his fast ball intelligently, saving it for the tight spots. He throws an overhand curve and a sidearm curve, each at two different speeds. His slider is showing up more and more as his confidence increases."

"Ramirez nods to Staefler, the catcher. He winds up and throws. Strike three! That's seven now. Knecht throws his bat away in frustration. The fans aren't too happy, either. Even the Cats' loyal crowd is beginning to boo. I don't think I've ever seen a team as completely stymied as the A's are today."

"I tell you, I almost wish I could go down there myself. Some of Ramirez' pitches look just too good. It makes me want to grab a bat and take a poke at one. His slow curves seem to hang there, inviting a good healthy cut. But, of course, from our vantage point we can't see what the batters are seeing. Ramirez must have tremendous stuff today. Not one Athletic hitter has taken a swing at his pitches."

● ● ●

When the eighth Athletic batter struck out, the fans stood and jeered. Marenholtz felt his stomach tightening. His mouth was dry and his ears buzzed. After the ninth batter fanned, staring uninterestedly at a mild pitch belt high, the stadium was filled with shouts and catcalls. Marenholtz couldn't be sure that they were all directed at the unlucky hitters.

Maybe I ought to hurry after Guerra, thought Marenholtz. *Maybe it's time to talk about that bowling alley deal again. This game is rotten at its roots already. It's not like when I was out there. We cared. The fans cared. Now they got guys like Grobert playing, they're nearly gangsters. Sometimes the games look like they're produced from a script. And Ramirez is going to topple it all. The kid's special, but that won't save us. Good God, I feel sorry for him. He can't see it coming. He won't see it coming. He's out there having a ball. And he's going to make the loudest boom when it all falls down. Then what's he going to do? What's he going to do?*

Rudy walked jauntily off the field. The spectators around Marenholtz screamed at the pitcher. Rudy only smiled. He waved to Marenholtz and pointed to Guerra's empty seat. Marenholtz shrugged. Ramirez ducked into the dugout, leaving Marenholtz to fret in the stands.

After the Cats were retired in the third, Rudy went out to pitch his half of the fourth. A policeman called his name, and Rudy turned. The officer stood in the boxes, at the edge of the dugout, stationed to prevent overeager fans from storming the playing field. He held his hand out to Rudy and spoke to him in English. Rudy shook his head, not understanding. He took the papers from the policeman and studied them for a moment. They were contracts that he had signed with Marenholtz. They were torn in half. Ramirez grinned; he looked up toward Marenholtz' seat behind the dugout. The man had followed Guerra, had left the stadium before he could be implicated in the tarnished proceedings.

For the first time since he had come to the United States, Rudy Ramirez felt free. He handed the contracts back to the mystified police officer and walked to the mound. He took a few warm-ups and waited for Kleiner, the A's lead-off batter. Ramirez took his sign and pitched. Kleiner swung and hit a shot past the mound. Rudy entered Kleiner's mind and kept him motionless beside the plate for a part of a second. The Cats' shortstop went far to his left, grabbed the ball and threw on the dead run; Kleiner was out by a full step. There were mixed groans and cheers from the spectators, but Rudy didn't hear. He was watching Gonzalvo take his place in the batter's box. Maybe Rudy would let him get a hit.

I am attracted to sports because I love excellence. I have a hunger to see anyone do anything well. A superior athlete is a joy to watch, even if his or her particular sport doesn't interest me very much.

Basketball provides the two kinds of excellence that sports offer in general. There is the basketball team composed of a flashy daredevil star and four competent caddies. There is also the team that has been put together into a marvelously functioning unit, showing off teamwork and precision rather than individual glory. Both teams can be winners, and both teams can be fun to watch. It's a matter of taste.

From Downtown at the Buzzer looks at the ultimate in one of these styles of play. The title is a bit of sportscaster's slang that describes a long-distance desperation shot in the final seconds that wins the game against all odds. The "game" in this story isn't the one played on the basketball court—at least, the truly important one isn't.

From Downtown at the Buzzer

THERE ARE A COUPLE of things my mother will never get to experience.

I mean, there are more than a couple, of course, but there are two things that I think of immediately. First off, my mother won't ever know what it's like to see twelve space creatures in blue suits and masks staring at you while you eat breakfast and wash walls and go to the bathroom. That I know. That I can talk about. My mother can't, and just as well, I guess. But believe me, I can.

The other thing is, my mother will never, *ever* know the incredible joy you get, this feeling of complete, instant gratification, when you jump into the air, twist around, and send a basketball in an absolutely perfect arc into the net maybe twenty-three feet away. You have somebody from the other team leaping up with you, his hand right in your face, but sometimes you have God on your side and nothing in the universe can keep that ball from going through that hoop. You sense it sometimes, you can feel it even before you let go of the ball, while you're still floating. Then it's just the smallest flick of the wrist, your fingertips just brushing the ball away, perfect, perfect, perfect, you don't even have to look. You land on the hardwood floor with this terrific smile on your face, and the guy who had his hand up to block you is muttering to himself, and you're talking to yourself, too, as you run down-court to the other end. You're happy. My mother will never know that kind of happy.

Not that I do, either, very often.

Now, this newspaper is paying me a lot of money for this exclusive story, so I figure I ought to give them what they paid for. But other magazines have paid others for their exclusive stories, and they might tell stories a little different from mine. That's because no one else in the security installation knew the Cobae so well as I did.

I'll start about a year ago, about a month before I saw my first Coba. I was a captain then, attached to Colonel James McNeill. Colonel McNeill was the commanding officer of the entire compound, and because of that I was given access to a lot of things that I really shouldn't have seen. But I saw those things, and I read the Colonel's reports, and, well, I guess that I can put two and two together as well as anybody. So from all of that, there wasn't much happening around the compound that I didn't know about.

The installation was in the middle of an awful lot of nothing, in one of the smaller parishes in southwestern Louisiana. St. Didier Parish. There was one town kind of large, Linhart, with maybe six thousand people, three movie theaters, a lot of bars. That was it for the whole parish, just about. South of us were towns full of Cajuns who trapped muskrat and nutria, or worked in the cane fields, or worked in the rice fields, or on shrimp boats or off-shore oil rigs, or netted crabs. They spoke a kind of strange mixture of English and a French no Parisian ever heard. All around us, and farther north, there were only farms. We were tucked away in an isolated part of the parish, with only a small dirt road leading to the one main north-south route. No one on the base had anything to do with the Cajuns; come furlough time or weekend passes, it made more sense to go to New Orleans, an hour and a half, maybe two hours east of us.

We didn't have a lot to look at except fields on the other side of the wire fence. It was summer nine months of the year. The base was landscaped with a large variety of local plants, some of which I don't even know the names of. Everything flowered, and there was something blooming almost every month of the year. It was kind of nice. I liked the job.

I liked it a lot, until the Cobae showed up.

Before that, though, I wasn't exactly sure why we were there. We were a top-security installation, doing just about nothing. I was kept busy enough with day-to-day maintenance and routines. I had been transferred down from Dayton, Ohio, and it never occurred to me to ask Colonel McNeill what the hell we were supposed to be doing, surrounded by a lot of yam fields, between the marshes on the west and the swamps on the east. I mean, it just never came up. I had learned a long time ago that if I did just what I was told to do, and did it right, then everything, absolutely everything would be fine. That kind of life was very pleasant and satisfying. Everything was laid out for me, and I just took it all in order, doing task one, doing task two, doing task three. The day ended, I had free time, at regular intervals I was paid. The base had plenty of leisure facilities. It was all just great for me.

Of course, I was a captain.

My main outlet during my leisure was playing basketball. There were very good gym facilities on the base, and I've always been the competitive type, at least in situations where winning and losing didn't have much of a permanent effect on my life. I enjoy target shooting, for example, because there is no element of luck involved. It's just you, the rifle, and the target. But if you put me down in a hot spot, with people shooting back, I do believe all the fun would go right out of it.

Forget it. There were always a few other people on the base, not always male, who liked to get into the pick-up games. Every once in a while someone would show up, someone I hadn't seen on the court for weeks. Mostly, however, there were the same regulars. Tuesday and Thursday evenings, those were the big basketball games. Those were the games that even I couldn't get into, on occasion. They were what you'd call blood games. I enjoyed watching them almost as much as I liked playing in them. Maybe I should have been watching a little closer.

All right, it was in the middle of August, and the temperature outside was in the low nineties, all the time. Every day. *All* the time. And the humidity matched the temperature, figure for figure. So we just stayed in the air-conditioned buildings and sent the enlisted men outside to take care of running errands. It takes a while to get adjusted, you know, from mild Ohio weather to high summer in sub-tropical Louisiana. I wasn't altogether adjusted to it. I liked my office, and I liked my airconditioned car, and I liked my air-conditioned quarters. But there were little bits of not-air-conditioned in among those things that got to me and made me struggle to breathe. I don't think I could hack it as an African explorer, if they still have them, or as vistor to other equatorial places where the only comforts are a hand-held fan and an occasional cool drink.

Terrific. You've got the background. That's the way things were and, like I say, I was all in favor of them just going on like that until I felt like dropping dead or something. But things didn't go on like that.

At the end of August a general showed up, trailing two colonels. They were in one long black car. In three long black cars behind the brass were the Cobae. I think it would be a good idea if I kind of went into detail about the Cobae and how we happened to get them dumped in our laps.

As I learned shortly after their arrival, the Cobae had appeared on Earth sometime in July. I forget the exact date. They were very cautious. Apparently they had remained in their ship in space, monitoring things, picking and choosing, making their inscrutable minds up about God only knows what. A paper that crossed Colonel McNeill's desk, a paper that I shouldn't have seen, said that one Coba appeared in the private apartment of the President. How he got there is still a mystery. An awful lot about the Cobae is still a mystery. Anyway, I suppose the President and his wife were a little startled. Ha. Sometimes on silent nights I like to imagine that scene. Depending on my mood, the scene can be very comic or very dramatic. Depending on my mood of the moment, and also what the President and his wife were doing, and how genuinely diplomatic and resilient the President was.

After all, remember that the President is just a guy, too, and he's probably not crazy about strangers materializing in his bedroom. He's probably even less crazy about short, squat, really ugly creatures in his bedroom. Picture the scene for yourself. Take a few seconds, I'll wait. See?

Well, the President called for whomever he usually calls

for, and there was a very frantic meeting in which nothing intelligent at all was said. There weren't contingency plans for this sort of thing. It's not often that the President of the United States has to wing it in a crisis situation. And this *was* a crisis situation, even though the Coba hadn't said a word, moved a muscle, or even blinked, so far as anyone could determine.

Okay, imagine everyone dressed and formal and a little calmed down now, thanks to things like Valium and Librium and Jack Daniels. Now we have a President and his advisors. *They* have a creature in a blue, shiny uniform and a mask over his face. It wasn't exactly a helmet. It covered what we call the Coba's nose and mouth, by liberal interpretation. There was a flexible hose from the mask to a small box on the chest. The President doesn't have the faintest idea what to do. Neither does the Secretary of State, who gets the job tossed to him because it seems like his department. The potato gets tossed back and around for a while. The Coba still hasn't done a doggone thing. As a matter of fact, no one yet has gotten around to addressing the creature (I think here I will stop calling them creatures).

Fifteen minutes after our world's first contact with intelligent life beyond our planet, someone has the bright idea to bring a scientist in.

"Who?" asked the President.

"I don't know," said the Secretary of State.

"What kind of scientist?" asked one of the advisors. "An astronomer? An ethnologist? A linguist? A sociologist? An anthropologist?"

"Call 'em all," said the President, with the kind of quick thinking that has endeared him to some of us.

"Call who all?" asked the advisor.

The President, by this time, was getting a little edgy. He was ready to start raising his voice, a sure sign that he was frustrated and angry. Before that, however, he chose to ask one final, well-modulated question. "There must be one person out of the millions of people in this damn country to call," he said. "Someone best suited to handling this. Who is it?"

There was only silence.

After a while, as the President's face turned a little redder, one of the advisors coughed a little and spoke up. "Uh," he said, "why don't we hide this joker away somewhere. You know, somewhere really secure. Then we assemble a high-power team of specialists, and they can go on from there. How's that?"

"Wonderful," said the President, with the kind of irony that has endeared him to a few of us. "What do you think the joker will do when we try to hide him away somewhere?"

"Ask him," said the Secretary of State.

Again there was silence. This time, though, everyone looked toward the President. It was a head of state meeting an important emissary kind of thing, so it was his potato after all. You can bet he didn't like it.

Finally the President said, "He speaks English?" No one answered. After a while the Secretary of State spoke up again.

"Ask him," said the S. of S.

"An historic occasion," murmured the President. He faced the Coba. He took a closer look and shuddered. That was the reaction we all had until we got used to their appearance. After all, the President is just a guy, too. But a well-trained guy.

"Do you speak English?" asked the President.

"Yes," said the Coba. That brought another round of silence.

After a time the Secretary of State said, "You've heard this discussion, then. Have you understood it?"

"Yes," said the Coba.

"Would you object to the plan, then?" asked the Secretary. "Would you agree to being questioned by a team of our scientists, in a confidential manner?"

"No," said the Coba, in answer to the Secretary's first question, and "Yes," to the Secretary's second.

The President took a deep breath. "Thank you," he said. "You can understand our perplexity here, and our need for discretion in the whole matter. May I ask where you are from?"

"Yes," said the Coba.

Silence.

"Where are you from?" asked the Secretary of State.

Silence.

"Are you from our, uh, what you call, our solar system?" asked the President.

"No," said the Coba.

"From some other star, then?" asked an emboldened advisor.

"Yes," said the Coba.

"Which star?" asked the advisor.

Silence.

It was several minutes later that the assembled group began to realize that the Coba was only going to answer yes-no questions. "Great," said the President. "It'll only take years to get any information that way."

"Don't worry," said an advisor. "If we pick the right people, they'll have the right questions."

"Pick them, then," said the President.

"We'll get to work on it," said another advisor.

"Right now," said the President.

"Check."

"What do we do with it in the meantime?" asked the Secretary of Defense.

"I don't know," said the President, throwing up his hands. "Put him or her or it in the Lincoln Bedroom. Make sure there are towels. Now get out of here and let me go to sleep."

"Thank you, Mr. President," said an advisor. The President just shook his head wearily.

I learned all of this from one of the advisors present at the time. This guy is now appealing a court decision that could send him to prison for five years, because of some minor thing he had done a long time ago, and which none of us understand. He's also writing a book about the Cobae affair.

I wonder how well the President slept that night.

The next morning when they came to get the Coba, someone knocked on the door (come to think of it, what made them think that a Coba would know what knocking on a door meant?). There was no response. The aide, one of the more courageous people in the history of our nation, sweated a little, fiddled around a little, knocked again, sweated some more, and opened the door.

Twelve Cobae stood like statues in the room. The aide shut the door and went screaming through the halls of the Executive Mansion.

Later, when the advisors questioned the twelve Cobae, they discovered that only one would reply, and only with yes or no answers. It was assumed that this Coba was the original Coba who had appeared in the President's bedroom the evening before. There really was no logical basis on which to make this assumption, but it was made nevertheless. No one ever got around to asking the simple question that would have decided the matter; no one thought the matter was important enough to decide.

You know what the strange thing about the twelve Cobae was? You probably do. The strange thing about them was that they all looked the same. I mean, *identical*. Not the way that you say all of some ethnic group look the same. I mean that if you photographed the twelve Cobae individually, you could superimpose the pictures by projecting them on a screen, and there wouldn't be the smallest difference among them.

"Clones," said one knowledgeable man. "All grown from the same original donor."

"No," said another expert. "Even if that were the case, they would have developed differently after the cloning. There would be some minor differences."

"A very recent cloning," insisted the first.

"You don't know what you're talking about," said the second. "You're crazy." This typified the kind of discussion that the Cobae instigated among our best minds at the time.

When the Cobae had been around for a day or two, the President signed the orders creating the top-security base in St. Didier Parish, Louisiana. I was shipped down, everyone else on the base was brought in, and for a little while we worked in relative comfort and ignorance. Then the day came when the general and his colonels arrived, with the twelve Cobae right behind. The four black cars drove straight to a barracks that had been in disuse since the installation was opened. The Cobae were put in there, each in its (I get confused about the pronouns) own room. Colonel McNeill was present, and so was I. I thought I was going to throw up. That passed, but not quickly enough. Not nearly.

The general spoke with Colonel McNeill. I couldn't understand their conversation, because it was mostly whispers and nods. One of the colonels asked me if the Cobae would be comfortable in their quarters. I said, "How should *I* know? Sir."

The general overheard us. He looked at the Cobae. "Will you be comfortable here?" he asked.

"Yes," said the Coba who did all the answering.

"Is there anything you'd like now?" asked the general.

"No," said the Coba.

"If at any time you wish anything, anything at all," said the general, "just pick up this telephone." The general demonstrated by picking up the receiver. He neglected to consider that the Cobae would have a difficult time making their wants known, limited to two words, yes and no.

A tough guard was put on the building. The general and the two colonels beat it back to their car and disappeared from the base. I looked at Colonel McNeill, and he looked at me. Neither of us had anything to say. None of this had been discussed with us beforehand, because the matter was so secret it couldn't be trusted either on paper or over normal communications channels. No codes, no scrambling, nothing could be trusted. So the general plopped the twelve Cobae on our doorstep, told us to hang tight, that scientists would arrive shortly to study the beings, and that we were doing a wonderful job.

It was a Thursday, I recall. After we left the building housing the Cobae, I went to the gym building and changed clothes. It was basketball night, Cobae or no Cobae.

I remember once, not long after the Cobae came to Louisiana, when Colonel McNeill asked me to show the aliens around. I said all right. I had gotten over my initial reaction to the Cobae. So had the men on the base. They were used to seeing the Cobae all over the installation. As a matter of fact, we became *too* used to seeing them. I'd be doing something like picking a red Jell-o over a green in the mess line, and there would be a Coba looking over my shoulder. I'd take a shower after a basketball game, and when I walked out of the shower room a Coba would be standing there, watching silently while I dried myself off with a towel. We didn't like it exactly, but we got used to it. Still, it was spooky the way they appeared and disappeared. I never saw one pop in or pop out, yet they did it, I guess.

From the arrival of the Cobae, our base became really supersecure. No passes, no furloughs, no letters out, no telephones. I suppose we all understand, but none of us like it, from Colonel McNeill down to the lower enlisted men. We were told that the country and the world were slowly being prepared to accept the news of a visitation by aliens from space. I followed the careful, steady progression of media releases, prepared in Washington. It was a fairly good job, I suppose, because when the first pictures and television news films of the Cobae were made available, there was little uproar and no general panic. There was a great deal of curiosity, some of it still unsatisfied.

I was starting to tell about this particular time when I was giving a guided tour to the Cobae. I showed them all the wonderful and impressive things about the base, like the high chain link fence with electrified barbed wire on top, and the tall sentry towers with their machine gun emplacements, and the guards at the main gate and their armaments, and the enlisted men going about their duties, cleaning weapons, drilling in the heat, doubletiming from place to place. If I had been a Coba, I think I might have written off Earth right then and there. Back to the ship or whatever, back into the sky, back to the home world.

The twelve Cobae, however, showed no sign of interest or emotion. They showed nothing. You've never seen such nothing. And all the time only the one Coba would speak, and then only when asked a question to which he could reply with either of his two words. He understood everything, of course, but for some reason, for some crazy Coba reason, he wouldn't use the words he understood in his answers.

I took the aliens through the gym building. I got one of the more startling surprises of my life. A game was going on; ten men were playing basketball, full court. It wasn't as rough as a Tuesday/Thursday game, but it was still plenty physical under the boards. I mentioned casually that this was one of the favorite ways of spending off-duty time. The Cobae stood, immobile, and watched. I began to move ahead, ushering them along. They would not move. I had to stay with the Cobae. I didn't see what interested them so much. I sighed. At that time, no one had any idea what a Coba wanted or thought. I say that as if we do now. That just isn't so, even today, though we're closer to an understanding. I had no way of knowing then that the basketball game would be the link between us and these travelers through space.

Anyhow, I was stuck with the Cobae until the game ended. After that, when the players had gone to the showers, I asked if the Cobae wished to see more of the compound. The answerer said, "Yes." I showed them around some more. Nothing else was interesting to them, I guess, because they just passed in front of everything, their expressions blank behind their masks. They never stopped again like they had at the basketball court.

Something about the game fascinated the Cobae. Of course, we've all tried to understand just what. People who in saner days wouldn't be caught dead inside a fieldhouse spent months analyzing basketball like it was a lost ancient art form. The rules of the game have changed a little since its beginning almost a hundred years ago, but the style of play has altered more considerably.

There are different sets of rules, though. You have professional basketball, college ball, high school ball. Minor variations among the different kinds of basketball exist to suit the game to the various levels of competition. Professional, college, high school.

And then you have playground basketball. When basketball was first invented, and during its first few decades of existence, all the players were white. In the professional leagues, this continued longer than on the lower levels. Why? Because of the same reasons that everything else remained white until the black athlete shouldered his way into a kind of competitive position.

For basketball, it was one of the greatest things to happen to the sport. The great pro players were white in the early years. Once blacks were allowed to play against them, the blacks began dominating the game. Bill Russell, Wilt Chamberlain, Kareem Abdul-Jabbar, Julius Erving, and plenty of others have caused a reappraisal of the old strategies.

Why have blacks taken over professional basketball almost entirely? I have a theory. Sure. But it's full of generalizations, and they're as valid as most generalizations. Sort of, you know. Pretty valid, kind of.

Where do these black ballplayers come from? From ghetto neighborhoods, from poor urban and rural communities. Not without exception, of course, but it's a good enough answer. In a ghetto neighborhood, say in New York, there just isn't physical space for baseball diamonds and football fields. There are basketball courts all over, though. They can fit into a smaller space. You can see a basketball rim attached to the side of a building, with groups of kids stuffing the ball into it, again and again.

Take white players. A lot of them come from better backgrounds. A white kid growing up in a town or suburb has a basketball hoop mounted on the garage. He plays by himself, or with a couple of friends.

On the ghetto playgrounds, basketball can be a vicious demonstration of one's identity. Six, eight black guys beneath a basketball backboard can turn the game into something almost indistinguishable from a gang war. Meanwhile the white kids are tossing the ball and catching the rebounds and tossing the ball. The black kids are using every move, every clever head fake, every deceiving twist of the body to show off their superiority. It's the only way many black youths have of asserting themselves.

One good way out of the slums is through sports. Mostly, that means basketball. The kind of basketball you learn on a ghetto court is unlike any other variety of the sport. It's the kind of ball we played on the base. I was out of my class, and I knew it. But I could play well enough so that I wasn't laughed off the floor.

The Tuesday/Thursday games were playground games, played under playground rules. There were no referees to call fouls; there *were* no fouls. It used to be said that basketball was not a contact sport, like football. Yeah. Try playing an hour with guys who came out of Harlem in New York, or Hough in Cleveland, or Watts in Los Angeles. Those guys know just how much punishment they can deliver without being too obvious. Elbows and knees fly. You spend more time lying painfully on the floor than you do in the game. Playground moves, playground rules. Hard basketball. *Mean* basketball.

I played with black enlisted men, mostly. Teams were chosen the same way as on ghetto courts. The people who show up for the game take turns shooting the ball from the free throw line. The first five to put the ball into the net are one team. The next five are the second team. Everyone else watches. Afterward the watchers could go back to their quarters without limping. Few of the players could.

I played often because I practiced my free throws. In off-duty hours I sometimes went to the gym alone and shot free throws for a while. I was good at it. I could sink maybe eight out of ten shots, most of them swishes—when the basketball went cleanly through the hoop without hitting the backboard, without touching the metal rim. All that you would hear was a gentle *snick* as the net below the rim moved.

I was a good shooter. By myself, that is, without another player guarding me, waving his arms, pressing close, without the other players shouting and running. You don't get such an open shot very often during a game. Without fouls, there are no free throws. During a game I was lucky to score ten points.

The games were an hour long, no breaks. That's a lot of

running up and down the court. Even the pros only play forty-eight minutes, resting some of those minutes on the bench, with plenty of time-outs called by the coaches, with breaks for half-time and fouls and free throws and television commercials. We played harder. We felt it. But on those rare occasions when I did something right, it was worth everything I had to take. It was worth it just to hear that *snick*.

There was an unwritten law: we left our ranks in the locker room. I wasn't a captain on the basketball floor. I was a white guy who wanted to play with the black enlisted men. Sometimes I did. After a while, when I showed that I could pretty well hold my own, they grudgingly accepted me, sort of, in a limited way, almost. They gave me a nickname. They called me "the short honkey."

About September the group of scientists had arrived and began their work. It went slowly because only one of the Cobae could be interviewed, and he still said only yes or no.

"Do you come from this part of the galaxy?" asked one man.

"No," said the Coba.

"Do you come from this galaxy at all?"

"No."

The scientist was left speechless. Two thoughts struck him immediately. The Cobae had come a very long way somehow; and it would be very difficult to learn where their home was. All the scientist could do was to run through a list of the identified galaxies until the Coba said yes. And the knowledge would be almost meaningless, because within that galaxy would be millions of stars, none of which could be pinpointed from Earth. The interviewer gave up the attempt. To this day, we don't know exactly where the Cobae came from.

I had, of course, made a report about the reactions of the Cobae to my guided tour, several weeks earlier. One of the demographers thought that the interest the Cobae had shown in the basketball game was worthy of exploration. He proposed that the Cobae be allowed to watch another game.

The game the scientists chose was a Tuesday night bell-ringer. "Bell-ringer" because if you tried to grab the ball away from the strong, agile enlisted men, you got your bell rung. The Cobae were seated in an area out of bounds, along with a team of specialists watching their reactions. Of course, there weren't many reactions. There weren't any at all, while the enlisted men and I shot free throws for teams. I ended up on a pretty good team. I was set for a hard game. The first team, mine, had the ball at the start. I took the ball out of bounds and tossed it to Willy Watkins. He dribbled downcourt and passed the ball to Hilton Foster. Foster was tall and quick. His opponent stretched out both arms, but Foster slithered beneath one arm, got around his opponent, jumped, and shot. The ball banked off the backboard and into the net. We were ahead, two to nothing.

The other team in-bounded and started to take the ball downcourt. I was running to cover my defensive territory, as loose and flexible as it was. We weren't pros. We just chose a man to cover and tried to keep him from scoring. There are lots of interesting ways of doing that, some of them even sanctioned by the rules.

Anyway, as the other team brought the ball down I saw an odd sight. Five of the Cobae had stood up and were walking out onto the basketball court. The scientists had risen out of their chairs. One man turned to the remaining seven Cobae and asked if the five wanted to play. There was silence. The speaker for the group was among the five.

"Do you want to join the game?" I asked the five. I couldn't tell which among them was the speaker.

"Yes," said one Coba. Behind the masks they all looked the same. I couldn't tell which Coba had answered.

"What do I do?" I asked one of the scientists.

"Ask them if they know the rules," said one.

"Do you know and understand how this game is played?" I asked.

"Yes," said the speaker.

I stood there for a while, bewildered.

"Aw, come on," said one of the black men. "Don't let those mothers screw up the game."

"They play," said one of the scientists. The blacks were obviously angry.

"All right," I said, assuming my captain's rank again. "My team against the Cobae. You other guys go sit down." The blacks who had been put out of the game were furious, but they followed my order. I heard a lot of language that the Cobae might not have understood. At least, I hope they didn't understand.

"*His* team. Huh," growled one of the men as he left the court.

"What we goin' to do with these blue bastards?" asked Foster.

"Play them loose," I said. "Maybe they just want to try it for a while. Don't hit any of them."

"Just like my mama was playin'," said Bobby O. Brown.

"Yeah," I said. "Five blue monster mamas."

The scientists were busily talking into their recorders and videotaping what was happening. I gave the ball to Watkins. He took it out and tossed it in to me. I started dribbling, but there was a Coba guarding me. He played close. I glanced over at Watkins, who was running downcourt beside me. He had a Coba guard, too. The Cobae had started in a full-court press.

Where had they learned about a full-court press?

I passed over my Coba's head to Foster. A Coba nearly intercepted the ball. Foster put a good move on his Coba guard, twisted around, and spun back in the other direction. It would have worked against me and a lot of the others on the floor, but he ran into another Coba, who had anticipated Foster's move. Foster hit the Coba hard, but he kept dribbling. The Coba reached out and swiped the ball away from Foster. "Goddamn it," said Foster.

The Coba threw a long pass to another alien downcourt. The second Coba was all alone, and made a nice layup for the first score of the game. The aliens were winning, two to nothing. I couldn't believe it.

The game went on for the entire hour. As it progressed, my team began to play harder and harder. We had to. The Cobae were quick, anticipating moves as if they had played basketball all their lives. Our shots were blocked or our men were prevented from getting near the basket, and we had to settle for long, low-percentage shots. The Cobae were playing with perfect teamwork, though. They had no difficulty finding one of their players open on offense. It didn't make any difference how we defensed them, one player was always maneuvering clear and the Coba with the ball always passed it to the open man (alien). After the first half hour, the Cobae were winning by a score of 48 to 20.

"Break," I called. "Take a rest." The black players walked off the court, muttering. All of them were glaring at me, at the aliens, at the scientists.

Monroe Parks passed near me. I could hear him say, "You can order me around all goddamn day, but don't mess with the game, you ofay son of a bitch." I said nothing.

I changed teams. The other men played the second half. I sat down and watched. The second half was about the same as the first. The Cobae were playing a tight game, perfect defense, amazing offense. They took no chances, but they were always in the right place. The final score was 106 to 52, in favor of the Cobae.

The scientists were just as confused as I was. I didn't care, though, right at the time. I went to the showers. The men showered, too, and none of us said a word. Not a sound. But there were some mean looks directed at me.

The following Thursday the five Cobae came to the gym for the game. The enlisted men started cursing loudly, and I had to order them to stop. Five black men played five Cobae. The Cobae won the game by 60 points.

The next Tuesday, the Cobae won by 48 points.

On Thursday, there wasn't a game, because only the Cobae and I showed up.

I wonder what would have happened if I had suggested to the speaker of the Cobae that I and two of his companions should play the remaining three Cobae.

Even though there were no more games with the Cobae, the scientific team that had come to study the aliens did not stop questioning me. It seemed to them that I was closer to the Cobae than anyone else on the base. I don't know. Against the Cobae, I averaged about 3 points a game. Maybe they should have talked to Foster; he got a pretty regular 10.

Colonel McNeill received regular reports from Washington about how the program to reveal the presence of the aliens on Earth was going. He showed me those reports. I read them, and I was at once amused and concerned. Well, after all, maybe I *did* know the Cobae at least as well as anyone else, including the specialists who had assembled at our installation. The newspaper and television releases grew from hints and rumors to denials and finally a grudging, low-key statement that there were, in fact, a few intelligent visitors from another galaxy in seclusion somewhere in the United States.

The immediate response was not too violent, and the fellows in Washington did a good job regulating the subsequent reactions. The Soviet Union came forward with a claim that they, too, had visitors from beyond Earth. The ruler-for-life of an African nation tried to seize headlines with a related story that didn't make much sense to anyone, and I can't even remember exactly what he said. One of the scientists asked the Cobac if there were any more of them on Earth, in addition to the twelve in our compound. The speaker said no. So if the Soviet Union had their own aliens they were from somewhere else, and we never saw them in any case.

The Cobae showed a preference for remaining in their quarters, once it became evident that the basketball games were postponed indefinitely (read, "as long as the Cobae were around"). The researchers put their data together, argued, discussed, shouted, cursed, and generally behaved like children. Colonel McNeill and I ignored it all from that point on, because we still had a security installation to run. The scientists and researchers were doing their best to bend our regulations whenever it was comfortable for them to try. The colonel and I came down hard on them. I guess they didn't understand us, and we didn't understand them.

So which group of us was better qualified to understand the Cobae?

Nobody, that's who. Finally, though, about the middle of October the nominal head of the investigating team called a meeting, to which Colonel McNeill was invited. I came along, because I was indispensable or something. The meeting began as a series of reports, one by every single professor and investigator in the camp. I can't recall another time when I was so bored. Somehow they managed to make something as awesome as creatures from another world boring. It takes a good deal of skill, many years of training, constant practice, and self-denial to do a job that huge. But boring it was. The colonel was fidgeting before the first man had gone through half of his graphs. He had plotted something against something else, and I wonder where the guy got the information. He had a nice bunch of graphs, though, very impressive, very authoritative-looking. He spoke clearly, he enunciated very well, he was

neatly dressed and well-groomed, and he rarely had to refer to
his notes. Still, I was ready to scream myself before he finished.
I don't remember a thing he was trying to say. In the weeks
that he had to study the Cobae, he apparently didn't come
across a single, solitary interesting fact.

Maybe that wasn't his department, I told myself. So I waited
for the second researcher. He, too, had plenty of visual aids.
He took a pointer and showed how his red line moved steadily
down, while his blue line made a bell-shaped curve. I waited,
but he was every bit as lacking in information as his prede-
cessor.

That's the way that it went for most of the afternoon. I think
that if I had been put in charge of those statisticians and, uh,
alienographers, I might have done a better job. I might be
fooling myself, of course, but I think I would have tried to
learn why the Cobae had come to Earth in the first place. No
one could give us a clue about that. Even with yes-and-no
answers, they should have been able to do that. Am I getting
warm? Yes. No. Am I getting cold?

I think the idea is to start big and narrow down until you
have the Cobae cornered, in an intellectual sense. Ask them if
they came to Earth for a definite purpose. Yes or no. If the
Coba answered no, well, they're all on vacation. If it said yes,
start big again and whittle away until you learn something.

But evidently that's not the way our men and women of the
study team worked. A large report was published eventually,
excerpts appeared in newspapers and magazines, but not many
people were satisfied. I'd still like to take my crack at the
Cobae, my way. But I can't.

So, in any event, investigator after researcher after pedant
after lecturer had his say. I got up after half an hour and went
to the back of the room, where two enlisted men were setting
up a film projector. Both men were black. One was a regular
basketball player I knew, Kennedy Turner, and the other's
name I don't recall. I watched them threading the film; it was
only slightly less boring than listening to the presentations. I
noticed that right beside me was Colonel McNeill. He, too,
was watching Turner thread film. After the film was wound
into the machine, the two men turned to a slide projector.

"You want to kill the lights, please?" said the woman on
the platform. Turner hastened to turn off the lights. "Roll that
first reel, please," said the woman. The other enlisted man

flicked a switch. I watched a few seconds of a basketball game. I saw myself embarrassed by the play of a short alien. "It seems to me, gentlemen," said the woman, "that these Cobae are governed by a single mind. I don't know how I can make the idea clearer. Perhaps the mind belongs to the Coba who always answers. But the visual input, *all* the sensory input of the twelve Cobae is correlated and examined by the central mind. That was what made the Cobac so effective in this game, although we know through our questioning that they had never seen anything similar before."

"A single governing mind?" asked a man seated in the audience.

"Yes," said the woman, "capable of overseeing everything that is happening to all twelve units of the Cobae multi-personality. The basketball game here is a perfect example. Watch. See how every human move is anticipated, even by Cobae players on the opposite side of the court. One mind is observing everything, hovering above, so to speak, and decisions and commands are addressed to the individual Cobae to deal with any eventuality."

(I'm editing this from memory, of course. We didn't know they were called Cobae until much later. We just called them beings or creatures or aliens or blue men or something like that.)

"I'd like to ask a question, if I may—"

The man was interrupted by the lights going on again.

"Not yet, please," said the woman. She stopped speaking and gasped. Everyone turned around. The twelve Cobae were in the back of the room.

The Coba speaker stepped forward. "Now you honkey chumps better dig what's going down," he said. "We got to tighten up around here, we got to get down to it. You dig where I'm coming from?"

I looked at Turner and his black companion. They were laughing so hard they could barely stand. Turner held out his hands, palms up, and the other man slapped them. Turner slapped his friend's hands. They were suddenly having a real good time.

I turned to Colonel McNeill. Everyone in the room was speechless. There was a long pause. Then the colonel whispered to me. "Uh, oh," was all he said.

*There will be a few people who would object to my including
The Exempt in this collection, on the grounds that running
isn't a sport or a game. The word "sport" seems to imply some
kind of competition. "Game" signifies play. Anyone who has
managed at least a quarter mile nonstop knows that play doesn't
enter into the matter at all. Pain, yes. Play, not a chance.*

*Other people would be quick to point out that the competition
is with one's self. These are the same folk who cling to the
delusion that the anguish of running is somehow beneficial for
the body. Two hundred years ago they would have applied
leeches for a headache.*

*When this story first appeared, some readers asked me about
the significance of the title. I do not recall what my answer
was at that time.*

The Exempt

BRIEFLY: A man whose name had been Hoyt Schermerhorn, in a sudden but intense fit of unhappiness, bought a round-trip ticket from New York City to New Orleans, flew down on Monday, got a newspaper from the day before, checked through the classified section, looked at eight apartments-for-rent, chose one, spent the night in a motel in the French Quarter, and flew home Tuesday afternoon. He told his wife, Suzy, to quit her job, which she did the next day. The representative from the Mayflower Van Lines Company gave them an estimate of costs to move their furniture to New Orleans; this was on Friday. The van came three hours late the following Wednesday. Schermerhorn and his wife watched their belongings disappear into the truck. Afterward, they packed their cat into a cardboard container and went to the airport. Seven hours later, near midnight, they arrived at their new home. The apartment would be empty of furniture for another four days. The landlord had left a mattress and a pillow on the carpeted floor for their use. The cat, released from the airline's cardboard carrier, cowered in the bare corners.

Schermerhorn was still vaguely unhappy, but he knew what he had to do in order to fix things. After the weekend he went about changing his name. He had prepared a list of names which he thought suitable and attractive. They were: Steven Ernest Weinraub, Sandor Courane, Billy Dean Glick, Robert Wayne Hanson, Justin Benarcek, S. Norman Moore, Bo Staefler, Rod Marquand, Robert L. Jennings. He showed the list to Suzy and asked her to choose. She decided quickly. She thought she would most like to be married to Robert Wayne Hanson. "There must be a lot of Bob Hansons around," she said. "That's an advantage, if ever you need one."

On Tuesday the landlord visited them. The furniture had been due to arrive, but hadn't. The landlord let them keep the mattress and pillow another night. As Hanson held the cat, a large gray Maine coon named Fish, the landlord opened the front door to let himself out. "Look out," said Hanson, trying to hold the twisting, squirming cat; Fish broke Hanson's grasp and ran for the door. Hanson put his foot in front of Fish, but it didn't do any good. The cat just lightly jumped over.

"It's all right," said the landlord. "She can't go anywhere in the hallway, anyhow."

"He," said Suzy.

"What?" said the landlord.

"Fish is a male," said Hanson.

"Here are your alternates," said the landlord, trying to give Hanson a spiral-bound notebook he had been carrying.

"What?" asked Hanson.

"Your alternates. You'll see. This apartment has some very nice ones. Most of them have a pool, a couple with built-in washer-drier. All of them have central air conditioning, except maybe fifteen or twenty toward the beginning. You know. There are always a bunch that really aren't good for anything. You got hand-sponged ceilings mostly, Japanese corkboard in the bathroom, a sunken tub, whatever you want within reason."

Suzy brought Fish back into the apartment and tossed him back toward the living room. The cat crept close to the doorway again. "I still don't know what you mean," said Hanson.

The landlord looked annoyed. "Where did you move from?" he asked.

"New York," said Hanson. "Brooklyn."

"Oh, hell," said the landlord. He looked disgusted now.

"And nobody's told you about your alternates? Well, damn it, I'm sick and tired of having to do it. The hell with it. Let somebody else do it, just this once. You're getting a phone, aren't you? Well, let the phone man explain it to you. Here. Call me if you need anything." He left Hanson with the notebook, with a bewildered expression on his face, and the suspicion that Hanson had bought his way into a madhouse. The landlord went out into the hallway and turned right, toward the elevator. Hanson and Suzy followed, turning left, toward Fish, who had taken the opportunity to flash by them.

"That's a relief," said Suzy.

"That's a relief," said her husband.

The next morning, Wednesday, their doorbell rang. Hoping that it was the van with their furniture, or, rather, the driver of the van, Suzy ran to the intercom. It took her a moment to figure out how to use it. "Who is it?" she asked.

"Phone company," said the intercom.

"All right," said Suzy. "Just a minute." She pushed the button which sounded a buzzer downstairs and unlocked the elevator door. Several seconds later, the doorbell rang again. "Who is it?" asked Suzy.

"Phone company," said the intercom. "You'll have to let me in. The elevator door won't open."

"I'll press the buzzer again."

A moment later: "No, ma'am. It won't open."

"Did the light stay on?"

"Which light?"

"The light on the elevator button," said Suzy.

"It's on now," said the phone company person.

"See, it's not there yet. You have to wait until the elevator gets there. Then the light will go off. Then you have to press the doorbell again. Then I'll buzz again. Then you can get in."

"Right," said the intercom. "The light's off." Suzy sounded the buzzer. A short while later, the man knocked on the Hansons' door.

"Phone company," he said. "For a while, it looked like you people were going to have to make do with nonverbal communication."

"What?" said Hanson.

"Nothing," said the man. "Where do you want your phone?"

"Where the other people had it, I guess," said Suzy.

"I'm supposed to talk to you about this," said Hanson, handing the phone company representative the spiral notebook left by the landlord the previous day.

The man glanced through the notebook. "These are your alternates, Cap." He looked up, stared at Hanson first, then at Mrs. Hanson. "I get it. You never lived in New Orleans before?" Both Hansons shook their heads. "For crying out loud," said the phone man. "I'm getting tired of doing this all the time. Why didn't your landlord explain it?"

"You can do it while you're installing the phone, if you don't mind," said Hanson.

"I wish I could offer you some coffee," said Suzy. "Our dishes haven't gotten here yet, and I don't have a thing in the house to give you."

"Why don't you run across the street and get some cold beer," said Hanson.

"That would be really fine," said the phone company man. He was on his hands and knees in the living room. Hanson sat down against a wall and watched the man work. Suzy went into the bedroom where she had left her keys and money. Fish just lay where he had been, posing bored and regal. "First, you have to understand that we don't tell anybody about these alternates unless they live here. It's not like we're trying to keep it a secret or nothing. It's just that, well, I mean, it's *our* city. If your landlord hadn't figured you to be all right, he wouldn't even have given you the notebook. You're New Orleanians now, and you're entitled to it."

"I'm quietly proud," said Hanson. Suzy came out of the bedroom and was leaving to go to the store. "Hurry back," called her husband. She just turned and smiled.

"First off," said the phone company man, "you got to understand that the city of New Orleans is the entropic center of this world at least, maybe the universe. All around the city, things are in a constant condition of flux. Things tend toward their primal chaotic state."

"I thought that had something to do with this being the Deep South," said Hanson.

"No, it goes beyond that. And the center of the center, to move quickly to the heart of the matter, the absolute exclamation point of possibility, is located in the French Quarter."

"That kind of figures," said Hanson. "We went down there

the night before last. Down to Bourbon Street. There wasn't nobody else down there but tourists and naked ladies on stage. We had a good supper at some restaurant. Nice place, but I can't remember where it was."

"Naked ladies will do that to you sometimes," said the phone company man. "Fortunately for us, the alternate center isn't on Bourbon Street." The man laughed. "Man, if it was, this city would *really* be something else. I think the reason Bourbon Street is as much like Bourbon Street is because the alternate center is as close to it as it is. If the center were, say, like in the Gunga Den on Bourbon Street, then Royal and Dauphine Streets would be like Bourbon Street is now, and Bourbon Street would be like I don't know what."

"What are you talking about?" said Hanson.

"The alternate center is on Royal Street, one block on the Mississippi River-side of Bourbon, between Canal Street and Iberville. It's inside Penny Land, a pinball and amusement place. You go in the front, turn right, walk over toward the wall. You'll see a row of pinball machines. Nearer the front of Penny Land is one of these booths where you go in and make a little record of your voice, you know? That's it."

"I don't know exactly what I was hoping for."

"You go into the record machine booth, pull the door shut, and punch the button for whatever alternate you want."

"I don't get it," said Hanson. Fish had come over and was nipping the phone company man's ankles, so Hanson picked the cat up and tossed him into the bedroom, then shut the door.

"Look, let me have that notebook. Here, see? Say you want Alternate Number 216. That's 'Small pool in the back, laundromat downstairs, central air conditioning in apartment, dishwasher, carpets stained irrevocably, large holes in the walls behind doors, unusual frequency of burnt-out light bulbs.' You know where these record machines have coin-return buttons?"

"I can find one if I have to."

"Fine. You hit that twice, then once, then six times. Number 216. When you get home, your apartment will be just like it says. It's almost like that now, except that you don't have the dishwasher, and you have an extra bedroom that Number 216 doesn't have. There are a lot of options. Some of them go beyond your apartment, you know. You can't ask for universal brotherhood or anything, but in some expensive neighborhoods and homes I've seen, you can kind of influence things like college football punt returns. Just read the notebook. You can change alternates whenever you want."

"Won't that confuse the neighbors?" asked Hanson.

Mrs. Hanson unlocked the front door and let herself in. "Hi, I'm back," she said. "Here's your beer." She carried a can into the living room and gave it to the phone man.

"No," said the man, "you're not changing the world. You're moving yourself from one to another. You have to be careful, though. If you punch a wrong number, sometimes you can end up in an alternate that doesn't have other alternates, or anyway no gate through to them, and you'll be stuck there."

"Has he explained about alternates, Bob?" asked Suzy.

"Yes," said Hanson.

"And your phone's in, too," said the phone company man. "Thanks for the beer. Study your notebook. You have some good alternates to choose from in there. Better than I have at home in Kenner. See you." Hanson walked with the phone company man to the door, and thanked him for all his help.

"That's a relief," said Suzy when the man had gone.

"That's a relief," said her husband. "Where's the notebook?"

After a while, during which both Hanson and his wife examined the alternates available to them—a joyful experience, very much like browsing at the age of eight through the Christmas catalog from Sears—the couple decided to take the St. Charles streetcar down to the French Quarter. Hanson mentioned the possibility of strolling along Bourbon Street again, but Suzy said that she had seen enough naked ladies on stages to last her quite some time. She suggested that they walk over by the river at Jackson Square, but her husband said that they might run into a degenerate, and after all, wasn't that why they had left Brooklyn? "There are degenerates on Bourbon Street, too," said Suzy.

"If we have to put up with drunks," said Hanson with a smile, "there's a better class of degenerate on Bourbon Street. We might as well have them with neckties."

"For sure," said Suzy. They laughed. They both knew that their real purpose was to explore the center of alternity in Penny Land on Royal Street. Afterward, no doubt, they would walk slowly by the strip shows on Bourbon Street, and toward Jackson Square and the river. Hanson and Suzy got along very well.

While Mrs. Hanson was in the bathroom, her husband leaned against a wall in the living room, waiting. The green carpet had already picked up tufts of fur from Fish, the conspicuous Maine coon. Gray fur from his back and white fur from his belly were the only decorations the apartment had. The gray fur looked like swiftly moving clouds threatening rain, rolling over the spring-green corn of Iowa. The white fur looked like frothy whitecaps on the wind-whipped green tea ocean of Japan. Hanson was content with these images, but when he tried to repeat them to his wife he failed. Instead he checked to make sure he had his keys, and they left the apartment to go downtown.

All these things Hanson recalled as he ran in the dark.

It was several months later, almost winter technically speaking, near the middle of November. He was quite a different man than the Hoyt Schermerhorn who had decided so abruptly to leave New York. Suzy had changed, and so had Fish. The alterations in their personalities were subtle and not yet finished. They never would be complete, so long as they lived in New Orleans.

"It's those alternates," thought Hanson. He was running two miles around the golf course in Audubon Park. It was about nine o'clock in the evening, and the park was deserted except for occasional cars parked off the narrow roadway, under the great, stretching, Spanish moss-tangled limbs of the dark trees. Hanson had just begun his nightly run, near the fountain and the unreadable floral clock at the entrance to the park fronting St. Charles Avenue. He made the first turn, running now with his back to the avenue, down the long straight road toward Magazine Street, with the shadowy open spaces of the golf course ahead of him. Most of the golf course would be on his left, a wide, empty area spattered with lonely trees. On his right was a narrow margin which was still part of the golf course, but which at that time of night was appropriated by parked lovers. Hanson saw the starlight and the bright coin of the moon reflected in the pond as he ran by, and the familiar artificial waterfall a bit farther on. Every night he thought the same thing at this point: "Good Lord, I have so much farther to go."

After a little while his breath began to come painfully. His chest hurt as if something in it had been torn and bloodied by the cool air and the exercise. He wheezed as he ran, and he tried to persuade himself to stop, to walk for a while and catch his breath. He had the same battle every night, and only the change in personality that he had gone through because of the record-making machine in Penny Land kept him going. That, and the god on his shoulder.

In the abandoned darkness Hanson looked at the stars. He loved the night sky. There were so many more stars to be seen here, in New Orleans, than there had been in Brooklyn. He had lived in New York off and on for almost five years, and most of those years had gone by without a single glimpse of some of his favorite constellations. The light in the city, the thick, man-made matter in the air, even his dislike of going out after dark in New York City prevented him. But in New Orleans things were different. They were *more* different about every day and a half, whenever Hanson or his wife visited Penny Land.

After he had run a fifth of the way down the straight section of the road, Hanson recognized his favorite constellation, Orion. The hunter lay on his back, just above a group of ancient trees, as if Orion had decided to nap a while before getting on with the labor of the evening. "It's beautiful," thought Hanson. "Nothing blocks my view of these stars. It's very wonderful. Especially when you consider how far away they are. When you think that some of these stars are trillions of miles away, if not farther, doesn't it seem unlikely that *nothing* has gotten between them and my eyes? Nothing at all, in all that distance? Good old Orion. Good old Orion's crooked belt, and the middle star." This star was Hanson's lucky star and also Suzy's, a factor they had in common which had kept them together when they had first met. "It's so clear," thought Hanson, "I can see Orion's sword. I never saw that in Brooklyn. And old Taurus looks like he's pinning Orion down, leaning on his chest."

It was the middle of November, but the temperature was still in the fifties at night. During the day it was in the upper sixties. Hanson and his wife often remarked happily about the climate, which they adored. Alternate number 154 would keep the weather about ten degrees warmer, but it would mean that their apartment wouldn't have a bathtub, a shower only. The Hansons agreed that if the winter should become unseasonably cold, it might be worth doing without the bathtub, and going down to Penny Land to punch number 154. It was an option open to them.

Hanson's chest hurt even more. The god on his shoulder tried to persuade him to stop. "You can skip a day," said the god, Hermes. "You ran a great two miles yesterday, didn't you? There's no sense in busting your back. Nobody's watching you."

"I want to run this course every night," said Hanson, puffing loudly. "Every night I can, unless something comes up. My legs were in terrible shape."

"Sure," said Hermes, crouched on Hanson's shoulder, small, like a toad at Hanson's ear. "But you ran so hard last night that you're still tired. You are tired, aren't you?"

"Yeah," said Hanson.

"You feel like stopping, don't you?"

"Yeah."

"You going to stop?"

"No."

Hermes sat down. The god had been holding Hanson's ear, but now he moved away and swung his legs over Hanson's shoulder. "See if I care," said Hermes petulantly. Hanson said nothing in reply.

Hermes had been part of the collection of details that belonged with Alternate number 867: two bedrooms, extra closet space, pool, laundromat in the building, quiet neighbors, low rent, convenience to several good restaurants within walking distance, movie theater twelve blocks from apartment building, personal relationships with several gods from the myths of classical antiquity, desire on the part of tenants to keep their bodies in optimum physical condition. Number 867 had many of the benefits that Hanson and his wife considered most desirable, at least among those available to them in the notebook. The only disquieting factor was the interference of the gods. But if that ever got too unpleasant, Hanson or Suzy could ride downtown and punch another alternate.

"You're different tonight," said Hermes a while later, as Hanson reached the halfway point on the first straightaway. This was about a third of a mile from the starting line.

"I'm always different," said Hanson, his legs beginning to ache. He wondered if tonight, after so many successful nights, he would be unable to finish the course. "I've noticed the changes for many weeks now."

"It's the alternates," said Hermes.

"Damn it," said Hanson, "I know that. I don't care."

"You don't care that you keep changing bodies and minds? Don't you wonder what the original you is doing these days?"

"I *am* the original me," said Hanson. "I'm not changing like that. It's the alternate worlds that are changing, every time I go into that record-making machine. The same me, the same Suzy, carry over from one alternate to the next. It's just that the process of choosing affects our personalities a little."

"I'd be afraid of where that kind of thing would lead," said Hermes.

"That would be *your* problem," said Hanson. "You could take a few fingers of Wild Turkey for a thing like that."

"Are you happier now?"

"Sure," said Hanson. "Of course."

"Are you really happier?"

"Sure," said Hanson. "Of course."

"You don't look happier," said Hermes. "You didn't look too happy before. That's why you changed your name. That's why you moved down here. You weren't really satisfied at all. I don't think, in all truthfulness, that you're the least tiny bit happier, after all that."

"I don't especially care what you think," said Hanson. A flag on a pole on the green of one of the golf course's holes waved at him, beckoning limply like Ahab's arm.

"You ought to care," said Hermes. "I'm a god."

"How can I take you seriously?" asked Hanson. "You're sitting on my shoulder, for the love of God."

"You'd be surprised what I can do from here."

Hanson didn't say anything. He was getting very tired, and he hadn't even gotten to the end of the straight section yet. He hadn't finished nearly half his run.

"I know what you need," said Hermes, laughing softly. "You need a mistress."

"I don't want a mistress," said Hanson.

"You want a mistress. Everybody wants a mistress."

"Suzy and I are very happy."

"How happy?"

Hanson sighed. "Look," he said, "the only thing we've disagreed on in a long time is the Rose Bowl a couple of years ago. I just couldn't get her to cheer for Ohio State. I sat there rooting for Ohio State, and she rooted for USC. I couldn't reason with her."

"How about ice hockey?"

"Well," said Hanson sadly, "you're right. Okay. I hate hockey, and she always watches it. But that's not very serious, is it? I mean, if that's the only crisis in our marriage?"

"You *need* a mistress."

"Suzy would never let me have one."

Hermes slapped his hand on the back of Hanson's neck. "Good grief," he shouted. The little god stood up and began pacing on Hanson's slowly jogging shoulder. "You do not consult with your wife about the choosing of a mistress, like you were deciding on a high-speed blender or something. Listen, I don't know if I can euphemize as well as you two. I mean, you guys are the Euphemism King and Queen of the sunny southland. You say, 'Suzy, there's something I want to talk to you about.' She says, 'Okay, Bob.' You say, 'There are certain things I consider important, and which you don't see as being as necessary to me as they are.' And then she says, 'And there are certain things I've always thought important to me, and which I've learned to live without to avoid making you unhappy.' And that's where you always give up. Because she's been so brave. How often do you have that pitiful battle, that amputated debate?"

"Every couple of months."

"Every couple of months," said Hermes scornfully. "And you been together, what?, going on seven years, right? Yeah. And every couple of months you have that same stupid scene. In all that time has Suzy ever heard, in specific and unambiguous language, just what 'certain things' you're talking about?"

"No," said Hanson. "She knows what I mean, though. I've made it pretty obvious."

"And have you ever found out just what she's foresworn for your peace of mind?"

"No," said Hanson, "and I don't want to know."

"You need a mistress."

"I got so much farther to run, why don't you just shut up for a while? I got so much farther. My God, I'm tired."

A cool breeze brushed Hanson's face from the river beyond the park. He knew that the breeze should be refreshing, and he was disappointed when he wasn't, in fact, refreshed. His arms were tired. They felt as if he had carried suitcases full of telephone books through the entire extent of the Superdome, from level to level, section to section. He let his arms fall and he shook his hands, but that didn't help very much. Hanson's legs were in better shape than before he began his running routine, and his lung capacity had increased. But his arms ached, constantly reminding him that his body was not entirely happy with the way it was being used.

"Whose idea was this?" asked Hermes. "This running. Who told you it was any damn good at all for you?"

"I don't know," said Hanson.

"I'll bet it was the vitamin C maniacs. You can't believe everything you read, you know. You ain't halfway yet. A little more, and you'll only be halfway."

"What are you trying to do?"

Hermes sat down again, swinging his legs and thumping his incredibly tiny heels against Hanson's collarbone. "I'm trying to steal your contentment. We gods aren't very contented. Just because we're gods doesn't mean anything. In the *Iliad*, do we sound very contented? In the *Odyssey?*"

"No, you don't."

"You could get for yourself something even the gods can't get. You could be contented."

"I am."

"You're not. But you could be."

"How?" asked Hanson, gasping loudly, running past the midway point on the short Magazine Street side of the rectangle.

"You've got a couple of hundred alternates, right? None of them overwhelmingly wonderful. You have to pay a lot more rent for those luxuries. But you could experiment. Punch for alternates you don't have listed. Visit them at random until you find one where, ah, conditions are better."

"Suzy comes with me, remember? I don't get a new Suzy with every alternate."

"You change a little every time, Suzy changes a little every time. Even Fish changes some. Who knows where you're headed? Godhood, maybe." Hermes laughed, a high-pitched giggle.

Before he turned his back on Orion, before reentering the park on the homeward leg, Hanson looked at the constellation. It had moved slightly on its own patch across the sky, and the change in perspective had lifted Orion up off the tops of the trees. It seemed to Hanson that the ancient hunter was slowly, slowly pushing the bull backward, making that gigantic beast give ground. Orion was forcing his indomitable will on that symbol of oppression, that symbol of pure, bestial power, irresponsible power, and of animal lusts. The stars themselves refuted Hermes' sophistry. "Look," said Hanson, panting, "the stars themselves—"

"I could cite other examples among the constellations to prove precisely the opposite," said Hermes. "And I could easily lift new constellations into the sky where adequate proof was lacking. How would you feel about spending eternity gesturing stiffly as a group of six, maybe seven white dots on a black background? It would be easy enough to arrange."

"'The constellation of Hanson,'" said Hanson. "It doesn't have quite the right sound."

"'The constellation of Schermerhorn' doesn't improve it much," said Hermes.

There was water on Hanson's left as he ran back toward St. Charles Avenue, toward the entrance to the park. A long, dark lagoon ran down the side of the golf course, which could still be seen dimly across the islands in the water. Among the trees on the islands Hanson saw small white forms, mostly stationary, some moving slowly. They were ducks which slept on the grassy earth beneath the huge live oaks. On his right was a pleasant area, broken up occasionally by a few small stands of trees. Cars were parked off the side of the road on both sides. No one was visible in any of the cars. Hanson smiled to himself.

"I got alternates, too," said Hermes, yawning. "I can give you better alternates than Penny Land."

"Why would you?" asked Hanson. He did not feel as tired as he did before. He always felt better once he turned the corner and began the last straightaway.

"I don't know," said the god. "It would put you in my debt. You're funny, Hanson. I don't know."

"Could you give me, say, a better view and free utilities?"

"I could give you good stuff, Hanson. The free utilities you can find for yourself. Look."

Hanson looked where Hermes was pointing, to the right, into the dark region of grass. A small area was lit, as if by portable floodlights. The place looked like a stage set, like the Shakespeare-In-The-Park stage in Central Park, back when he had been Hoyt Schermerhorn. The stage set looked like their old apartment in Brooklyn. Hanson slowed his running; he could hear his own voice coming from the little bright place on the grass. He could hear Suzy's voice. As he got closer, he saw that they were both sitting on their old couch, which they had left in the Brooklyn apartment, rather than move it down to New Orleans. "Here's what I'm going to do, Suzy," said the other Schermerhorn.

"What, Hoyt?" asked Suzy. Hanson could already remember the conversation as it had taken place a few months before.

"I decided that we ought to move to New Orleans."

"Why?" asked Suzy, naturally startled. "Aren't you happy here?"

"No," said Schermerhorn. "I'm vaguely unhappy. And after we move, I think I'll change our name, too. I've made up a tentative list of names I think suitable and attractive."

"That might be fun," said Suzy.

"I'm glad you feel that way," said Schermerhorn. "I'm sure glad hockey season is over with." The lights in the area faded as Hanson ran past. He looked over his shoulder, but there was nothing in the park but grass, trees shrouded with Spanish moss, and a few bald spots on the ground.

"That really happened, of course," said Hermes.

"Sure," said Hanson. "I remember it."

"I wanted to make sure that you did. I can let you have anything you've ever had before, anything you might be nostalgic for. Nobody's rich enough to afford alternates that can do that for them. But I like you, Hanson. I just wanted you to know that."

"I appreciate it."

"How come Suzy took to changing your name so fast?"

"Oh, she knew that it wasn't the first time I changed my name. I've done it before."

"What was it before Hoyt Schermerhorn?"

"It's on the list I made. Suzy didn't know which one, but I thought I'd give her a chance to pick it. Then I'd know that my original name was the right one for me, after all."

"Did she?"

"Yeah."

"You look like a Bob Hanson," said Hermes. "There must be a million of them around."

Another area of the park lit up, ahead of Hanson. It was the inside of a bar. "What's that?" asked Hanson. "I don't recognize that."

"That's something you haven't had yet," said the tiny god, standing again and holding tight to Hanson's earlobe. "It's a bar in the French Quarter."

"That's me there. And Suzy."

"Well," said Hermes, "let me explain. That woman's name is Suzy, all right, and she looks remarkably like your wife, but she isn't. She's a stranger. A coincidence. I can make one of those anytime you want."

"So," said the other Hanson in the bar scene, "what's happening?"

The pseudo-Suzy looked up slowly and smiled. "Anything you want," she said in a low voice. She slid her hand along the bar and touched Hanson's fingers.

"Well, uh, can I buy you a drink?"

Suzy didn't say a word. She lifted Hanson's hand and kissed his fingers. She put one of his fingers in her mouth.

"That's enough," said the real Hanson to Hermes.

"Quiet," said the god. "Watch the show."

The mock Hanson seemed agitated. "You wouldn't want to go somewhere else, would you?" he asked.

Suzy just looked at him. After a moment she slowly pulled the finger from her mouth. "Where did you have in mind?" she asked.

"I could walk you home," he said. "We could take a cab."

Suzy smiled and shook her head. "I have a boyfriend at home," she said. "He wouldn't appreciate you."

Hanson frowned. "I have a wife at home, too."

Suzy laughed and stood up. The lights faded. Hanson looked back, but again he could see nothing. He was about halfway along the last stretch. He was nearly finished with his run.

"You can't get that nohow, pushing buttons in Penny Land," said Hermes.

"If I go downtown now," said Hanson thoughtfully, "I could push for Number 512. That's built-in home entertainment center, speakers in every room, built-in microwave oven, cut pile carpeting, and a bowling alley where the parochial school is on Napoleon. Also, of course, no mythical personalities bothering me."

"You have to go downtown," said Hermes. "You have to have exact change."

"I'll give them the extra fifteen cents."

"I can't believe how unhappy you are, Hanson. Man, are

you unsatisfied."

"Tempt me, tempt me," said Hanson, laughing hoarsely. "I love it."

"You're also tired," said Hermes. "Don't kid me. You're incredibly tired."

"You may also note how I only have a little farther to run. I am incredibly tired. I am also nearly finished."

"I'm glad *you* said that, not me. Do you know how this would end up, if this were a contemporary novel? If this were a seriously intended art film?"

"Yes, indeed, guide of the dead. With a poignant final scene. Sit down. My ears are stinging. It's cold."

"Sorry. Yeah, with a poignant final scene. You know what? I'd win you over, that's what. Not loudly. No Faustian sky-splitting, earth-shaking, fires of Hell. No, if this were, say, any of your regular books or movies, you'd just think about that last vignette, see, with that other Suzy in the bar. Maybe you'd mutter to yourself a little, you'd look back again and again, hoping to catch another glimpse of her. You'd run right by the exit, you'd keep running, right around the first turn, Orion would be over your head a bit higher in the sky, the first flag on the golf course would be flapping in the wind, urging you on, I'd be dancing on your shoulder, laughing. The picture would fade out with you running, running with me, around again forever. Very symbolic. Cut to black, then end titles. It could be done just as well on the printed page."

"Sure," said Hanson. "Here we are." He turned into the exit lane and jogged past the fountain. There were two cherubic boys sitting on turtles on either side. In the middle was a tall woman, naked from the waist up, with a bird and a duck. It didn't make any sense. Hanson ran by it and, like every night, tried to figure what it might represent. Perhaps somewhere there was an alternate with a fountain that wasn't so ridiculous.

"You're very unhappy, Hanson," said Hermes.

"So what?"

"You're dissatisfied."

"I just ran two miles," said Hanson. "Could you run two miles?"

"You're different. You've really changed."

"I know that. I told you so."

"You're still changing. You can't stop it now. You're just going to change, Hanson."

"That's a relief," said Hanson, stopping on the sidewalk, waiting for the traffic to let him cross to the streetcar tracks.

"Yeah, that's a relief," said Hermes angrily. He jumped down from Hanson's shoulder. Hanson turned and watched the tiny god stalking back into the black expanse of Audubon Park.

There are two kinds of story that are most likely to intrigue me, both as a reader and as an author. The first is the story of obsession; Moby Dick, for example, or The Count of Monte Cristo. A character with such an idée fixe can be so fascinating that he can lead me through whole chapters of duller material, for the sake of another glimpse of the working of his anguished mind.

The second story line that most often produces powerful narratives is the account of great loss. Some analysts explain that any story about people who have suffered an irrevocable loss has its basis in our subconscious desire to return to the security and peace of our prenatal life. Therefore everything from the expulsion of Adam and Eve from the garden of Eden to the typical science fiction story of life after a nuclear holocaust is mere symbol for the trauma of birth.

That should neatly explain 25 Crunch Split Right on Two, except that I don't buy it. This story is about football, but more importantly it is about a man who finds a way to recover his great loss. An expensive way.

25 Crunch Split Right on Two

ELDON MACDAY, No. 23, 6 foot 1, 225 pounds, a running back from Arizona State, realized where he was. It was a frightening discovery not merely because he was sitting at a round table in the dim private dining room in a restaurant in Euclid, Ohio. And not merely because he ought to be, really *should* be lying face down in the odd-smelling artificial turf in the new McGuire Coliseum in Cleveland, beneath a defensive end and an outside linebacker. That didn't upset him much, either; after all, the restaurant was a great deal more restful. The detail that really tore at MacDay's composure was his wife's presence at the table. His wife, Louvina. His wife, who had died over five years before. She was eating a steak, supposedly a strip sirloin, and he could tell that it was excessively rare, just the way she always ate them. He could see the wine-red juice pooling up around the meat on her plate.

"That ain't no real strip sirloin, Lou," he said.

"I know," she said, smiling. "I don't specially care."

"Just so's you like it," he said.

"I like it fine."

"All right." MacDay was getting more frightened. He wasn't supposed to be in their favorite old restaurant. He wasn't supposed to be in Euclid at all. But even worse, Louvina wasn't supposed to be *anywhere*.

"You sure you don't want some wine, honey?" he asked.

Louvina just smiled again. He hadn't seen that smile in five years, but it still made him feel the same way. MacDay shuddered. The waiter came to the table and asked if everything were all right; MacDay knew just what the man was going to say. He knew, without looking, that the waiter's shirt would be hanging out behind. MacDay stared at the tablecloth, but after a few seconds, though still afraid, he looked up. The waiter was walking slowly away. His shirt was just the way MacDay remembered.

"Are you feeling all right, Eldon?" asked Louvina. MacDay recalled that, too. The first time, though, five years ago, he hadn't known why she had asked it.

"I'm fine," he said softly. He knew that the next thing she'd say would be, "Why aren't you eating?"

"Why aren't you eating? Don't you like the steak?"

"It's all right, Lou," he said. "I just ain't hungry."

"But this is a celebration, baby," said Louvina. She paused, a forkful of baked potato, sour cream, and chives held in abeyance while she looked at him almost shyly. "You know what we be doing tonight, Eldon?"

MacDay looked startled. He stared at his wife; her expression changed to bewilderment. MacDay *knew* what they were going to do that night. He *knew*.

And just as he opened his mouth to reply, he was hit by the Comets' middle linebacker, a rookie subbing for the regular who had been hurt early in the second quarter. MacDay had been kneeling in the artificial grass, one of the Comet defensive players hanging onto MacDay's ankles, another Comet player sprawled across his back. MacDay's mind cleared slowly; first, he felt the sharp point of the football jammed into his forearm near the elbow; then he felt the cold string of the Cleveland winter air, a contrast from the controlled temperature of the restaurant. He opened his eyes, and the difference in light from the shadowy dining room made his head hurt. Then he felt the lingering shocks of the tackle, he heard the fading sound of the official's whistle, the voices of his teammates and the Comet players, then the background moan of the sixty thousand people in the stadium. He heard the voice of the Browns' quarterback, Tom Bailess, shouting, "Late hit! Late hit!" and the officials disagreeing. The Comet players got to their feet and walked toward their defensive huddle. MacDay opened his eyes wide and shook his head, then stood up and trotted to the Browns' huddle.

"All right," said Bailess, "second and seven. You all right, Mac?"

MacDay nodded. He felt a little bewildered, but you can't explain something like that to a head coach like Jennings.

"Okay," said the quarterback. "Thirty-eight Sweep split right. On three. Break!" The Browns' offensive team clapped once in unison and went into formation. MacDay was glad his running mate, Sonny Staley, the small halfback from Colgate, was getting the ball; Bailess could probably see that MacDay had been shaken up a little on the last play. MacDay was getting a rest, if he could accept blocking the Comets' 260-pound defensive end as a breather.

There was little time to think about the strange vision he had had only a matter of seconds ago. Already it was beginning to vanish, to fade in his memory. It had been only the collision, MacDay told himself; his head had hit one of the Comets, or the ground. He had been knocked out for a second or two. Now, though, while he watched Bailess set up under the center, he had too much to think about. The quarterback, seeing the other team's defensive alignment, might decide to change the play at the last moment. MacDay listened closely to the signals; Bailess followed the Browns' digit system, calling out first the kind of formation the Comets were using on that play, then a single digit, then a two-digit number. If the digit were different than the "hut" number chosen by Bailess in the huddle, the Browns' players were alerted that a change was being made. The number that followed would indicate the new play. Any other digit would be a dummy, to keep the Comets guessing.

"Blue," shouted Bailess. "Three, thirty-seven. Three, thirty-seven." No change in the play. "Hut . . . hut. Hut!" On the third hut, the Browns exploded into concerted action. The Comets followed immediately. Bailess took the snap from center, spun around out of the way of the two guards pulling from their position, blocking in the direction of the sweep. Bailess faked a handoff to MacDay, who hit the line of scrimmage just after the guards ran by. Behind him, MacDay knew, the quarterback had given the ball to Staley, who was following the guards around right end. MacDay hit the Comets' big defensive end, who was trying to push him aside and get at the ball carrier. MacDay threw himself at the man low, hitting him just above the knees. The Comet player fell forward, pushing MacDay with him for a short distance. MacDay twisted, and he saw that the defensive man would hit him while MacDay was lying on his side. "Oh, hell," thought MacDay. "Here comes a shoulder separation." The man fell on him heavily, knocking the breath out of MacDay.

"Are you all right?"

MacDay opened his eyes. His chest and back ached so badly that he couldn't catch his breath. His wife was looking at him with a worried expression. "You okay, Eldon?" she asked again.

"Sure, Lou," he said. He wasn't so upset as he had been before. In fact, he was grateful for the quiet moment, even if it were only a split-second dream on a cold football field.

"I said, you know what we be doing tonight, Eldon?"

"I know, baby," he said. He ate a piece of his steak. The game always worked up a terrific appetite in him.

"Well, I got a surprise for you." Louvina smiled a bit timidly and reached down to the floor, where she had put her purse. "I got a present for you, honey."

It wasn't going to be a surprise; MacDay knew just what she was going to take out and give to him. Still, it was sweet of her. He wanted to act surprised, for her sake. "Aw, you don't have to get me no presents, Lou," he said.

"Here," she said. "'Cause of what you got for me." She handed him a small black box. He opened it, and there was the gold ring with the garnet. He always wore that ring; the only time he took it off was before a game, when he had his hands and wrists taped. It was sitting on the shelf in his locker right now. Or, rather, the "now" he recognized; this episode in the restaurant was coded in MacDay's mind as "then." He took the ring from the box, making startled sounds and saying just the same words of thanks he had said . . . "then." He looked inside the band, and there were the words *Eldon + Louvina*. He put the ring on his finger.

"Don't say anything. Let me look at you."

Louvina hadn't said that. MacDay blinked, saw the bright blue cloudless sky, heard the odd hush in the stadium, saw the faces of teammates, officials, and the Browns' team physician. "Oh, hell," murmured MacDay.

"I said, be quiet," said the doctor. The man pointed a pocket flashlight into MacDay's eyes. "There's only a minute and fifty-four seconds left," said the doctor. "You're out of the game." He turned to one of the assistant trainers. "Get the stretcher."

"Don't want no stretcher," said MacDay. "Let me walk off."

"You feel strong enough?" asked the doctor.

"If I ain't, there has to be two guys on the bench I can lean on. I ain't going to be carted off like some goddamn stiff." Two of the Browns' players supported MacDay, and they walked slowly from the field, up the tunnel to the locker room. The spectators applauded furiously, in the mildly unpleasant way they do only when someone is hurt, in solemn but short-lived respect for his "courage." MacDay paid little attention to their ovation.

The doctor ordered MacDay to rest on a training table for a few minutes. One of the clubhouse men came with a pair of longnosed scissors and cut the tape from MacDay's hands. Beneath the tape, on MacDay's right hand, was the gold ring, the present from Louvina. "Oh, God," whispered MacDay.

"You really hurting?" asked the clubhouse man. "I been listening in here. I heard you really got your bell rung."

"Frenchie, you want to do me a favor?"

"Sure, Mac. What you want?"

"You go into my locker and get my rings. Both of them, the wedding band and the garnet ring."

"Sure, Mac," said Frenchie. "They'll be on the shelf?" MacDay nodded. The other man went to the locker, and MacDay watched as he looked around for the rings. In a few seconds he came back. "Here you are."

MacDay thanked him and took the rings. He put the wedding ring on his left hand. He held the garnet ring for a moment before he examined it. It was identical to the one he was wearing. "Frenchie," he said, taking off the other garnet ring and handing both of them to the equipment manager, "can you tell the difference between these two?"

"Huh? No, they look the same to me. This one's heavier, I think, isn't it? No, I guess not. No, Mac, you got me. Here, this is the one you was wearing." Frenchie handed the two rings back.

"Okay, Frenchie," said Mac, "thanks."

"Hope you feel better," said Frenchie. He left MacDay and went about his own duties.

"Just a headache," said MacDay, very quietly. "And something pretty damned freaky." He waited for the doctor to come back and finish his treatment.

The sounds of the crowd came into the locker room, though muted by distance and MacDay's own fatigue. He was still charged with nervous energy, worked up in the course of a week's preparation for this first game of the season. He wanted to go back out on the field, back into the game. He felt useless, lying on the training table, listening to the play-by-play of the end of the game on Frenchie's radio. His whole life was geared to taking the ball from Bailess and running at the other team; everything else was wasted time. He lived alone now, ever since Louvina's death. He didn't party with his teammates, rarely even spoke to anyone connected with football except in the context of the game itself, at practice or on Sunday afternoons. After the season ended, no one knew what MacDay did or where he went. That was his private business, he felt. But no one knew how empty he was, how pointless and futile, when he wasn't running the ball.

MacDay had arrived at training camp in the same manner as in the previous several seasons: unannounced, unexpected, but nevertheless precisely on time. He said little to the other team members, to the coaching staff, even to the friendly, familiar employees of Hiram College, where the Browns trained. He was given his dormitory assignment and told that he would be rooming with a rookie running back, J. D. Lieger, MacDay's first white rommate. MacDay didn't even shrug; he just wanted to get into his gear and start working.

The training sessions were hard, much more strenuous than the regular season routines. Many of the veteran players had let themselves balloon up, fat and soft, during the off-season. The rookies had no idea of the kind of work that was expected of them in the professional world. Most of the players grumbled; MacDay said nothing, and his coaches had few complaints about his performance. He was ready to play the first regular season game on the morning he arrived at camp.

The weeks of training camp passed slowly for MacDay, just as they had every year since Louvina's death. He was impatient for the real tests to begin. But he never let down, even when he was worn out with fatigue and the boredom of repetitious drills.

On the eighteenth of July, about two months before the first game of the season the Comets, Coach Jennings announced at the breakfast assembly that the team had been the victim of some petty thefts. Jennings said that he was certain that the thief was a player, and that he expected that man to come into Jennings' office and apologize. The coach spoke some more about pride and integrity, then sighed and sat down. At three o'clock, just before the daily afternoon calisthenics, Jennings said that the thief had not had the guts to show up. In a low voice the head coach said, "Well, then, gentlemen. Grass drills." Every member of the Browns' team knew what was coming; every one of them would have loved to have gotten at the man responsible—except, of course, the guilty man himself and Eldon MacDay.

Grass drills, or up-downs, were a conditioning exercise consisting of running in place, knees pulling as high as possible, for from fifteen seconds to half a minute. Then Jennings yelled "Down!" and the men threw themselves down to the grass, all together, so hard that an observer could hear but one sharp smack as their bellies hit the ground. Immediately, the coach yelled "Up!" and they all jumped to their feet, running in place again, doing this over and over, usually twenty-five times. By then, most of the Browns, veterans and the youngest rookies, were hardly able to stand. Jennings would give them a couple of minutes to rest, and then go on to a new exercise.

Today, however, was something special. The coach called "Down!" forty times, then fifty. While the players were running in place, exhausted, gasping, struggling just to keep their legs moving, Jennings said they'd stop when the thief made a public confession. No one said anything. Jennings shouted "Down!" After a few more repetitions, several of the players were left lying on the ground, too weary to lift themselves up again. The count reached sixty. Then sixty-five. MacDay began to see a haze forming in front of him. He felt as if he were working in a warm, sleepy fog. The bright, hot sun paled in the sky; the day darkened. MacDay was wrapped in a protective faintness, and the only outside influence that penetrated was Jennings' voice: "Down!" Seventy. Only a few players were still going. Some men were vomiting on the grass. Some didn't move at all, helpless and moaning. Seventy-five. MacDay was by himself, the last one on his feet. Jennings shouted his orders for MacDay alone. MacDay didn't know that. He was fascinated by what his oxygen-starved brain was showing him.

He saw a strange, wonderful scene around him. The grass field had disappeared. The college and the entire summer world had vanished with it. He was still running in place, jumping up and down at the head coach's command, but MacDay had forgotten that. The darkness had swallowed him up, then gradually lightened a little to show him the inside of a restaurant. He saw a table, and he saw Louvina. He saw his wife, just the way she had been on the afternoon before she had been . . . hurt. Nothing moved. Louvina seemed frozen, looking at him with an odd expression. She seemed so real that he could touch her. The table and chairs, the other people in the place—MacDay could turn his head and observe everyting to the smallest detail—all seemed caught in a suspension of time. He felt tears coming to his eyes. He wanted to hold Lou one last time. He wanted to say something to her. He opened his mouth to speak, but all that emerged was a hoarse groan. His legs would hold him no longer. The light failed again, and MacDay fell to the ground.

"Ninety," said Jennings respectfully. "And down." MacDay couldn't hear.

When MacDay came to his senses, he saw that the rest of the team had broken up into squads and were working on their specialties. Someone had put a wet towel across his forehead. He thought about Louvina, about the vivid, static tableau he had entered. His body was angry with pain, but he didn't pay attention to that. He wished that he could have just touched Louvina, just a little. But he hadn't been able to move nearer to her.

MacDay remembered that first flashback as he lay on the training table, staring at the gray soundproofed ceiling. The game with the Comets had ended, and he could hear his teammates coming up the tunnel, yelling and congratulating each other. "That's one," he thought. "If they's all that easy, we gonna have a *good* time." He tried to take his mind off what had happened to him on the field, but his thoughts kept going back to Louvina.

During the previous summer at the training camp, he had never been able to speak to her. The flashbacks that he had experienced there were all exactly like the first—as though he had walked onto a stage set or an exhibit in a wax museum. Even during the preseason games, when he had three or four flashbacks during the course of each game, he was never able to break out of the paralysis that held him helpless in the restaurant. The flashbacks happened less and less frequently; it took MacDay a while before he understood what made them happen at all. At first, on the occasion of the grass drills, they were brought on by extreme physical exertion. After the first episodes, it had been four days before he had another, while he had been working at the blocking sleds.

The temperature went up over ninety-five degrees, but the coaches never seemed to notice. They all stood around with clipboards, shouting. It seemed to MacDay that the coaches had their speeches written down for them. Maybe they had scripts on their clipboards; one coach yelled, "You ain't gonna get weather like this, come December!" about every twenty seconds. Another coach kept repeating, "Keep your head up! Head up!" The third coach, his voice gravelly hoarse, just chanted, "Drive! Drive! Drive! Drive!" MacDay was grateful when the dark haze began to form around him, shutting out the realities of the drill.

The flashbacks required pain, he learned. But during that stretch of weeks before the first regular game, the flashbacks were frustrating to him, for all that they gave him more incentive to work. The flashbacks cost more in exertion, as if his mind and body were building a tolerance to fatigue. If he repeated the amount of work that had given him a flashback the day before, he would only succeed in wearing himself out. He had to increase the pain. And, if he did that, all that he'd get in return was the same photographic vision. He wanted more, but he didn't know how to get it. He wanted to go to her, he wanted to touch her face one last time.

Then, that afternoon, on the field with the Comets, it had happened for the first time. He had seen Louvina move, he had sat down at the table across from her. They had talked, he had stared into those eyes that had been taken from him. He was too surprised to know what to do; still, the matter was out of his hands, it seemed, because he couldn't do anything that he hadn't done in that situation years ago. Nevertheless, he was awed and grateful. And he wanted more. He still hadn't touched her.

He had not told anyone yet about the flashback episodes. He was glad that he hadn't, now, because they seemed to be something different than he had first guessed. Working as the Browns did at training camp, MacDay could pass the episodes off as some kind of mental strain, some deficiency in diet perhaps. Now, though, the garnet ring moved the circumstance into an entirely different realm. He couldn't tell anyone, after that. The decision had been made for him. It also compelled him to try harder to visit Louvina again, as often as possible. It wasn't a dream or hallucination. MacDay knew that he was truly going back to her, back those five empty years. He much preferred sitting in that restaurant with her than doing whatever he had to in the present.

"You took a pretty good pop, huh, roomy?" said J. D. Lieger, MacDay's roommate, as Lieger came into the locker room.

"Yeah," said MacDay. "That happens to you sometimes."

"So I'm told," said Lieger. "I hope I get to find out one of these days."

"You gonna have to beat out some gentlemen, if you gonna play," said one of the Browns' defensive backs.

Lieger grinned. "Ain't that why I'm here?" he asked.

"Naw," said Bailess, the quarterback. "You're here so our real runners don't have to get hurt taking back kickoffs and punts. You're what we in the trade call 'cannon fodder.'"

"What's that?" asked the rookie.

"Look it up," said Bailess. "Hey, Mac, how you doing? We missed you."

"Didn't sound like it on the radio," said MacDay. "I'm fine. Damn doctor forgot about me. Either I'm all right, or I'm dying."

"Let me know which before practice on Tuesday," said Coach Jennings. "Here, this is yours." He tossed MacDay the game ball. MacDay only nodded. The other players congratulated him, but MacDay just thanked them quietly, swung his legs off the training table, and went to his locker to get undressed and showered.

On Monday, MacDay relaxed in his apartment, thankful for the day off following the victory over the Comets. He watched television for most of the afternoon, then went out to dinner by himself. He had an idea to drive out to Euclid to visit their old restaurant, but after he entertained the notion for a few seconds he grew unaccountably nervous. Instead, he drove to a large shopping center, ate dinner at a mediocre Chinese restaurant, then sat in a theater for a double feature. He left about a third of the way through the second movie.

The week's practice began again the next morning. He reported to the stadium, and the doctor gave him a quick examination. MacDay showed no sign of injury, for which he was grateful. He had more goals to work for than ever before, and his prime objective would have to be secret from Coach Jennings and his staff. Fortunately, the reaching of that goal was by the same route as the achievement of his more orthodox aims.

If getting hit hard was what it took for MacDay to return to Louvina, to see her move and smile and speak, then he was eager to pay that price.

"Okay," said Coach Jennings briskly, "let's go in and look at the films of the Comets' game. I know that was just the first game of the season, and the newspapers have given you the benefit of the doubt. They say it's too early for the squads to have hit their best strides, or whatever those guys are writing these days. I know the game was just Phoenix, who haven't won a game since the dawning of Western civilization. And I know that we killed them. Nevertheless. *Nevertheless,* gentlemen, I'm sure that every one of you will find something instructive about these movies. Because every one of you did something crummy. The coaches will be circulating among you, to point up moments of special interest, to learn your views and opinions, and mainly to make sure that none of you gentlemen are falling asleep." MacDay sat alone, and he studied the film closely; he watched his own performance, which was creditable—139 yards gained in 27 carries, with one touchdown. Even Coach Jennings gave him a few compliments, a rare honor indeed. MacDay watched the actions of the linemen and the other blocking backs, trying to become even more familiar with them, even more efficient a part in the machine that was the Cleveland Browns.

But the movies were a torture for MacDay, as well. He was glad when they ended, when the team went out for calisthenics and drills. He worked through these, getting the pains and aches out of his muscles. After lunch Jennings had scheduled a couple of hours of scrimmages, beginning with a light workout, no tackling, and ending the day with hard-hitting exercises. MacDay was ready to hit.

"Look, Mac," said the head coach at lunch, "I don't want you to think that I'm handing out special favors. I don't do that kind of thing. You know that. But you put out a hundred percent Sunday, and I know that you'll give everything today, too. You're that kind of player. If I had forty-five players like you on the roster, the Browns wouldn't need me at all. So what I was starting to say was, I want you to use your own judgment. I don't want you to hurt yourself in practice on account of the rah-rah talk I use. That's just for the other clowns, to get them to perform. If you don't feel up to working out full this afternoon, lay off a little. Forget the scrimmages. Why don't you just run a couple laps? Tomorrow's good enough."

MacDay was a little startled. To his knowledge, the coach never spoke like that to anyone; the coach had waited until everyone else had left the cafeteria before he began, so that the players wouldn't think that he was playing favorites. It had been Jennings' experience that athletes rarely understood the real intentions of their coaches.

"I'm fine, Coach," said MacDay. "I ain't even hurting none."

"You're sure?" asked Jennings. "I mean, it don't do us no good to have you being brave today, and being out for Cincinnati on Sunday."

MacDay smiled. "Trust me, Coach," he said. Jennings only nodded, slapped his running back on the shoulder, and left the table. MacDay carried his tray to the service window and followed, out to the field.

The scrimmages started easy, about twenty minutes of touch-tackle plays run by the offense against the defense. Most of the players enjoyed this part of the workout every week; MacDay now thought it was the most irritating thing about his job. He longed to feel the hard jolt of a tackler cutting him down, or the deliberate shock as he himself blocked out a defensive player. After a while, Jennings began putting the Browns through plays under conditions more like the real game. MacDay was glad.

"All right," said one of Jennings' coaching assistants, "Mac, let's try a 20 Strong."

MacDay nodded. This was the play he had hoped for. He

would take the ball from Bailess and run straight up the middle, right for the middle linebacker. Theoretically, the center would be controlling that man, and the rest of the line would be blocking straight ahead. MacDay would get no other blocking help, either from his halfback or the tight end. He would be by himself, and if any of the linemen missed their assignments, MacDay would be cut down, quickly. Bailess called the signals, took the snap, and jammed the ball between MacDay's arms. The latter lowered his head and bulled his way through the line. The linebacker spun around the center and was waiting for him. MacDay hit him at full speed. He was hoping. . . .

It didn't work. After the play, the middle linebacker gave MacDay a hand up. "Wow," said the man, "you put a hell of a hit on me." MacDay only grunted.

"No way, Warrick," said the assistant coach to the center. "That linebacker got around you like you was planted on Arbor Day. Can you try it again, Mac?" MacDay nodded. They ran the play again, and this time MacDay hit the linebacker as hard as he possibly could. This time, for a moment, a short while, he caught a glimpse of the darkened restaurant, the table, Louvina. Then, instantly, it disappeared. He was already getting to his feet.

"Let's try the 37 Plunge," said the coach. In this play, Bailess gave the ball to Sonny Staley, and MacDay ran ahead of the ball carrier, blocking the outside linebacker. MacDay hit his man harder than usual for a scrimmage; the linebacker complained, but MacDay couldn't hear. He was seeing a clear tableau of the restaurant scene. Again, nothing in it moved.

So it went for the rest of the day, and the following days of that week before the Cincinnati game. MacDay took his hits agressively, but all that he got for his pain was the same vivid but motionless tableau he had experienced during the training season. He had to have something special happening in order for him truly to go back there; it was only under real game conditions, when his emotional state or his physical energy provided an essential catalyst. So then, he realized, he wouldn't be able to visit Louvina until the Sunday game. He was disappointed, but at least he was beginning to understand the ground rules of the situation.

At last, after days of tension relieved by occasional unsatisfactory flashbacks, MacDay went to the McGuire Coliseum for the game with Cincinnati. During the pregame preparations, he experienced an intense anxiety and anticipation, unlike anything he'd ever known before in his career. At one point, his hands shaking so much that he was barely able to dress, he considered asking the team physician for something to calm him. But the word would get back to Coach Jennings; the head coach would be displeased, MacDay knew. Jennings would wonder about any player who wanted to be quieted down before a game.

"This is for Lou," MacDay thought, as he and the other Browns charged out of the locker room, down the tunnel toward the field. "If I got to break my neck to talk to her, I'll break my neck."

The Cincinnati defense was not as tough as the Phoenix team had been the week before. Coach Jennings was screaming excitedly on the sidelines, and the Browns' players not on the field were standing just out of bounds, shouting encouragement to their teammates. It looked as though Cleveland would be able to take a quick lead over their divisional rivals and that the game might be decided for good before halftime. This disappointed MacDay somewhat. If that were the case, it was possible that the Cincinnati defense might let down even more; the Bengal players would feel that it was meaningless to risk injury in a losing cause. In that event, MacDay would have to take the game to them. He took the ball on one play and ran through a hole in the Cincinnati front. He saw the linebackers sliding down the line in pursuit. His instincts told him to cut back to the inside; his mind and his desires made him continue to the outside. A Bengal player hit him from the side, knocking MacDay's legs out from under him, and a second Cincinnati player blasted him out of bounds.

"Well, how do you like it?"

"I don't know what to say, Lou," said MacDay, before he was even able to focus his eyes. "How did you know what size?"

Louvina laughed. MacDay just stared at her; she was so happy that it hurt him, in a way. He remembered that she was dead, that she would die not so very long after they left the restaurant; for these last few years he had hated the world, the people in it, he had even hated God for letting someone with so much love to be obliterated in such an offhand manner. He genuinely didn't know what to say to her, and he was glad to be bound by the situation. His self of five years past was in control, and he was just a spectator. But he was thankful for even that much. "It was easy, Eldon," she said. "You had that old ring you got for playing in the College All-Star game."

"Yeah, sure," he said. "But, damn it, honey, you didn't have to do it. I don't need a ring like this."

"Of course not," she said smiling. "If you needed the thing, I wouldn't have waited until now to give it to you. I love you, Eldon."

Even five years ago, even unaware of what was to happen, the previous MacDay had been unable to reply for a moment. "I love you, too, Lou," he said at last, quietly. He reached across the table and took her hand. MacDay felt an over-powering emotion as their fingers touched. "Yes," he said to himself, "that's Lou. That's just the way I remember her."

"Listen," she said, "I'll be right back. I been crying all over my eye stuff here. I got to go fix it up."

"That's silly, Lou. You look fine. I don't want you to leave me here alone." MacDay's sentiment made every word of hers, every gesture painful, but infinitely wonderful.

"Oh, I'll be right back, I said," she said, rising from her chair. "I'm way ahead of you on the meal, anyway."

MacDay stood, too, and held her before she turned away to find the ladies' room. He wanted to go after her, but his previous self wouldn't allow it. He took two steps back to his chair, and turned his ankle. It didn't hurt very much, but the memory of it happening the first time made the situation even more real to MacDay than the garnet ring had done. He sat in his chair, his mind a shifting mixture of feelings. He ate some of the steak, then rubbed his ankle, which was getting sore.

"Your ankle bothering you?" asked Bailess.

"It's fine," said MacDay. "I turned it a little making my cut."

"I didn't see much cut," said one of the Bengal players scornfully.

"That's why my ankle's giving me hell," said MacDay. Then he turned his back and went to the Browns' huddle. His ankle did bother him a bit, and he limped off the field when J. D. Lieger ran on to replace him.

"Thanks, roomy," said Lieger. "This is my big break."

MacDay nodded wearily. Jennings' backfield coach came

over to see how badly MacDay was injured. "Just turned it a little," said MacDay.

"You want the doc to look at it? Spray it cold or something?"

"Hell, no," said MacDay. "Let me catch my breath, and I'll be back in. I don't want no smart-ass kid like Lieger breaking one for no touchdown, not while I'm sitting on my butt." The assistant coach shrugged and reported back to Jennings. MacDay thought about his twisted ankle. It appeared that garnet rings weren't the only souvenirs he could bring back from the past. The thought entered his mind that . . . later . . . after they left the restaurant. . . .

"All right, come on, let's go!" he shouted at the Browns on the field. It was third down and six yards to go for a first down. Bailess took the snap and ran back into the pocket, set up, then threw an incomplete pass to Lieger, who had circled out of the backfield. MacDay hadn't really been worried about losing his job to the kid, and he was sorry that Lieger hadn't been able to hang onto Bailess' pass. The Browns would have to punt it away.

"It worked," he thought. "I saw her again." His mind raced from one thought to another. He began to realize again what might happen when the scene developed further. He shook his head to stop those thoughts, and tried to concentrate on the game.

Just before halftime MacDay went back into the game. On the second play from scrimmage he was given the ball on the 20 Strong, the run up the middle. He was intent on executing the play correctly, as always, but his main objective had changed. Rather than gaining yardage, his purpose now was to hit the middle linebacker as hard as possible. In this instance, it meant that MacDay had to do some quick shifting to get a good shot at the man and not draw the wrath of the coaching staff. He lowered his head and butted the linebacker. The man gave a little ground, then wrapped his arms around MacDay. The two struggled. MacDay cursed loudly, because he hadn't earned the flashback he wanted so badly. "What the hell's the matter?" said the linebacker, as a second Bengal player came over to assist on the play, "you'll get your hundred-yard day, all right." The two Cincinnati players toppled MacDay, and the second man managed to knock the ball out of his hands. MacDay scrambled for the fumble, but a Cincinnati player recovered it.

The Bengal players jumped up and shouted. The Browns walked slowly from the field. Bailess slapped MacDay back.

"Okay, Mac," said the quarterback. "Even I blow one, once in a while."

"Not the way I did," said MacDay, upset that Louvina had been denied to him.

"Aw, it wasn't so bad," said Bailess. "Why, I seen fumbles kicked back and forth all the way from one end zone to the other. Yours was just a *little* fumble."

"Yeah," said MacDay as they reached the sidelines, "but it probably means we won't get back in the game until the second half."

"Yeah, is right," said Bailess, grinning. "Good boy."

Late in the game, with the Browns leading by a score of 31 to 13, with second down and five yards to go, Bailess called for a long pass. He looked around at the players bent over in the huddle and said, "63 Fly split right. On three."

"Shoot, man," said Nathaniel Coggins, the wide receiver. He spat on the artificial turf. "Hey, man, there's only three minutes left in this game. What you think they gonna do in three minutes? Why you want me to run my ass off? What for, man? You ain't careful, I just might accidentally pull a hamstring or something."

"Shut up," said Bailess. "Break!" They all clapped, and went to their positions.

"You don't never pull no hamstring when we're winning games," said one of the linemen to Coggins.

"Yeah," he said, "you right. I forgot." The play went off, but the pass was overthrown. The next play was 25 Crunch split right, MacDay carrying through the hole between left guard and tackle. He knew that time was running out; he had failed to get another flashback all afternoon. He was determined to do it now. He took the handoff from Bailess and charged into the Cincinnati defenders. A hole opened up for him, and in a few steps he was through. He raced down the length of the field; only a weak-side safety stood between him and a touchdown. MacDay gave a little fake with his head, then paused. The pause was just enough to let the Cincinnati player adjust. Jennings saw from the sidelines that MacDay seemed to have given up, and the head coach shouted; MacDay couldn't hear. The safety hit him high, and another defensive player recovered quickly enough to hit MacDay again, spinning him off his feet.

MacDay held his head. He felt terrible. He had quit, he had deliberately permitted that safety to crack him, when MacDay had had a certain touchdown. It was going to be difficult to explain. He wondered about the silence around him. Had his actions been that obvious? He lifted his head, and he was reassured.

Louvina was coming back to the table, accompanied by three other men. MacDay had worried; he always worried when she talked to strangers, whatever the situation. But he *knew* who these men were. He knew, but he realized that it didn't make any difference. He could only watch this time.

"Eldon," she said, "these here men are from Jackson. They say they saw you play ball at Hanson High."

"That's right, Mr. MacDay," said one of the men, taller than the football player. "On West Third Street, around the corner from Mrs. Perkins' diner. You remember?"

"Sure," said MacDay. Five years ago he had suspected nothing. He had only wanted to eat his meal in peace.

"We were wondering if we could coax you and your wife into having a drink with us after you finish," said the first man.

"I'm sorry," said MacDay.

"Oh, it's all right, I think," said Louvina. "After all, this man tell me he used to bring your ma the paper. I mean, just this once, it'd be all right, wouldn't it, Eldon?"

"I understand that you're probably always bothered by fans," said the second man. "But my son is probably your biggest rooter. Next to your wife, of course." He laughed briefly. "I have this football in my hotel room. I bought it for my boy, Cledis. I was really hoping you'd sign it for him."

"It be okay with me," said Louvina. "Maybe it'd help the boy some. You're always saying how you want to do something for the community."

"All right, all right," said MacDay impatiently. He pleaded with his wife silently, his five years of helpless hindsight just as ineffectual now, trapped in his second chance. The five of them stood up; the third stranger, silent through all the conversation, took out a wallet and paid MacDay's check. Then they left the restaurant. Louvina walked with her arm through MacDay's; the two of them walked behind the three men.

"I'd like to ask you a question, Mrs. MacDay," said the tallest of the strangers. "Why do you think your husband plays football? I mean, why does he go out there, week after week, and put himself in a position to get dangerously injured? One play after another, he runs right into a bunch of other men who are trained to cut him down. And winning a stupid football game can't be worth all that, can it?"

Louvina laughed. "They ask him that all the time. And Eldon always says the same thing. I don't say it as good as he do, but it has to do with wanting something bad enough. Eldon want to be good, is what he want. He want to be the best."

"That's not the reason I take all the pain," thought MacDay sadly. "It's for you, Lou. I hurt for you."

"No," said the tall man, "that's not why he goes out there and gets bruised. I hate to contradict you, Mrs. MacDay, but he goes out there because he gets paid a hell of a lot of money."

"Not all that much," said MacDay sourly.

The men ignored him. "And what do you think, Mrs. MacDay?" asked the second man. "If he gets paid so much for taking a risk, don't you think if we got paid ten times as much, we'd take a bigger risk?"

"What do you mean?" asked Louvina, frightened by the man's tone.

They had been crossing the parking lot of the restaurant. The silent third stranger had left their group to get his car. Now the tall man grabbed Louvina, and the second man caught MacDay in a tight hammerlock. The third man drove straight for them. "You see, MacDay," said the second man, "we gonna make sure you don't feel like playing. You won't take our money, and you won't listen to our threats. Chuck there, why, you'll pay attention to him. He's going to be very persuasive."

The tall stranger waited until the car was only a few yards away, then he pushed Louvina in front of it. MacDay twisted free of the man holding him. He saw Louvina fall in front of the car. He heard her screaming, he saw her huge eyes, bright and staring, looking straight at him. "Goddamn it, not again," thought MacDay. He tried to run to her, but the second man tripped him. As MacDay fell, he never lost contact with Louvina's eyes. They seemed to grow even larger. He heard her, still crying. "Please, God," shouted MacDay, "not her!"

"What?"

MacDay could only groan. The heavy chest of drawers lay across his legs. He couldn't move. He just stared at the pieces of the broken mirror on the floor. He saw his face, contorted by pain.

"What did you say, roomy?" It was Lieger, calling from their other room. "What are you doing out of bed? The doc—" The rookie came into the bedroom, stopped, and ran to where MacDay lay twisted on the floor. He hauled the massive chest up off MacDay's legs. "Are you okay?"

MacDay just shook his head. He knew his legs were shattered, just as Louvina's had been. Crushed. He knew it would be nothing short of a miracle if he would ever stand on them again, let alone walk. "God," he muttered, "you got a great sense of humor."

"What?" said Lieger frantically. "Wait, I'll call the doc. You been out since you got popped in the fourth quarter. Jennings figured you'd rather come to here than the hospital."

"Sure," said MacDay faintly. "Hey, J. D., you better get the hang of picking your spots. You ain't gonna get all your spots picked for you. Not like this."

"You just wait, Mac," said Lieger, dialing the phone. "We'll get you to a hospital. You need it now."

MacDay knew that a chest of drawers couldn't have so thoroughly destroyed his legs. But how could he explain that he'd been run over by a car, five years in the past, in his own bedroom? Jennings would never understand. "That's it," thought MacDay. "No more games, no more seeing Lou. No more seeing Lou. Seen her die twice, now. That's enough, I guess."

"You'll be all right," said Lieger, who was near hysteria.

"It's all right," said MacDay to himself. He was curiously peaceful. The pain in his legs seemed to be a solid object, with a separate existence of its own. It didn't throb or stab; it was constant, rolling on with MacDay's own life. That made it easier to ignore. "It's all right. I been dead for five years already, anyhow. In a way. Ain't had no soul for five years. Been in Hell for five years. So for a few weeks, God has to lift the lid off Heaven for me, just to make me sweat. God, you sure a *bad* dude."

"You're crazy, Mac," said Lieger.

"Didn't know I was talking out loud."

"Sometimes, you're just plain crazy. No offense."

MacDay didn't answer. He was looking into the shards of mirror all around him on the floor. All he could see were eyes, huge eyes, the eyes of a dying person. He wasn't sure whose.

The Pinch Hitters *appears in this book as a—you will pardon the expression—pinch hitter for another story, one which has not yet been published by the editor who purchased its first publication rights. It's a terrific little story, and I wish I could tell you about it, but I promised to wait. Too bad.*

I set out originally to put this collection together with stories about different sports and games, without using the same sport twice. This is another baseball story—but only in a strict sense. I talked myself into using it by considering The Pinch Hitters *to be about science fiction and science fiction fandom. That's an entirely different game, as anyone who's ever been to an sf convention knows. So it only took a few minutes of rationalization to squeeze* The Pinch Hitters *in here under the wire. I had a third story I could have used, a dynamite prizefighting story, but it was printed under a secret pseudonym. That's another shame. Too bad.*

When I wrote The Pinch Hitters, *I used the names of four of my best friends. In the early 1970s we had a kind of Bloomsbury Group of our own, getting together to criticize each other's stories and entertaining ourselves with highly intellectual pursuits of one kind and another. It was suggested by a well-known editor that I ought not to use their real names in* The Pinch Hitters *and, because he was paying me a lot of money, I didn't. I'm taking this opportunity to salute these good pals of mine, who appear in major roles in the following story: Gardner Dozois, Jack Dann, Joe Haldeman, and Jay Haldeman. It is left as an exercise for the reader to decide which actual person is represented by which fictional character.*

The Pinch Hitters

THE TELEPHONE RANG, and the noise woke me up. I reached across the bed to pick up the receiver. I was still half asleep, and something about the dimly lit hotel room disturbed me. I couldn't identify the trouble, though. "Hello?" I said into the phone.

"Hello? Is this Sandor Courane?" said an unfamiliar voice.

I didn't say anything for a second or two. I was looking across the room at the other twin bed. There was someone sleeping in it.

"Is this Sandor Courane?" asked the voice.

"It often is," I said.

"Well, if it is now, this is Norris."

I was silent again. Someone was claiming to be a very good friend of mine, using a voice that didn't belong to Norris. "Uh huh," was all that I said. I remembered that I hadn't been alone the night before. I was at a rather large science fiction convention, and I had met a rather nice young woman. The person in the other bed, still asleep, was a large man I had never seen before.

99

"Where are you?" asked the person who claimed to be Norris.

"In my room," I said. "What time is it? Who is this?"

"This is Norris Page! Have you looked outside?"

"Norris," I said, "I can't think of a single reason why I would waste the effort to walk across the room. And I don't know how to say this, but, uh, you don't sound at all like Norris, if you know what I mean. My clock says it's eight-thirty, and that's a rotten time to wake somebody up at a convention. So I think I'll just hang—"

"Wait a minute!" The voice was suddenly very urgent. Much more urgent than a voice generally gets at a science fiction convention. I waited. The voice went on. "Look out the window," it said.

"Okay," I said. I'm moderately obliging. I got up. I was wearing thin green pajamas, something I have never owned in my entire life. I didn't like that discovery at all. I walked quietly by the stranger on the other bed and peered through the slats of the venetian blinds. I stared for a moment or two, then went back to the telephone. "Hello?" I said.

"What did you see?" asked the voice.

"A bunch of buildings I've never seen before."

"It's not Washington, is it?"

"No," I said. "Who is this?"

"Norris. It's Norris. I'm in New York."

"Last night you were in Washington," I said. "I mean, Norris was here in Washington. Why don't you sound like Norris?"

There was a short, exasperated sound from the voice. "You know, you don't sound like you either. You're in Boston."

"Boston?"

"Yeah. And Jim is in Detroit. And Larry is in Chicago. And Dick is in Cleveland."

"I feel sorry for Dick," I said. I was born in Cleveland.

"I feel sorry for all of us," said Norris. "We're not us anymore. Look at yourself."

I did. Beneath the pajamas, my body had become large and hairy. My tattoo—I have an Athenian owl tattooed on my left forearm—was gone, and in its place was a skull with a dagger through its eye and a naked lady with an anchor and a snake. There were certain other pertinent revisions in the body. "Wow," I said.

"I've been up since six o'clock running this down," said Norris. "The five of us have been hijacked or something."

"Who did it?" I was feeling very unhappy about the situation.

"I don't know," said Norris.

"Why?" I was starting to feel very frightened about the situation.

"I don't know."

"How?"

"I don't know."

I was beginning to feel annoyed. "Since six o'clock, huh?" I said. "What *have* you found out?"

Norris sounded hurt. "I found you, didn't I? And Jim and Larry and Dick."

I got the same cold feeling at the base of my spine that I get when I have to have blood taken. "We're scattered all over the United States of America. Last night we were all in the same lousy hotel. What happened?"

"Take it easy." When Norris said that, I knew we were all in trouble. "It seems as though we've been, uh, transported back in time too."

I screamed, "What?"

"It's 1954 out there," said Norris.

I gave up. I wasn't going to say another word. When I started the day, I was sleeping very nicely. Every time I opened my mouth, it only encouraged Norris to tell me something else I didn't want to hear. I decided to clam up.

"Did you hear me?" he asked.

I didn't say anything.

"It's 1954 out there. You've been transported back and put in the body of, uh, wait a minute, I wrote it down, uh, Ellard MacIver. Do you know who that is?"

I felt cold again. "Yes," I said, "he was a utility infielder for the Red Sox. In the fifties."

"Right. You have a game today against the Athletics. Lots of luck."

"What am I supposed to do?"

Norris laughed, I don't know why. "Play ball," he said.

"How do we get back?" I shouted. The man in the other bed grumbled and woke up.

"I haven't figured that out yet," said Norris. "I have to go.

This is long distance. Anyway, this week you play the Tigers, and you can talk it over with Jim. He's in the body of, uh, this guy Charlie Quinn. Second base."

"Wonderful," I said. "Terrific."

"Don't worry," said Norris. "I have to go. I'll talk with you later." He hung up.

I looked at the phone. "Terrific," I muttered.

The other guy propped himself up in the other bed and said, "Shut up, Mac, will you?" I just stared at him.

I realized that I should have asked Norris whose body he was in. I shrugged. Maybe Jim would know.

A few days later we had the situation completely sorted out. It still didn't bring us any closer to solving the problem, but at least it was sorted out. This is the way it looked:

FAMOUS SCIENCE FICTION WRITER	IN THE BODY OF	TEAM	POSITION AND BATTING AVERAGE	
Sandor Courane (me)	Ellard MacIver	Boston Red Sox	Inf.	.221
Norris Page	Don Di Mauro	Chicago White Sox	Left Field	.288
Larry Shrader	Gerhardt 'Dutch' Ruhl	New York Yankees	1B	.334
Dick Shrader	Marv Croxton	Cleveland Indians	Center Field	.291
Jim Benedetti	Charlie Quinn	Detroit Tigers	2B	.254

I didn't like it at all. Not batting .221 and being thirty-six years old (I'm not thirty-six, but MacIver was, and he was in danger of losing his job next spring, and if we didn't get home soon, I'd have to become a broadcaster or something).

That morning I went to the ballpark with my roommate. His name was Tony Lloyd, and he was a huge first baseman. Everyone on the team called him "Money." His most memorable attribute was explaining how Jackie Robinson wouldn't survive the walk from the clubhouse to the dugout if the National League had any men with guts over there. I didn't listen to him much. Anyway, we had a game scheduled for two o'clock, but the Red Sox were headed for a mediocre finish to the season and that meant that everybody was taking all kinds of extra practice and hustling around and pretending that they cared a hill of beans about the outcome of every game.

I, for one, was excited. I was scared out of my skin too, but I was excited. I followed Lloyd into Fenway Park—the gate guard gave me a nod, recognizing my borrowed body— and stood for a while in the dressing room, just staring at things. I'd always wanted to be a ballplayer when I was a kid, of course, and now . . .

And now I *was* a ballplayer. Sort of. A sort of ballplayer, a bench-warming antique of a ballplayer who was hitting just well enough to prove he was still alive. I wondered why, if I were going to be transmiggled through time and space, I couldn't have ended up in the body of, oh, Ted Williams, say, whose locker wasn't far from mine. I stared at him; I stared at everybody else; I stared at the towels; I stared at the soap; I stared at the contents of my locker. *My* locker. My locker as a member of a professional baseball team. There were pictures of beautiful women taped to the inside of the door. There were parts of the uniform that I couldn't even identify. I had to watch a couple of other guys getting dressed to see how they worked. I think the guys noticed me watching.

After I got dressed I walked through the long, cool tunnel under the stands and emerged in the dugout. Before me was a vast, green, utterly beautiful world. Fenway Park. And they were going to let me go out there and run around on their grass.

I took my fielder's glove and trotted out toward second base. I know how to trot. I was in a little trouble once I reached where I was going. I said hello to men I didn't recognize. Someone else was hitting ground balls to us and we were lazily scooping them up. Well, anyway, *they* were; I was letting them hit me on the elbow, the knee, and twice on the chin.

"Hey, look at the old man," said some kid, backhanding a hot rocket of a grounder. "You going to be around next year, old man?"

I felt angry. I wanted to show that kid, but there wasn't anything I could show him, with the possible exception of sentence structure.

"He'll be around," said another kid. "They're going to bury him out under center field." Another grounder came my way and it zipped between my feet and out onto the grass. The kids laughed.

Later I took some batting practice. This was 1954, of course, and the batting practice was pitched by a venerable old ballplayer whose name had been a legend when I was a boy. I told him that I wasn't feeling very well, and he took some of the stuff off his pitches. They were nice and easy, right over the plate every time, and I hit some liners around the stadium. I pretended that they would have been base hits in a real game. It felt great. After I finished, Ted Williams stepped in and demolished the bleachers.

And then the fun began. The game started. I vaguely remembered hearing a kind of pep talk from Lou Boudreau, the manager. I guess they played the "Star Spangled Banner," but I don't remember that. And then, before I was even aware of what was happening, I was sitting in a corner of the dugout, watching, and we were in the third inning of the game. Frank Sullivan was pitching for us, and Arnie Portocarrero was pitching for Philadelphia.

Right then, if someone had asked me, I might have declined to go back to the seventies, back to typing up fantasies to pay my rent. Why should I? I could stay in 1954 and get paid to play baseball! Eisenhower was President. The space race wasn't even to the starting gate yet. Ernie Kovacs and Buddy Holly were still alive. I could win a fortune betting on things and waiting for Polaroid to split.

But no. I had a responsibility to the science fiction world. After all, science fiction might well do without me (just let it try), but Norris and Jim and Dick and Larry were here too, and I had to help my friends, if I could. But could I? Why were we here, what had zapped us more than twenty years into the past?

And then I had a terrifying thought. What all this meant was that more than twenty years in the future, in New Orleans, some man named Ellard MacIver, a failure of a baseball player with very little to recommend him, was sitting down at my typewriter and continuing my writing career. No! I couldn't bear it! If anyone was going to ruin my career, I wanted it to be me.

On Sunday night we rode the train out to Detroit. It was a rotten trip. I hadn't gotten into any of the three weekend games with Philadelphia, which was just as well. I was extra baggage to the Red Sox, carried along in case a hole opened up and swallowed four-fifths of the team down into the bowels of the earth. I was looking forward to talking with Jim. Sure, 1954 had its good points—I think I counted about six of them—but, all in all, I had decided that we had to get out of the mess somehow, and as soon as possible. I had a contract outstanding with Doubleday, and I didn't want Ellard MacIver writing that novel. If he did and it won a Hugo, well, I'd have to join the Navy or something.

Fortunately, Jim was in the same frame of mind. Jim is a great guy normally, but his situation was driving him crazy. He was supposed to be a second baseman, a starting second baseman, and he had fallen on his face three times trying to pivot on double-play balls. Also, his batting had gone into a slump (understandably enough), and he didn't like the body he had been put into. "You think the old one gave me trouble," he said, "this one complains if I eat Wheaties."

We had lunch at my hotel on the afternoon of the first game of the Detroit series, Tuesday. "Have you had any ideas about who's doing this to us?" I asked him.

"Is somebody doing this to us?" he asked.

I looked at him blankly for a moment. It hadn't occurred to me that all of this might be a function of the Universe, instead of an evil plot. That made me feel even worse. "Look," I said, "we have to believe that we can get out of this somehow."

Jim ate some more oatmeal. "Fine," he said, "we'll believe that. What next?"

"The next logical step is to assume that if this is being done to us, that *someone* is doing it."

Jim looked at me like he suddenly realized that I was just a bit dangerous. "That's not the most spectacular reasoning in the world," he said.

"Well, we have to make that assumption. It doesn't make any difference who it is. The main thing is that we flip things around the right way."

"Boy, do I hate this oatmeal," he said. "Wait. What if we flip things, and we end up somewhere else? I mean, like in the bodies of apple salesmen in the thirties. Don't do anything we'll regret."

"I won't," I said, because as yet I couldn't think of anything at all. "If anyone can figure this out, Larry can."

"Right," said Jim, smiling suddenly. "We'll let Larry figure it out. You and I write sort of surreal fantasies. Larry is the real nuts and bolts science fiction type. He'll know what to do."

"Right," I said. We finished eating and went out to the ballpark. I sat in the corner of the dugout during the game and watched Jim muffling around second base.

The next series was in Cleveland, my hometown. I thought about visiting my parents and seeing myself at seven years old, but the idea was vaguely repellent. I reminded myself that I'd have to see my younger brother at five years old, and that settled the matter. I went to a movie instead.

I talked with Dick several times, and he said that he'd heard from his brother, Larry. Larry is a good old rocketship and ray-gun kind of thinker, and we were counting on him to help us out of the predicament. "What do you think?" I asked Dick Shrader.

"Well," said Dick, doing something I'd never seen him do before—take a handful of chewing tobacco, mix it with bubble gum, and stuff it all in one cheek—"unless I have a bad slump the last few weeks, I stand a good chance of finishing over .300. I'm going to ask for thirty thousand next season."

"Dick," I said loudly, "you're not paying attention."

"Okay. Thirty-five thousand."

Clearly there would be no progress at all until the series in New York, when Larry and I could go over the matter in great detail. I guess, then, that I can skip the next several days. Not much happened, really, other than a series with the Orioles during which I got to bat (a weak ground-out), and I had an interview with a newspaperman who thought I was Jimmy Piersall.

Following the first game with the Yankees, Larry and I went to a small restaurant where he wouldn't be recognized. We ordered dinner, and while we waited we talked. "How do you feel about this guy Dutch Ruhl taking over your writing career?" I asked.

"Doesn't bother me," said Larry, gulping some beer. Larry breathes beer.

"Why not?" My hopes rose. I thought he had found a solution.

"Well, if we get out of this, there won't be any problem, right?" he said, swallowing some more beer.

"Right," I said.

"And if we don't get out of it, well, I'll just wait around

and come up behind him and take my career back."

"That's twenty years from now!" I said.

Larry didn't look disturbed. "Think of all the ideas I'll have by then," he said. "I'll do 'Star Trek' in 1960, and *2001* in 1961, and *Star Wars* in 1962, and—"

"What are you going to do with Dutch Ruhl?"

Larry knocked back the last of the beer. "Was there a Dutch Ruhl writing science fiction when we left?"

"No."

"Then there won't be."

"But there was somebody in the body of Larry Shrader, maybe you, maybe not. How are you going to prove *you're* Larry Shrader?"

Larry looked at me as though I were in some way tragic. "All I need are my driver's license and my Master Charge."

"Got those with you?"

Now Larry looked tragic. "No," he said.

"Who could stand to gain from this?" I wondered, as Larry signaled for several more beers.

"Who?" he said, in a hollow voice.

"Who?" I said.

There was a slight pause, and then we looked at each other.

"Who could stand to gain from the sudden disappearance of, well, if I do say so myself, the cream of the newer generation, the hope and future of science fiction?" he said, a little smile on his lips.

"Well," I said, "apart from the Dean of Science Fiction . . ."

"In conjunction with the Most Honored Writer of Science Fiction," said Larry, laughing a little.

"Acting in concert with the Acknowledged Master of Science Fiction," I said.

"With the aid of two or three others we might name," said Larry.

"Why would they do this to us?" I asked.

"Why, indeed? It's the natural reaction of the old dinosaurs when they spot the first strange mammals bounding through their jungle. But it's a futile action."

"How did they do it?" I was still bewildered.

Larry was not. These things were always marvelously simple to his agile mind. That was why he was hitting .334 for the Yankees and I was chewing gum for the Red Sox. Larry was on his way to becoming a dinosaur in his own right. "They accomplished it easily enough," he said. "They got us here the same way we're going home. By typewriter."

"You mean—" I said, my eyes wide with astonishment.

"Yes," said Larry, "what *is* reality, anyway?"

Before the veal marsala came, we had the solution to our problem. We weren't vengeful, though, because we have to set the tone of the future. That's a heavy burden, but we carry it gladly.

"Now what?" said Larry, drinking some beer for dessert.

"Now we go home. We can go now, or we can wait around here in 1954 for a while, for a kind of vacation."

"We'll take a vote," said Larry, because he's a four-square kind of guy.

Well, we did take a vote, and we decided to go right home, because some of us had library books overdue. Getting home was simple. It was like Dorothy's Ruby Slippers—it was there all the time. We all gathered in Washington, because that's where we had last been together. We all sat together in a large suite in the same hotel where so many years in the future there would be a science fiction convention. We had Cokes and beer and pretzels and potato chips. We had the television on ("The Stu Erwin Show"), and we messed the room up some. "Remember," said Norris, "not one word about baseball. Only science fiction."

"Just science fiction," said Dick Shrader.

We started talking about money, of course. We talked about who was paying what, and that led to a discussion of editors. When we realized how violent our passions were growing we changed the subject to "The Future of Science Fiction," and then "Science Fiction and the Media," and then "Academia and Science Fiction." Just about then a short, heavy man came into the suite with a camera and took Larry's picture. The man sat down and listened. We offered him some pretzels. We talked about "The Short Fiction Market," and two wild young women dressed like characters from a trilogy of novels came in to fill the bathtub with some viscous fluid. We didn't offer them pretzels. We talked about "Science Fiction as a Revolutionary Weapon," and two writers and an agent and four more fans came in, and it was getting noisy, and Jim called down for some ice, and I went into the hall, and more fans and more pros were coming toward the room, so I went to the elevator and went up to my room. I opened the door carefully.

The light was on and I saw that there was someone else in the room. I was ready to turn away, but I saw that it was the same young woman who had been with me at the start of the adventure. I looked down, and of course I was in my old body (it's not *that* old, really, and it's a little worn, but it's mine) and everything was all right for the moment. We were victorious.

Breakaway, of course, is a story about ice hockey. I have to admit that it took me a long time to learn to appreciate hockey. I thought the game lacked one of the essential qualities that drew me to sports: precision. As far as I was concerned, skaters were forever gliding past the puck on the ice, or passing to people who weren't there, or muffling clumsily with each other against the boards. Even the fights were tiresome, or so I thought. All those guys could do was drop their sticks and clutch each other's jerseys. They wobbled around and couldn't throw a punch and stay upright at the same time. I felt that if it caused them so much trouble, they should just forget about the ice and get off the skates altogether.

My friends prevailed upon me, however, and I gave the sport chance after chance. One winter spent, for God alone knows what reason, in Cedar Knolls, New Jersey, I learned to my horror that all professional or collegiate sports were practically inaccessible. That winter, starved for vicarious victories, I watched a couple of dozen high school hockey games. Since then I have not dismissed the sport as I once did. I learned that skill and precision were involved as much as in any other team game. If some hockey players look less ept than others, it is only that competing while mounted on skates is basically unnatural. Like playing soccer underwater.

In Breakaway *I took the hazards of the game and made them a million times worse. Just for the hell of it.*

Breakaway

OLD NUMBER 12 stood by a port and looked down at the playing field. The port, for some reason, was shaped like the rounded rectangle of a CRT screen. It gave you the feeling that you were watching television, even while you stared out at real life. It had the effect of creating boredom and dissatisfaction, something the ship's designers never foresaw, because real life never moved so fast or so frantically as television. After thirty seconds at the port, you had a sneaking desire to change the channel. There was no way to do that, of course, and then you'd remember that you weren't watching television, that you were instead aboard an orbiting plastic and steel ball, and you were so far from home that sometimes your eyes stung with tears.

Václav Zajac, Number 12, turned away from the port. There really wasn't anything to see: a pale green-white world of ice turning in the dim light of a distant cold sun. He leaned against the bulkhead, feeling the machinery of the orbiting station thrumming in the wall at his back. He chewed his lip and stared at the deck without seeing anything in particular. He was avoiding the locker room, and he didn't want to take another glance through the port. There wasn't much else to do. That was one of the main troubles with the station: there was really nothing to do.

"Hey, Jackie," called another player. "You coming?"

"Sure," said Zajac. He didn't look up. The other man went into the locker room. Zajac studied the rippled sole of one shoe. Finally he took a long breath, exhaled slowly, and followed the other through the pastel green door.

Only the lack of personal decoration set his locker area apart from any of the others. Some of the players had adorned theirs, added bits of individuality, audio dots and holoscenes that were intended to portray something about their owners' tastes. The fact that most of these scenes were the same—running to ghostly, beckoning women apparently afflicted with respiratory difficulties—didn't diminish their value. Zajac's locker space was bare except for his uniform suit and a few toilet and training articles on the shelf. He never felt the need to express himself by decorating his person or his belongings. He believed that his personality and his essential nature were well-enough defined downstairs, on the playing field. On the ice.

Václav Zajac was right about that. There wasn't another hockey player in the Havoc Force amateur league with his reputation and statistics. He didn't need tiger stripes on his faceplate to unnerve an opposing defenseman. That defenseman was already frightened of him, and had been since before the opening faceoff.

He sat on the bench in front of his locker and listened to the cheerful conversation of his teammates. They were excited and just a little artificially high-spirited. They were beginning to wind themselves tighter, to allow their controlled hysteria to get them to the competitive peak they would need to play the game down below. Zajac didn't participate in their jokes and shouts and laughter and curses. He waited quietly until he felt ready, and then he began to dress. He had always been sober, oddly silent and disturbingly distant, even as a young rookie many years before. He stood up and took a roll of broad tan adhesive bandage from the shelf. He began strapping his ankles. Around him in the locker room soap and protective cups and wet towels flew through the air. If Zajac noticed, he showed no sign. The younger men respected him, but they played around him. Their missiles defied his air space, but no one ever presumed to include him in the locker room play.

The Condors were the station's entry in the Havoc Force Hockey Association, Second Quadrant champions for the last four seasons, league champions twice in that period. Zajac was a major reason for that success. His ice time was the only real life he knew. The endless days he spent monitoring the emptiness around the frozen rock of Niflhel seemed like punishment, with the occasional reward of liberty two hundred fifty miles below, on the nightmarish surface of the little world.

The game today was against the Rome IV Stingers, a weak team from the Third Quadrant. Rome IV was an outpost halfway across the spiral from Niflhel, and the two teams had never played each other before. Zajac, as he finished taping his ankles, wasn't even curious about them. He hadn't watched any of the tapes of the Stingers' previous games. He hadn't even studied the defensemen he would be facing. It didn't make any difference who they were, he thought. When he got down there, on the familiar but deadly pale green ice, he would own the game. He would establish his dominance early, and he would skate and score at will. He told himself this over and over, in a kind of self-hypnotic way. It was as important to his readiness as his physical condition and equipment.

The ice hockey tournament had been invented by the psych maintenance division to deal with the peculiar claustrophobia that always threatened to turn into an epidemic at the isolated outposts. They couldn't prevent the panic that gripped people who felt themselves lost and permanently abandoned in space, but if the hostile environments and lonely scenes could be made more familiar, the experts said that maybe the screaming red horror would diminish and eventually all but disappear. It was a nice theory, and it even worked after a fashion. None of the hockey players, for instance, ever felt the choking terror growing in them while they glided over the ice fields of Niflhel. The game was great therapy. It was fun, there was an exciting and considerable welcome relief from the tedium of their passive military duties. Down on the ice all was well. But in the shuttle ride back to the station. . . .

The temperature on the surface of Niflhel was only a little pocket change of Kelvin, just enough to register on the meters, to differentiate the dusky world from the near-absolute of the surrounding interstellar medium. The place had once been a marvelous laboratory where gases that could be liquified under difficult circumstances on Earth were found in solid prairies of unusual ice, or pools of sluggish liquid with dreamlike properties. Niflhel would have been of immense interest to physicists and chemists except that since the expansion through the spiral, worlds of this kind had become so common they were no longer even named: silent, lifeless planets circling so far from their central sun that the stars was just a glimmer of divorced energy in the daytime darkness of the sky.

Zajac put on a thin set of long underwear, made of cotton all the way from Earth. He chose only the best when it came to his equipment. He had tried snythetic fiber underwear as a rookie and it had almost cost him his life in a game on a forgotten and nameless world in the First Quadrant. His suit's climate sensors had failed briefly. The synthetic material didn't soak up his perspiration and tended to trap body heat. Zajac had almost stifled and dehydrated within the protective armor of his game uniform.

The suits were the most sophisticated pieces of equipment the technical teams could devise. They were lightweight, made of a dynaprene material that gave almost as much freedom as everyday clothing, yet insulated and protected the wearer against the harshest environments in the spiral—or anyway against most of them. The dynaprene had a little trouble dealing with certain atmospheres of very high pressure and very low pH. But in the general realm of conditions, the suits were miracles of efficiency and comfort. Because of them, people inhabited places that were bluntly uninhabitable, a paradox the human beings resolved by ignoring it. The suits were specially modified for the athletes. They were a little larger, a little roomier, in order to fit in pads for shins, ankles, elbows, and shoulders. These fiber and foam pads were snug, comfortable, and didn't restrict movement in the least.

Clothed in the suit, Zajac sat on the bench and waited. His helmet, his gauntlets, and his skated boots still rested on the shelf. He was finished dressing and there was nothing more for him to do until it was time for the team to head for the shuttle. None of the others had even begun getting into his suit. Zajac closed his eyes and breathed slowly. He relaxed. He felt mildly happy, as though something marginally pleasant was just about to happen, like a healthy sneeze or a good yawn.

He remained confident about his performance during the game, but he didn't think about it any longer.

"Jackie, the rest of you jokers, listen up." Zajac opened his eyes. The coach had come into the locker room. It must be almost time, thought Zajac. "These guys we're playing today are basically your everyday type of clowns," said the coach. "But that doesn't mean you don't have to pay attention to what you're doing down there. They're clowns and princesses, but they've scored a few goals, too. So watch yourselves. Check them hard a few times right in the beginning, and they'll probably skate clear of you the rest of the day. All right?" There was a murmur from the younger players. Zajac had heard all of this many times before. The coach gave the same speech before every game; every other team in the association seemed to be made up of clowns and princesses.

"Any change in their lineup?" asked Moro, the Condor goalie.

"No, so just go with the game plan. Keep the puck down at their end, don't pay any attention to their crazy defense. They do that a lot, I don't know why. Maybe they think it will confuse you. It's probably why they're always losers. Almost always. So just play your own game, control the puck, move it up and put it in. Get that first goal, and they'll have to play catch-up the rest of the day. You know that you can skate rings around them, they don't have anybody who can catch even Anangi, here." There was a sharp, quick laugh from the players, and Number 11, Bashako Anangi, spat angrily. He was a Condor defenseman not famed for his winged skates.

"Anything else?" asked the coach. He didn't look like what a coach ought to look like. He didn't have a big cigar or a Condor cap on his head. He wasn't wearing an old sweatshirt or a natty suit or ancient sneakers. He wore a white lab coat with an ID badge clipped to a lapel, and a headset and microphone over his thinning blond hair. He looked more like a communications technician, and when he wasn't coaching the hockey team, that's what he was.

There was a silence. The coach looked around the room, then clapped his hands. "So let's hit the ice," he said.

Zajac stood and stretched. The others hurried to complete their dressing. He took his gauntlets and boots and helmet and walked in his stockinged feet across the carpet of the locker room to the corridor leading to the shuttlecraft. Inside the shuttle he took his place on the long padded seat. He was all alone. There was a loud humming in the shuttle; it annoyed him and he tried to block it out. He busied himself. He went to the rack of hockey sticks against the aft bulkhead and found one of his. He used a low lie Victoriaville, a number four. He carried it back to his seat and rubbed the blades of his skates against the stick, dulling them a little. You had to do this for every game; if the skates were too sharp, they tended to stick to the ice, rather than cutting and gliding. You'd have a restricted stride and a little trouble turning. On ice, on water ice back on Earth, this would be inconvenient and might cost a player and his team eventually in the final score. On Niflhel, where the ice was made of complex hydrocarbons frozen harder than steel by the fearful coldness of space, that kind of inconvenience could develop into a perilous situation. One of the secrets of the game—not much of a secret, really, because every player in the league understood it well enough—was that you had to keep moving. The weight of the person pressed the skates into the surface, the pressure melted a molecular layer of the hydrocarbon ice under the blade, just enough to allow the skate to slide along. If the skate stood there a millisecond too long, though, it froze in place and Niflhel had itself a brand new surface feature. The skates could be loosed from the boots, being held there by the same dileucithane tape that closed the uniform gauntlets and boots. But that meant the player, skateless, would have to run and slide over the ice, on the broad boot bottoms, and it was unlikely that anyone could travel that way more than three steps without falling. The layer of melted hydrocarbon ice under a human foot made virtually a frictionless surface. And a fall in that situation could prove fatal.

So the players kept moving. Even the goalies, who wouldn't see action nearby sometimes for the greater part of the game, even they skated back and forth, around and around their domains, rather than become brittle, frozen statues on the face of the little green world.

After a few minutes five other Condors filed into the shuttle. They took seats and waited. The coach didn't come with them; there wasn't a single thing he could do for the team down on the surface of Niflhel. From the station two hundred fifty miles above he could monitor the game and make decisions. The rest of the team, the substitutes, stayed behind with the coach, ready to be ferried down when they were needed. The starting six players looked at each other, just a little nervously. Zajac felt a little tension, a little tightening of his shoulders, a little tingling in his head and hands. It would have distressed a rookie, but it was vaguely pleasant to Zajac. He welcomed it. He had learned long ago to use every bit of his pre-game agitation, to channel and focus it all.

"Well, Jackie, what do you think?" Zajac turned to face Gill, Number 16, the starting center. Zajac had no close friends, but he had played alongside Gill for more than five years and they had a kind of wordless communication on the ice, a coordinated effort that derived from intelligence and long experience. Conviviality counted for little on the glacial plain.

"No problem," said Zajac. His face was expressionless.

"Right," said Gill, "no problem." He seemed a little uncomfortable, as though, despite knowing Zajac's mood and manner, he wanted to make a deeper, more personal contact. "How do you feel?"

"Fine," said Zajac. "I feel good. You?"

Gill was quiet for a moment. He knew that he was being outmaneuvered. Whatever he said, Zajac would reply with just the right words to kill the conversation. Even when Zajac asked about Gill's condition, he did it in a way that demanded a meaningless answer. "Great," said Gill sadly, "really great. I got to tape." He busied himself taping his stick, winding the pearl gray dileucithane tape around the flat part of the stick's blade, just where he would want to keep the puck as he moved it down the ice toward the Stingers' goal.

The trip down took almost thirty minutes. Zajac used the time to finish checking out his suit. He put on the boots and skates, tucking the ends of the suit's legs into the high tops of the boots, then winding gray tape tightly around the ankles of the boots. Kileucithane tape had the molecules of its sticky stuff polarized on one side. When the tape was stretched tight and wrapped over itself, no man alive was strong enough to pull it apart. A weak electric current, however, applied from within the suit, released the hold and the tape became just a dull-colored length of rough cloth. There was no way to pull the boots off without first removing the tape; Zajac's foot would pull off first.

Next he checked the neoprene laces of the boots and the tape that held the skates themselves tight. In the first year of the association, players used skates brought from Earth made for use under Earthlike conditions. The rawhide thongs held moisture, froze as solid as a rope of glass, and shattered under the first application of stress. Men suffered because of that small unforeseen aspect of the eternal winter. It didn't take long, though, to find replacement materials that wouldn't be affected by the temperatures near absolute zero. Dynaprene, neoprene, and dileucithane performed perfectly. Or, at least, well enough so that no one had perished on the pale ice fields since their introduction.

Zajac nested his helmet into the locking rings around the neck of his uniform suit. He heard the buzz and click of the helmet's circuits cutting in. He saw the projection of the playing field at the top of the faceplate, a rectangular map laying on its long side with two vertical slashes for the goals and a vertical stripe for the center line. The map represented the whole field of play, which was huge, immense compared to the hockey rinks on Earth. The rectangle marked out on the surface of Niflhel measured one mile by three.

Zajac touched on the receiver and switched from one channel to another. On the first channel he heard two of his teammates talking to each other, telling grotesque stories in two languages. On the second channel there was only static; later he would be able to hear the communications of the Stingers' players, scrambled so that none of the Condors could intercept their strategy. On the third channel there was gentle music, instrumental versions of show tunes from faraway stage successes and popular entertainers. During the game on the fourth channel he would be able to hear the coach's directions; now there was only the sound of slow, regular breathing, a kind of irritating whistling, and the coach's unconscious humming. Zajac switched to the fifth channel and listened to the internal communications of the orbiting station.

A red warning light flickered on his faceplate, indicating that his suit's integrity was breached. Of course that was true, since he hadn't put on his gauntlets and closed the sleeves of the uniform. He did that, winding the dileucithane tape around his forearms. He was now sealed into the suit, and he made a quick check of the life support circuits. Every gauge showed green, healthy, fine, perfect, ready to go. Zajac clutched his stick and waited for landfall.

The shuttle set down in a great silent explosion of clouds of methane and formaldehyde liberated from the craggy face of Niflhel. The hydrocarbons sublimed instantly, invisibly, from ice to gas, leaving ringed depressions of melted frost which solidified immediately into pocked craters. Václav Zajac climbed out of the shuttle and skated away in long, lazy curves. The shuttle shook and flared and lifted back into the black sky, but he didn't watch it go. The men from the Niflhel station were delivered one by one to their starting positions on the ice. When they left the shuttle they skated around in circles, getting the feel of the hard ice again, enjoying the freedom and the peace, welcoming the change from their devastatingly dull jobs in orbit. They waited for the arrival of the Rome IV Stingers. They didn't care how long that would take.

"Here they come," said a voice over Zajac's receiver. He looked up and saw another shuttle—or maybe the same one, he couldn't tell.

"Okay, boys, line up," said Gill, who was the team's captain. "Niflhel Station, this is Gill. Plug in the position markers, please."

"Right, Maxie," said a voice from the station. Zajac's faceplate lit up with seven colored dots, laid over the rectangular map of the playing field. Five of the dots were green, and represented the positions of Zajac's teammates. One dot was orange, resting on the center stripe, and marked the puck. One dot was fiery red, and showed Zajac's own relative position. When the Stingers hit the ice, they would show up as blue dots. The system was necessary because for extended stretches of play some of the players would be out of sight of each other.

Even with the suit lamps and the photo amplifiers in the helmets, the upper limit of visibility was slightly under twelve hours. The game lasted fourteen hours by the clock on the orbiting station. A skater's endurance was figured at about eight hours; after that his judgment and precision began to suffer, to deteriorate so rapidly that very shortly he had difficulty merely keeping himself upright. It was the coach's job to keep track of his players' condition by monitoring their vital signs and analyzing their performance during the game. Substitutions were made carefully, protecting the players and preventing the other team from seizing an advantage. The coach's role was vital. The game was more than a battle to wrestle a neoprene puck into the other team's cage; it was a deft balance of strength and conditioning, of skill and shrewd guesswork and decision.

Václav Zajac skated in the twilight at his wing position. He was stationed at a point one mile from his team's goal, where Moro patroled the six-foot-wide net, and a half mile from the center line. He was at one wing, a quarter mile from Gill at center, a half mile from Pete Soniat at the other wing. A half mile behind him were the two defensemen, Seidl and Brickman. He saw their green dots on his faceplate, wavering about as they skated around waiting for the game to begin. The orange puck still rested at center ice. There would be no faceoff as such; referees were of little value on a playing field of three square miles. They couldn't hope to follow all of the action and catch all of the penalties. The game would begin when a signal bell sounded in their helmets, triggered by an association observer and impartial umpire aboard the orbiting station. As for fouls—there weren't any. The play sometimes got a little testy and just a little physical, but real fights were infrequent because the suits were so well padded and insulated that a punch did little damage.

The bell rang. Gill shot off his mark toward the stationary puck. His opposite number on the Rome IV team raced toward him. Zajac and Soniat angled toward the center, skating easily. There was no chatter on the first channel; Zajac switched to channel four, to hear the coach. "All right, boys," said the coach, "let's go, let's go." The coach didn't have anything terribly cogent to suggest yet; it was all cheerleading until somebody got hold of the puck. That wouldn't be for a few minutes, because Gill had a half mile to skate before he could begin to locate it.

"They're fanning out, Jackie," said the coach. When he had something important to say, he could broadcast on both channels one and four.

"Right, I hear you, coach," said Zajac. He saw on his faceplate the rapid movement of the Stinger wings heading out from their starting position. They were going to flank the Condors' front line, gambling, banking that their center would come up with the puck and then they'd be past the Condors' first line of defense without a struggle. Of course, if Gill reached the puck first the Stingers would be in bad shape. "Pete," called Zajac to his other wing, "what do you want to do?"

"What's it look like, Maxie?" asked Soniat.

"Too soon," said Gill, huffing a little as he sprinted toward the center line.

"Maxie has it," said the coach calmly. "The projection is that he'll reach the puck forty-four seconds before their boy."

"We'll be through them," said Soniat.

"Sixteen strong side," said the coach, calling the play.

"Okay," said Soniat.

"Right," said Gill.

"Did you hear that?" asked Zajac. The two defensemen behind him answered that they did.

"That's assuming Maxie doesn't fall on his face getting there," said Moro from his lonely goalie post.

"Uh," snorted Gill.

The two wingers, Zajac and Soniat, were converging on center ice. When the three Condor players got sufficiently close together, they would appear as one large blue blur on the faceplates of the Stingers. The puck would be a muted glow submerged beneath them. One of the Condors would carry the puck toward the Stinger goal and the others would swing away, but it would be a moment before the dots on the faceplate maps would separate enough for the Stingers' defensemen to know who had the puck and in what direction he was going. Those seconds would mean a considerable headstart. Under normal circumstances it would be almost impossible for the Stingers to chase down the puck carrier. Only superb play and a good deal of luck would save them. The Condors would converge again in the area of the goal, so the Stinger goalie would not have advance warning of where the puck was coming from. He would see three streaking Condor skaters, and have no notion which man would be the attacker. They would come at him from straight on and from oblique angles to the right and left, and he would be helpless until the final instant of the approach. Then everyone watching the game would learn what the poor man's reactions were like.

Soniat would take the puck off to the left, crossing the routes of Gill and Zajac. The three would weave their way down the ice, skating apart as far as an eighth of a mile and then returning, passing the puck to each other whenever one of the Stinger defensemen seemed to analyze the pattern too well.

The play was a good one. The trouble was that it just never got off the ground.

"Damn it to hell," muttered Gill in Zajac's ear.

"What's wrong?" asked the coach.

"The damn puck isn't here."

"Oh boy," murmured Seidl, "he missed it."

"I was off by less than a hundred yards," said Gill.

"Get moving, Maxie!"

"Too late, he's got it," said Gill. "Look out, here he comes."

"We see him," said Zajac. Because he and Soniat had been closing in, they weren't far from the Stinger center's path. Gill hooked around in vain pursuit, but Zajac closed in on an angle that would intercept the puck carrier before either of the Rome IV wingers could arrive to help out.

"Take it away, take it away," called Moro. Calling out encouragement was about all he had to do at this stage of the game.

"I'll get the son of a buck," said Gill. He was still trailing Zajac, who was shortening the distance between himself and the puck carrier. After a minute he announced that he had visual contact with the Stinger center.

"Crease the bastard!" cried the coach. The game transformed him from a pleasant, amiable technician into a half-crazy commander who lusted to get out on the ice himself.

"Exactly what I'm going to do," said Zajac. Some players would have skated alongside the opposing player, trying to fish the puck away with swipes of the stick. Zajac's technique was a little more direct, and accounted for his intimidating reputation. The two men skated directly at each other; for a while it seemed that the Stinger center didn't know Zajac was coming. Then he must have been warned, because he looked up and jerked as if startled. He began skating away from Zajac, but Zajac was faster. He closed the gap between them, coming in from the Stinger's side. He let himself glide past the man a few feet, planted one skate, and swung around. Zajac took off after the puck carrier and caught up to him in five or six powerful strides. They skated silently together, matched stroke for stroke. The Stinger protected the puck by changing his stick to his other hand, keeping the puck out of range of a slashing reach by Zajac, but that wasn't Zajac's plan. He, too, transferred his stick to his outside hand. He raised his left arm to shoulder height, then brought it down and back, catching the Stinger skater in the chest with his elbow. The man leaned backward, arms flailing, off balance. Zajac gave him a slight push, and the nameless man toppled over on the ice. Zajac slapped the puck away a few feet, skated after it, then changed direction and began cutting smoothly back toward Maxie Gill, the center line, and—one-and-a-half miles beyond—the Stinger goal.

"You got it?" asked the coach.

"Sure," said Zajac, not even breathing hard, "no problem."

"No problem," said Gill.

"Way to go, Jackie," said Brickman.

"Sixteen strong side?" asked Soniat.

"As before," said the coach. "Nice playing, Jackie." Zajac aimed for his rendezvous with Gill and Soniat.

The play developed exactly as it had so many times on the coach's animated board. Zajac brought the puck up, fed it to Gill. Zajac crossed over to the left wing, Gill continued up the middle, then passed the puck to Soniat. Soniat drove toward the goal, and Gill slipped into the right wing. Soniat crossed left, abandoned the puck to Zajac, and Zajac skated toward Gill. The puck leapt from blade to blade, and the puck carrier swooped and changed. The three men wove a braided pattern in the ancient chill of Niflhel. Soon the Stingers were faced with a problem. Only two defensemen, and then the goalie, stood between the three Condors and the first score of the game. The Stingers would have to make a choice, and a speculative one at that. It would be a poor decision for both defensemen to gang up on a single charging Condor lineman, so each picked one of the three and intercepted. One of the Rome IV skaters went after Gill, and the other decided upon Soniat. At that precise moment, however, Zajac had the puck on the right wing, and undeterred he sped through the last of the Condor defense, unhindered now toward the goal.

"Nothing to it now, Jackie," said Gill, a little short of breath.

"Breakaway, breakaway!" chanted the coach. He had offered a minimum of thoughtful guidance, but so far this game hadn't needed any.

"No one to stop you now, Jackie," said Soniat. "We checked these fools hard. You're in the clear."

Alone. All alone on the pale green ice, beneath the unwavering stars of a stranger world, Zajac skated, exhilarated, cheered and warmed by his own skill and luck and daring. A little over a mile to the goal, according to the rough estimate he could make from his faceplate map. Then would come the final dramatic thrill of deking the Stinger goalie out of position, the silent man-on-man confrontation and the slamming home of the puck, the flash of the neoprene stick and the clean flight of the puck into the corner of the net. He pictured the goalie lying sprawled vainly across the ice, and Zajac celebrating all alone, all alone until Gill and Soniat joined him for the cross-country journey back into position for the next faceoff....

All alone. It was the time of the game that Václav Zajac loved the best. He luxuriated in the feeling of solitude, of purposeful activity, of being the focus of energy in the dynamic effort. He leaned forward and skated with long, powerful strides. He looked around him to the close horizon: there was nothing to see, no other people, no physical features of dramatic interest. The photo amps in his helmet showed him just smooth glass underfoot and velvet sky above, the gliding orange puck and the diamond chip stars. This was exaltation. Perhaps this had always been the utter joy of the sport, since the days when Indians skated on frozen lakes with the ribs of elks bound to their feet. When Zajac had been a small boy he had played shinny, battling a small rubber ball across the frozen river of his native Moravia. He had learned the game, learned the techniques, subjected himself to the necessary conditioning, accepted the demands and rewards, at an early age. Now, separated from those games by many years and uncountable miles, he was still getting the same intoxicating sensation as he ripped the puck away from the other team and set out alone toward the goal. He was inexorable. He was overpowering. He was alone.

He skated with his head up, his knees slightly bent. He kept the puck ahead of him, moving it forward with little taps, first to the left, then to the right. The feeling of pure speed was like a passionate embrace. He wanted it to go on and on, never to end, and it wouldn't end, not until he climaxed the overwhelming surge down the ice with the conquering drive into the goal. Even then the excitement would linger, fading a little of course, but the giddy arousal would remain, spoiled only by the arrival of his teammates and their chattering congratulations. That always ruined it a little for Zajac, but it never destroyed the experience completely. The race was always his, and he lived for it alone. Now, on the home ice of Niflhel, he exulted.

"Let's go!" said Brickman, who was miles behind, completely out of the action, who had nothing to do but skate about somewhat bored and watch Zajac's green dot streak toward the goal on his faceplate.

"Okay, Jackie, okay!" said the coach.

Zajac grimaced and changed the channel. He listened to the soft, lilting, excruciating music for a while.

He was thinking about the move he was going to use on the Stinger goalie. His mind wasn't on his skating, on the immediate condition of the playing field. He didn't see the frozen ripple, the small raised scar on the glacial floor. He didn't know it was there until his skate hit it with a numbing shock. There was a raw grinding feeling, and then Zajac was flying flat in space, falling. He landed heavily on his left side, his left arm pinned under him. There was a noiseless push of liberated gases; it was as jarring as a blow to the jaw in a beer-soaked brawl. Then everything was still. Everything was very quiet. Everything waited. Zajac was stunned and probably dying, but he didn't know it yet. He was caught in a billion-year-old trap, and he hadn't even heard it spring shut. He would have to learn the rules one by one, the hard way, and if he was going to survive he had no time to lose.

"Oh, hell," he said. He took a deep breath.

No one answered. No one wondered what had happened.

"I guess I'm all right," he said.

No one asked him what he meant.

"Coach?" he said.

The black coldness waited.

"I fell pretty hard out here but I'm okay. I can feel the puck. I'm lying right on top of it. Give me a minute to catch my breath." He felt warm. Actually, as he calmed down a little, he felt hot. His suit wasn't cooling him off enough. He wondered what was wrong. He tried to sit up, to take a quick inventory of his monitoring systems. He learned with an ice-cold shiver of fear that his helmet was frozen fast to the rock-solid ice. He nearly dislocated a shoulder trying to raise his head.

Zajac was afraid. He had never before felt this particular kind of fear, this awareness of the nearness of death. It was so close, the end of his life, that he could not see how he could avert it. He knew he couldn't deke death with a good feint in one direction, then go skating off free and clear in another. It would take more than that. He didn't know what it would take, and that thought terrified him. He needed help, and that thought mortified him. But his terror was greater.

"Coach?" he called. He waited in vain for a reply. He

switched channels. "Maxie? Pete?" There wasn't even the sound of static. He went back and forth through the five channels: there were four channels of utter, terminal silence, but channel three was coming through clearly. The damned music, sweet strings and a binging triangle playing a sprightly march. It was a paralyzing insult added to his calamity.

"Hey, coach!" Zajac screamed. His voice sounded raw and harsh to himself, and the effect was ominous. He was in trouble, that was definite, but he was ashamed that he was losing control so quickly. He forced himself to calm down, to think. He carefully appraised his situation.

Evidently he wasn't receiving his teammates' communications. That didn't mean, though, that they weren't receiving his. "Coach, Maxie, Pete, if anybody can hear me, I had a tumble and I'm frozen onto the ground. My helmet and my shoulder. I landed on a couple of the trade-off buttons and they melted the ice, and then I got caught in it. I can't hear a thing. I can't hear you, and I can't see where you are. My faceplate map isn't functioning. I don't know what to do. You're going to have to come get me, because I can't move. I only have one arm free, and the trade-off buttons are going to be overworked, trying to compensate for the coldness of the ground. So hurry." He stopped talking. He felt a little foolish, not knowing if anyone could hear him.

What next? He didn't know. The climate control would be raising the temperature of his suit as the internal heat bled away. Eventually the heating unit would fail, and then it wouldn't be long before Zajac, suit and all, would be lifeless solid human ice. He didn't know how much longer the suit's unit could function.

As he waited, an unpleasant thought returned again and again: his only hope was that he'd be found and rescued in time. The prime concern, therefore, was that if the others weren't receiving his calls, and if neither his suit nor the puck were sending out signals, they would never stumble across him in time. And stumble across him is what they'd do—eventually. If they ever found him at all, they'd trip across his marblestiff corpse in the dark.

There was no way of judging how quickly the time passed. The sun—the dim, distant star that barely held Niflhel in its weak grasp—cast no shadows on the enemy ice. Zajac couldn't see that sun from his sprawled position, so he wouldn't be able to observe it as it cut its way through the strange constellations. He doubted if he'd be alive long enough to notice much stellar movement in any case. There was nothing else within sight that could help him in any way. There was nothing else at all but ice, endless ice, murderous ice.

Zajac waited and studied himself closely for any sign of panic. The notion that at the end, as he began to feel the sting of death creeping along his rigid limbs, he might lose control of his mind was more repellent to him than the threat of death. He feared madness more. Though his suffering would be limited by the mercilessness of the environment, he swore that he would choose an immediate end by his own hand rather than descend muttering and weeping into insanity. It occurred to him that his promise was one he might not want to keep at that final instant, or even be able to remember.

There were many things to regret while he waited between life and death. He thought about his joyless childhood, about the unkindness he had often shown others, about the broken vows and broken dreams, about all the things of a lifetime that are without meaning and are given importance only by an ultimate realization that they can now never be corrected. Zajac felt contempt for his own remorse, because he knew how shallow he was. Even as the tears slipped from his eyes, he laughed skeptically. "You don't mean a word of it, Jackie," he whispered. "Try to die like a man." Whatever that meant. . . .

This gelid vista would be the last thing he would see: a jagged horizon, low ridges of pallid green shining in his suit's lamplight, ice of a color he had seen sometimes in a young woman's eyes, a sky as black and empty and devoid of hope as Hell—and wasn't Hell described just like this? A lake of ice, rather than pits of flame? And Lucifer frozen in the middle of it, immobile and bitter? The comparison made Zajac laugh aloud, and it was not a healthy laughter, with just the faintest tinge of hysteria. It brought his wandering thought to a sudden focus. His experiment with fancy ended abruptly.

Was there anything that he could do to release the helmet from the tenacious ice? His hockey stick lay on the rough surface not far from his outstretched right hand, within reach. Zajac didn't believe he could use it to chip the helmet free; the neoprene was tough, but not as hard as the ice. Still, he reached

out and grasped the end of the blade, then drew the stick near.
He would never be able to use it to pry the helmet loose, either.
The stick would snap like a dry bone.

If he were to live, to free himself from the frozen tomb, he
needed an audacious idea. In order to find the key, he needed
all the coolness of thought on which he prided himself. And,
he admitted, he might need all the crazy reasoning of desperation, as well. In the same way that he might have proceeded
to fix a leaking faucet at home, he took it by the numbers.

How could he get free? By removing himself from the ice,
of course. How could that be done? By getting rid of the ice,
by breaking it or melting it. Could he break it? He had already
decided the answer to that was no.

That left melting.

What could melt the ice? Under these circumstances, only
the heat inside his suit. The warmth from the trade-off buttons
was melting the ice in that immediate area, leaving a bowl-
like depression under his left side, but his helmet was too far
away and there was no way of delivering the heat from between
his shoulders to the necessary point.

Was there another way of transferring heat from inside his
suit to the place where the helmet was welded to the ground?

Zajac didn't have an immediate answer. More accurately,
at first he didn't want to examine the only solution that did
present itself.

"Well," he murmured after a moment, "there is a way." He
had a flickering, half-formed notion.

It was unpleasant. It was very unpleasant.

The idea grew, and Zajac realized that there was every
reason to believe it would work. But the more clearly he understood what had to be done, the more grotesque and awful it
seemed. Yet it was a choice between sacrifice and certain death.
Rational thought demanded—

Zajac pressed the button in the handle of his hockey stick.
The dileucithane tape wound around the blade immediately lost
its adhesiveness. With his free hand he removed the relaxed
tape from the stick. Now it was ready to be used again, and
he was careful not to foul it in tangles because he would never
be able to untwist it, and that would be the end of him. He
transferred an end of the tape to his left hand and clumsily
wrapped the length of it around and around his right arm, just
above the tape that sealed his right gauntlet to his sleeve. He

pulled the tape as tight as he could, so tight that he knew he was shutting off the circulation in his arm.

It occurred to Zajac that if he managed to save himself and then stay alive until he could be rescued, he might look back on this nightmare and realize that there had always been a simple and easy way to solve the crisis. If there were he couldn't see it now, and as he became more frantic he cared less about what he would think in the future. The terrible present over-shadowed all that. Maybe he would curse himself for a fool. Maybe his teammates would be shocked by the means he had selected to save himself, when there was some other obvious method he had overlooked. Zajac's mouth was very dry, and there was a loud buzzing in his head that distracted his attention. He was near emotional collapse, and he put the thought of hypothetical painless answers in the back of his mind. He had not been able to find one, and so he was compelled to follow the path he had chosen.

His right hand tingled with a myriad sharp pinpricks. He closed his eyes tight and tried to calm his agonized thoughts. The pain in his hand became a throbbing that he couldn't ignore. Needles of pain stabbed up his arm from his fingertips to his shoulder. It was time to act, but the process of summoning courage and strength was more difficult than he had imagined. "Come on, Jackie," he whispered, "just do it. Do it or you'll die right here."

His left thumb found the button on his right gauntlet. He pressed it, giving as he did an odd, high-pitched cry. The tape on the gauntlet went dead. He unwrapped it quickly and flung it away. He ripped the gauntlet off with his left hand and shrieked as the unbearable cold attacked his exposed hand. He grabbed at the back of his helmet, twisting as much as he could so that he could reach the frozen bond. The remaining warmth in his freezing hand turned the ice to thin and poison gas. He rolled over, and his helmet was free. He sobbed loudly and rose to his knees. His right hand remained on the ice where he had rested.

Zajac got to his feet, staggered, stumbled, fell again to his knees. He felt dreamlike, a little dazed. He felt no pain; that meant that he was in shock. He was alive, but he didn't know for how long. The ragged end of his forearm was exposed beyond the tourniquet of tape, and the killing cold would soon crawl through his veins like serpent's venom. He was very cold. He looked back to where he had lain prisoner. His right hand, his strong hand, was blanched white as new snow in the glare of his lamp. The thumb had snapped off. The light flashed from a gold ring on the fourth finger. Zajac's eyes opened wide and he stared, sickened. He clutched his ruined arm to his chest. Suddenly, like a vast and overpowering expulsion of evil, he vomited inside his helmet.

With an effort he got to his feet again, a bit unsteady on his skates. Freeing the helmet had been only part of the problem, although he hadn't wanted to think about the rest until now. He was faced with the difficulty of staying alive until he could find the other players. Evidently they couldn't find him, or they would already have come to his aid. His uniform suit wasn't transmitting its signal. The puck, though, ought not to have been affected. He remembered, however, that he had been on top of it the entire time. It was likely that its position had just reappeared on the faceplate maps of both the Condors and the Stingers. If Zajac were lucky, they'd all be sprinting toward him that very instant, and they'd be there to call for help in a few minutes.

If he weren't lucky, of course, the puck was as lost as he, and therefore he'd have to find his own salvation. He grimaced. That was the way it had always been, the way he had always preferred. He was too lightheaded from shock and loss of blood to recall how only a short time before he had rejected that delusion.

In the singlemindedness of his condition, Zajac decided to head for the Stinger goal, the nearest place where he could be certain of finding another person. He tried to find traces of his passage across the ice before his accident, to get an idea of the direction of the goal. The ice was so hard that his tracks were almost invisible, but he caught them in the oblique beam of his lamp. He saw the small wrinkle of ice that had caused his fall, and he mouthed a vicious Slovak curse. He picked a place on the horizon, a tiny landmark of three sharp spires of ice, and skated weakly toward it. He estimated that the goal should be only a bit more than a half mile beyond it.

His right arm, from the shoulder to the torn end, felt paradoxically warm. The rest of the body was colder than before, and he shook with chills. He tried not to think about the loss of his hand, but the image of it lying abandoned on the ice kept occurring to him, and he had to fight down new sickness again and again.

After fifty yards he realized that he was carrying his hockey stick. "Stupid," he said to himself. He dropped it to the ground, and then came to a halt. "What I ought to have is the damn puck." The puck may or may not have been transmitting. If it were, it would give the others his position. It was worth taking along. He bent down and picked up his stick, then turned and went back for the puck. It took him several minutes to find it; he spent the whole time muttering angrily. When he located the puck he started off again toward the Stinger goal, holding his stick lefthanded, stickhandling the puck across the ice. He was too confused to realize that he could simply have carried the puck in his left hand, that he didn't need to obey the rules of hockey: for Václav Zajac, that game ought to have been over. But his thoughts were sluggish and wrapped in a kind of muffling peace. At intervals a great, sharp, piercing pain broke through the fog, the first tentative bits of the massive anguish to come. Clumsily, holding the hockey stick in the crook of his right elbow and guiding it with his left hand, Zajac maneuvered the puck toward the indifferent horizon.

Zajac wandered in the dream delirium that accompanies serious bodily trauma. He patted the puck along, directing all of his attention to that small chore, forgetting for the moment what had happened to him and where he was going. The only thing that seemed to matter was nudging that neoprene puck forward in a straight line. At one point he assembled his senses enough to ask himself why this task was so vital. He had no ready response. It had something to do with the game. He recalled the game well enough, and the team and the station. He tried to imagine what everyone was doing back aboard the station. He wondered if they were following his progress, if they were excited or concerned or completely bored. The game must mean very little to the others aboard the station, he realized. To them it was only a pattern of glowing points of color on a two-dimensional map. How involved could they be with that? The action was rapid, as the orange dot sped toward one end of the rectangle or the other. But there was no indication that these points of light even presented living players. As far as the people on the station knew, the hockey team may never actually have been delivered to the surface of Niflhel. The games might really be played at a keyboard console in another room.

If that were true, though, Zajac mused, why did he hurt so terribly? And what the hell was he doing?

The numbing clouds in his mind dispersed to several bright, clean brass notes. It was the music again on channel three. This time, however, Zajac welcomed it; it was reassurance that he wasn't alone in the world. He had begun to feel like the last survivor of his race, or like a solitary spirit of the cosmos awaiting physical reality. He listened to an appalling trumpet improvisation based on the Horn Call from *Siegfried*. In addition to the trumpet there was a piano, a snare drum, a string bass, a vibraharp played with a heavy hand, and a guitar. The music pulled Zajac along, and he was grateful for it. Utter silence would have killed him, would have persuaded him that he was tired, that he shouldn't bother to go on, that an attempt to prolong his life was an affront to the entire entropic basis of the universe. But human beings had shouldered aside that silence and filled the space with sappy music, and that accomplishment heartened Zajac. He would not surrender until he, too, had made a mark equal to that trumpet solo.

Less than a quarter mile from his goal the agony dispelled all the soft sleepy thoughts. He saw and felt with a clarity that unnerved him. He was isolated as few people ever had been. He had been singled out, he was marked, and he had been made ready for death. His futile struggles were worse than useless—they were humiliating. How could Václav Zajac believe that he had the resources to repel all that a hostile world chose to throw at him? It was arrogance of the sort that hastened death.

Movement caught his eye. He looked up from the ice and saw a man in the green and white uniform suit of the Rome IV Stingers about a hundred yards away. It was their goalie. The man waved at him. Whether the goalie was signalling concern or boastful challenge Zajac couldn't tell. Even if the receiver in his helmet were functioning, the two men wouldn't have been able to communicate. Zajac took a better grip on his hockey stick and skated for the net. He was so dazed that his highest priority was scoring the goal. He forgot his own terrible condition. He slanted over on a path that would take him past the goal net at about a forty-five degree angle. He didn't worry about rocketing the puck past the goalie on the first pass; he wanted to get a look at the man's moves, his defensive tendencies.

Zajac's eyes tried to peer through a red haze that exploded into golden points of light. He heard his own heartbeat and the roaring of his blood, and the noise bore the hollow echoes heard usually only in dreams and drunkenness. The world seemed to pulse around him, to grow larger and then shrink so there was barely room for Zajac to breathe. In all the universe there was only Zajac's troubled brain, his bewildered senses, and the unwanted freight of ghastly pain. His terror had dissipated, replaced first by fatigue, then by mindlessness, finally by a growing resentment. His anger was directed entirely toward the Stinger goalie, whose duty it was to thwart him. Zajac desperately needed to slam the puck home, but now he doubted if he was strong enough to accomplish it.

Two familiar skaters in Condor uniforms approached him from the left wing. "Maxie, Pete," he said, sighing. He left the puck on the ice: he didn't need it any longer. They had found him.

Zajac skated in a wide loop toward the goal, then toppled forward. He sank to his knees, blinded by the throbbing pain. It was now a rhythmic beating that filled his entire consciousness. He stood again, unaware that he did, and he moved blindly over the ice. He cried softly to himself, and in a short while the pain subsided. It didn't vanish completely, but the hammering was pushed down to a manageable level, and allowed Zajac to clear his head.

He looked around and saw the goalie, who seemed unusually intent on Zajac. It had been compassion, then, that the man had been expressing. That made Zajac feel good. He expected to see the Stinger player crouched, wound tight, motionless as a stalking cat waiting for the first glimpse of the puck. Instead he was moving slowly over the ice, toward Zajac. Zajac waved his left arm wildly, ignoring the increase in pain, trying to tell the foolish goalie that everything was all right, that the worst had happened and Zajac was no longer worried, that the goalie had better tend to his own troubles because Gill and Soniat were speeding toward the open net, passing the puck between them. Zajac, not thinking clearly, tried to shout, "Get back to the net, you damn fool!" The effort cost him, and he was struck down by an angry slash of pain. He lay still for a moment, an indefinite length of time. When his awareness returned, the goalie was only fifteen feet from him. Soniat had one arm in the air, Gill had the puck on his stick, in front of the goal. He did not take the shot. He swooped by and swung around, toward Zajac.

Zajac smiled placidly to himself. He rose to his knees, and he knew then that he was exhausted, used up. He might never skate away from that spot. He leaned on his stick and watched. He tried to see the face of the Stinger goalie through the man's faceplate, but it was obscured. Zajac listened to the music; it was partially drowned out by the drumming in his head. Gill skated close by, and Zajac wanted to wave but he couldn't. Gill dropped the puck by Zajac's side. It skidded a few inches and came to a stop against his knee. The goalie was bending forward, reaching out a hand, helpless, perhaps frightened. Gill was gesturing to Soniat, evidently suddenly aware of Zajac's desperate state. Soniat skated toward them. Gill pointed first to Zajac, then into the black sky. Zajac nodded; yes, yes, he understood, they were coming for him.

Zajac was fading. He wondered idly, as if he had no personal stake in the answer, if the shuttle would arrive in time. He looked up at the stars, then at Gill, then at the puck beside him. He pushed the puck with his stick, more than slapped it, awkwardly, from his kneeling position. An angry noise began to burr in his head. Gill was waving an arm wildly but Zajac never took his gaze from the puck. It slid straight and true for the far side of the empty cage, and it seemed to take forever to cross the distance. It skimmed over the victorious ice, and as Zajac struggled to clear his vision, the puck came to rest at last, home in the corner of the goal.

So tell me, what would a book like this be without a racing story? Therefore, I proudly present The Horse with One Leg, the story of a horse and the girl who loves him. When this story first appeared, the editor who bought it had to do a little tap-dancing to justify it as science fiction. He called Lucky a "mutant horse." Well now. Who am I to say otherwise?

Before I sold this strange piece, I submitted it first to a major mainstream magazine that publishes modern fiction. It was rejected with the comment that the story was "too sentimental." That's about all I'd like to say at this point about major mainstream magazines. The Horse with One Leg is satire flirting dangerously with parody. I plan to do a sequel some day, about the offspring of the puppy mentioned in the final paragraph. The title of that story will be The Spherical Dog. So you can start getting ready for that now.

The Horse with One Leg

POPS AND MOMMA weren't home that night, I remember. I can recall that I felt completely abandoned. They *should* have been there; they certainly knew that it was nearly time. I was only eleven years old then, much too young to have to face any sort of major crisis alone. Pops and Momma had done quite a thorough job of keeping me carefully sheltered. As an eleven year-old girl growing up on an Ohio farm I knew nothing of the terrors of the wider world; indeed, even the more intimate and unavoidable mysteries of my own body were officially nonexistent.

And, as these things always seem to occur at the *worst* possible time, it was a Thursday night: Jimmy, Pops' hired man, was off, no doubt miles away in Kepton with his fancy lady. It was unusual that Pops and Momma would leave me alone entirely, but I seem to remember that the occasion was grave enough to make this necessary. In any case there I was, alone in the old white house, with Calpurnia ready to deliver.

About seven o'clock I fixed myself a sandwich from the leftover chicken and went out to the barn. It had been a beautiful, clear day, with little wind and an unseasonably warm sun, but by sundown the sky had clouded over. Now the wind had risen, and the poplars in the yard rustled and bent in the darkness. I felt a strange and unpleasant coldness inside, and though I realized that it came from being left alone, and from worrying about Cal, it grew worse and worse. In the night blackness I felt as though I were walking through a dream, and the chicken sandwich brought tears to my eyes. I was startled by the bare bulb glaring above the door to the barn, but once I was inside I felt *real* again, although hardly more secure.

I stood by Calpurnia's stall, leaning on the half-door and testing my thoughts. I watched myself rather dispassionately, feeling fear (a new experience in my young and insular existence), loneliness, and worry about a creature other than myself (an emotion equally as untried). Cal shook her beautiful chestnut head at me, and her dark eyes shone in the dim light. I said a few words to her, more to make myself feel better than to soothe her troubled maternity. I had never felt such an intense mood of impotence before. I was so helpless, and the fact that I myself was in no personal danger did not alleviate my worry. When I had finished the dry sandwich, I went back into the house. Perhaps if I stayed there, everything would happen quietly, without me, and it all would turn out well. If not, when I awoke in the morning Pops or Jimmy would be taking care of Cal. Perhaps if I closed my eyes it would all go away.

About nine o'clock I began to get sleepy. I turned off the radio and washed the dishes so that Pops and Momma would be proud of me when they came home. Just before going upstairs to bed I felt a sudden pang of apprehension, and I decided to go outside again to check on Cal. It had finally begun to rain, and the drops were cold and falling heavily, so that I had to put on my shiny yellow raincoat and hat. It was supernaturally dark now; even the light from the barn weakened and died before reaching my eyes as I stood on the back porch. The blackness was divided now and then by the jagged country lightning, and the following thunder did nothing to calm my guilty fears.

There was a strange silence in the barn. The other horses were standing in their stalls, apparently unaware of any change in the nightly routine. But their hooves did not stamp in the damp air; there were none of their usual low neighings of greeting; I heard scarcely more than the swish of heavy equine tails. Blaze and Ginger did not even raise their heads. I could almost taste the atmosphere of anxiety. I hurried to Cal's stall, afraid of what condition I might find her in.

She had dropped her foal during the previous two hours. He lay beside her on the floor of the stall, hungrily nuzzling his mother. Calpurnia seemed well, weak but proud and happy. I wept, and the tears were a curious mixture of relief and horror. Cal's foal had only one leg.

That's how Pops and Momma found me, they say: asleep at the foot of Cal's stall door. Pops carried me into the house and put me to bed, and I suppose that the next morning he discussed with Jimmy the best way of disposing of Cal's freakish son. In any event, he slipped some word of his intentions to Momma at breakfast, and I must have reacted with outrage.

"Why, Pops, you can't just get rid of him!" I said. "He's *Cal's*, and he's so . . . so little!"

"He's lucky enough that he was born with at least one leg to stand on," said Pops in his gruff way. And that's how Cal's foal was named. Lucky he was then, and Lucky he was to remain.

So poor Lucky stayed, and as the weeks passed we all came to love him, his strange appearance and ways endearing him to our whole family. Even Pops, usually the most practical of men, soon ceased complaining about the expense of feeding Cal's one-legged prodigy. We talked about Lucky very often, and when we weren't working around the farm one of us was generally looking in on him in Cal's stall. In these early days, before he learned to get around by himself, he required the help of one of us to stand, or else he spent the day lying on his side on the straw. Pops and Jimmy together propped him up against the side of the barn so that he might get the benefit of the sunshine and fresh air, but otherwise he led a lonely and secluded life. It was in these first weeks that I often thought that he might indeed have been better off had Pops disposed of him immediately. But always a soft voice within me answered that surely every one of Nature's children had the same right to life, and that we had made the only correct choice in letting him live.

One day, while I was helping Momma put up some fruits for the winter, Jimmy came running into the house, grinning and gasping for breath. "Come on outside," he said. "You have to see your Lucky." Both Momma and I wiped our hands clean and followed Jimmy out to the barn.

Lucky, who as I have said normally spent the day in the stall or merely leaning against the barn like some strange field implement, was standing alone in the middle of the yard. He looked so comical there, balanced on his one fragile leg, that both Momma and I began to laugh. "How did he get there?" I asked.

"Must of got there by himself," said Jimmy. "Your father and I were both too busy to help him. We noticed him just now when we knocked off for lunch."

Lucky tossed his head up and down, as if in agreement. He looked at me for a short while, and then he did an odd thing: he bent his one leg at the knee, falling low toward the ground but maintaining his balance. Then he hopped. He did this again, and again, until he was standing next to me, rubbing his lovely head on my arm. I was so happy that I threw my arms around his neck to hug him, and he and I toppled over together. The scene must have been somewhat ludicrous, for both Jimmy and Momma laughed; but for me it was the happiest moment of my young life. No longer was my brave, spirited Lucky a helpless sport of cruel Fate.

At first I don't suppose that I had any intention or goal in mind as I worked with Lucky. He was just Lucky, my Lucky, and he was more than a pet. He was a real friend, one who somehow seemed to know what I was thinking and what I wanted. Jimmy helped me to train him, and Lucky never seemed to mind the extra burden of a saddle, and he stood patiently when I mounted him. This was potentially a difficult operation, for someone had to hold Lucky upright while I vaulted to his back. If no other person was available I leaned him against some handy object.

I began by "walking" him around the pasture, guiding him with the reins and getting him used to taking my directions. He was soon able to keep a steady and surprisingly quick pace with his bizarre hopping. He would bend, dip, and jump, coming to a complete stop and making sure of his footing before repeating the series of motions. The more we practiced, the less time elapsed between successive jumps. We certainly must have presented a curious picture to Pops and Momma, who always watched from the kitchen window or the back porch. It surely must have been peculiar to see me riding that misshapen one-legged beast, but never again did I hear them suggest that Lucky ought to be disposed of before getting his chance to prove his capabilities.

Thereafter Jimmy and I worked with him every day, building up his confidence, his speed, and his stamina. When the first winter snow fell he was already holding his own with our other young horses, showing more and more leadership potential as he hopped about the pasture. Then, shortly after his first birthday, happened the event that was so drastically to alter our lives.

We were visited by old Colonel Jennings, a retired horse breeder from Kentucky and a boyhood friend of Pops' father. He was staying with us for a few weeks, during which time he expressed an interest to see any promising racing stock in the neighborhood. Although he himself was no longer breeding horses, his nephew still ran the Colonel's famous stables in his name. Momma jokingly referred to Lucky, and the idea so intrigued Col. Jennings that we all went outside. I saddled Lucky, and when we hopped out of the barn I could hear the Colonel gasp. Of course by now the sight of me riding a horse with only one leg was not particularly unsettling to Pops, Momma, or Jimmy, but the Colonel wasn't really prepared.

"No," he cried, throwing his hands up before his face. "Take it away; it's horrible, horrible!" Lucky and I hopped over to him. I smiled down at the Colonel.

"Watch this!" said Jimmy, as I dug my heels into Lucky's sides. He hopped off at a great speed, and we stopped at the far end of the yard. The Colonel was staring silently. Lucky hopped and spun at my command, and then we raced back across the yard.

"Amazing!" said the Colonel. "Did you train him yourself, young lady?"

"Well, Pops and Jimmy helped," I said.

"Amazing. Simply amazing. Would you consider selling him? I could give you quite a good price."

"Oh no," I said. "He's *Lucky*, he's my horse!"

The Colonel smiled at me. "I understand. I too was young once. But here is what I will do for you. Judging from what I have just witnessed, your Lucky is already one of the fleetest animals that I have ever seen, and I've seen all of the great ones. With proper training, and the help of God, we'll have him ready for the Big Race. That is, if I have your consent."

The Big Race! With the prize money, Pops and Momma would at last be able to afford the corrective braces for my teeth. "Oh yes! That would be wonderful! Could I ride him in the Race?"

"No, I'm sorry, Suzy," said the Colonel with a chuckle, "they don't let girls ride in the Big Race. But we'll let you have your pick of my boys for the jockey. We'll need a specially understanding lad for Lucky, won't we?" and the Colonel winked at me.

I was so happy that I couldn't answer. Lucky, in the Big Race!

Weeks passed, during which the Colonel's staff of expert trainers and handlers turned the little horse into a professional competitor. At first every one of them expressed doubts that Lucky could ever do it, but as they came to know him they loved him, because his gallant heart could never admit defeat. He seemed to understand immediately that his duty was to run the course ahead of the other horses, because *I wanted him to*. He worked and he strained for me. Sometimes it was heart-breaking to see him after one of the practice sessions, his tongue lolling from the side of his mouth, panting while he rested against the wooden railing. It was impossible of course for him to take his weight off his one foot, and so he had to stop at more frequent intervals than the other horses. But never did he give the trainers reason to suspect that he was shirking.

The summer passed. It was now early autumn, time for the Exposition and the Big Race. Pops worried about scraping together the $200 for the entry fee, declining a loan from the Colonel. Finally Momma donated the money from her secret fund in the cookie jar. If Lucky won, we would get first prize— $1000, which we would share with the Colonel. Our part of the money would almost eliminate all of Pops' financial worries.

The day of the Big Race was clear and crisp. I sat in the first row of the stands with Pops, Momma, Jimmy, and the Colonel. The fair was so exciting: flags, bands, interesting people, good things to eat; but I remember little of that now. All that I knew was that it was the day of the Big Race.

The horses were announced one by one, and they were led

out to the starting gate by their trainers. The jockeys sat straight in the saddles, dressed in their bright silks. The crowd cheered each horse as it took its place. But Lucky, given the number five post position, was omitted. I looked at Pops, who shook his head to indicate that he didn't understand either. The Colonel stood up and patted my shoulder. "Don't worry," he said. "I'll find out what's happening."

He returned a few minutes later, smiling broadly. Apparently the stewards thought that Lucky's entry was some sort of bad joke, and decided to scratch his name from the list. The Colonel, a very well-known and respected gentleman in racing circles, persuaded them that it wasn't a joke after all. I can imagine how astonished they must have been. And just as the Colonel returned to his seat, the announcement was made: "Ladies and gentlemen, the number five horse, Lucky, ridden by Johnny Angelo." Lucky hopped his way to the starting gate, but there were no cheers. Instead, the crowd sat in hushed bewilderment.

And then they were off! Lucky needed a few seconds to build up his momentum, and of course by that time he was well behind the last horse. He trailed the pack down through the far turn and into the backstretch. Looking from the club-house stands across the grassy oval, Lucky appeared among the sleek horses like a wooden torso mounted on a pole, an animated merry-go-round ride. But he couldn't stand to run last, not with his mistress watching. Halfway through the backstretch he was running fifth in a field of eight. I could imagine with delight the dismay of the jockeys on those three horses as Lucky hopped by, boldly on the outside.

I was on my feet cheering him on. Pops and Momma and Jimmy were shouting, too, and I had never seen my father so excited before. The Colonel just sat silently, smiling confidently and nodding. As we watched, Lucky moved up on the outside, passing the fourth horse. He now trailed the front three by some four lengths, and I had no doubt that, given enough time, he could catch even them. But they were already coming into the clubhouse turn, with less than the final five furlongs to go. Now was when Johnny Angelo was supposed to let Lucky make his move. I gripped the railing tightly, and I found myself almost pleading. "Come on, Lucky. Now, do it *now*," I whispered; but still he hopped along at the same four-length handicap.

All at once he opened up. As the horses passed right in front of us he moved by the third horse. I screamed, turning to Pops and Momma. Momma wăs crying, and even the Colonel was cheering now. Then I heard the shouting of the people in the stands: it seemed to me that every single one of them was pulling for my Lucky, surely the saddest underdog that ever ran a race. Most of them had bets on other horses, but these were forgotten in the cheering for the most unlikely long-shot of all time.

Lucky's solitary hops were coming faster and faster now. Johnny Angelo was leaning far up on his neck, urging him on, and they moved to the inside, along the rail. Halfway down the homestretch they slipped by the number two horse, and found themselves only half a length behind the leader. The roar from the spectators was deafening, but nowhere as loud as the pounding of my own blood. Lucky edged up neck to neck with My Rocket, the leader, with less than a furlong left to run. They stayed that way until just before the finish. With a last, valiant effort, Lucky made a prodigious hop, and he broke the tape just ahead of My Rocket. He could not regain his balance and he stumbled, spilling Johnny Angelo to the ground. I was yelling and weeping with joy, and Pops was busily congratulating the Colonel. The people in the stands were chanting Lucky's name.

But then I saw that Lucky had not gotten up. He lay still in the middle of the track, where several of the other horses behind him had had difficulty avoiding trampling him. I ran to him, with Jimmy and the Colonel and my parents right behind. The Colonel's trainer was already examining him.

"He really exerted himself for you, you know," he said. "He pushed himself harder than he ever had before, harder than Nature ever intended."

"But will he be all right?" I asked fearfully.

"He's just a bit winded, as far as that goes. He'll get over that in a few minutes."

"Oh, thank goodness," I said, smiling through my tears.

"But," said the trainer, "but the real problem came from his fall. He's broken his leg. Fractured it rather severely. He'll have to be . . . disposed of."

I stared dumbly for a few seconds. Lucky raised his head weakly and nuzzled my hand. I looked into his soft brown eyes for a short while, and then I turned away to cry. I don't remember the cheering of the crowd, or the prize money or loving cup, or the reporters seeking interviews. I just remember sobbing piteously against the Colonel's expensive plaid corduroy vest.

A few days later Pops came home with a cute collie puppy. She stayed with us for several years, and she was real nice.

Which brings us to the strangest story in this collection. Heart-stop takes place in the small town of Gremmage, Pennsylvania, a place I invented early in my career. I've written several stories set there, all of them decidedly odd. The best way to describe Gremmage is that it's the way Oz would be if Kafka had written the book.

The story is about chess, but a particular form of the game called "fairy chess." Problems in fairy chess have been popular for many years; the authors of these problems have the freedom to change certain pieces and principles while maintaining all the other rules of the game. The fairy chess game, then, is unbalanced compared to the strict laws of normal chess, but perfectly logical within its own framework. That is one of the possible definitions of insanity.

Chess has been used as a metaphor for life more than any other game. Chess in particular, and games in general, mirror the confrontation and competition implicit in all human rela-

tionships. If you want to know what Heartstop *means, if anything, and what this entire book is about, listen to James Jones in an interview in* Writers at Work, Third Series, *edited by George Plimpton:*

> *I think games are significant in people's lives because in a game everything is clearly defined. You've got the rules and a given period of time in which to play; you've got boundaries and a beginning and an end. And whether you win, lose, or draw, at least something is sure. But life ain't like that at all. So I think people invent and play games in order to kid themselves, at least for a time, into thinking that life is a game; in order to forget that at the end of life there is nothing but a big blank wall.*

That explains the sports aspect of these stories. It is science fiction's job to climb that wall and peek over.

Heartstop

IN THE NEARBY TOWNS, places like Indian Bog and Leeper, they still talk about "the Gremmage murders." In the town of Gremmage itself, though, they don't talk about them at all. Those murders happened a long time ago, and there are always new people and new things happening in Gremmage.

This is despite the fact that Gremmage has to be one of the most neglectable places in all of Pennsylvania, if not the country. There isn't even a good-sized shopping center to drive around in. When a man wants to teach his daughter how to park her Mustang, he has to take her five, ten miles away just to find the right kind of yellow lines. And that's today. It was even worse fifteen years ago.

Now there's an interstate highway that skirts the town; there's an exit, but it's diabolically placed, about thirty yards on the far side of an overpass, so you can't see it coming. Between the overpass and the exit there is a small green sign that says *Gremmage*, with an arrow. Of course, at interstate speeds, you have maybe a squint and a half from the time you leave the shade of the overpass until you're to the sign. If you read the thing, before you finish the two syllables and pointer you've passed the exit. And there's a bush growing up in front of the green sign, and it doesn't look like the highway people are going to do anything about trimming it. So either you know where you're going and look for the exit, or you get off completely by accident and stupidity. In either case, you deserve what you get.

But, again, that's *today*. Fifteen years ago, a traveler didn't even have that obscure green sign. A weary salesman could only stop along the narrow blacktop road and try to get information from a farmer. "Yeah," the farmer would say, "there's a town a ways from here, maybe seven or eight mile. I can never remember the name of it, though. You just go on here 'til you come to it." The farmer would pause, relishing the bewildered, unhappy look on the salesman's face. "You'll recognize the town," the farmer would say slowly. "There's a cannon on the square. These here farms don't have no cannons, nohow." The farmer wouldn't grin until the salesman had climbed back into his dusty car and driven off toward Gremmage.

At least the information was accurate. Fifteen years ago, Gremmage *was* about seven or eight miles from a lot of farms. And the salesman wouldn't have any trouble at all, once he located the town. Fifteen years ago, before the interstate, there weren't any motels, no Holidays Inn, no Qualities Court, no Howard Johnsons. So the poor salesman would be little cheered by the sight of the meager row of shops along Ridge Street. Particularly if it was after six o'clock (three o'clock on Saturdays); then there wouldn't be a single store open, where he could even find out about hotel rooms. Except the diner, of course. Mrs. Perkins' diner was pretty dependable. So that's where the salesman ended up, out of desperation.

There was a slight haze of burnt grease in the diner, but otherwise it seemed like a pleasant enough place. Mrs. Perkins didn't have the time to bother much with decorations. The result was an establishment that was plain without being sterile. The atmosphere was purely hick town (no, not rural. Really and truly *hick*). The salesman, after too many hours on the road, found it nearly refreshing. Almost.

"Can I take your order, sir?" asked the waitress. The salesman looked up tiredly. The girl was young, high school age, probably working part-time in the diner to earn money for movie magazines.

"Can I see a menu?" asked the salesman. The girl nodded and reached past the salesman to pull the menu from its place behind the napkin container. There was nothing listed on it that could set Mrs. Perkins' diner apart from any of several thousand like it anywhere in America. That was one of its charms. It was almost a reflex action for the salesman to order the baked meat loaf, mashed potatoes, green beans, and coffee. He always studied the menu, and he always ordered the same thing. His wife, back home in Stroudsburg, always ordered eggplant Parmesan. His son always ordered cheeseburgers. But there was some kind of exotic, wistful hope that someday someone would come up with something tremendously exciting on his menu. The salesman always wondered, if that were ever to happen, whether or not he'd order it.

Some minutes later, the waitress brought the meat loaf dinner. The salesman muttered a thank you. The waitress did not go away. She stood by his booth; the salesman wondered what he had done wrong. "You're new in town, aren't you?" she asked.

He just looked at her. He didn't say anything.

"The reason I say that, I know just about everybody in Gremmage," she said. "It's not that big of a town."

"No," said the salesman, chewing his food slowly, "no, it's not."

"Are you from New York?" she asked.

"Stroudsburg."

"Oh." She fidgeted nervously. The salesman was sure that she was going to ask him for something. She was pretty enough, he guessed, in a way that would be immature whatever her age. Her hair was a dull carrot color, tied into two short braids. Her face was so lacking in memorable features as to be indescribable. She spoke in a low, husky voice which the salesman found vaguely unpleasant. "Do you have business here in Gremmage?" she asked.

"No, none at all. I was just seeing the sights." The girl stared for a moment, then laughed. The salesman smiled. "I was wondering, though," he said, "if there was a hotel around here. I don't feel much like driving any more tonight."

"No," said the waitress. "No hotels. But if you go over to

Aunt Rozji's she'll probably have a guest room vacant. She usually does."

"Is she your aunt?"

The waitress shook her head. "We all call her that. She's old enough to be *anybody's* aunt."

"All right," said the salesman, "I'll try that. Can you give me directions? Maybe I can drop you somewhere."

"No, that's okay," said the girl. "Thank you. I don't get off here for a while yet. But if you want to wait a few minutes, Old Man Durfee comes in every night about now. He could take you over there. Aunt Rozji doesn't like to rent her rooms to just anyone, you see. But if Old Man Durfee took you over there, and if you told her that I sent you, why, I guess it would be all right."

"Old Man Durfee, huh?"

"Yes," said the waitress. "Why don't you have a piece of pie while you're waiting?"

"A piece of pie, then," said the salesman, sighing. "While I'm waiting for Old Man Durfee. Who'll take me to Aunt Rozji. This is a very folksy town you have here."

The waitress smiled. "Thank you. It's not very big, though."

"No," he muttered, "it's not very big." She went back behind the counter and brought him a piece of apple pie and some more coffee.

"Do you want your check now, Mr., uh, Mr.—"

"Newby," said the salesman. "My name's Newby."

"Well," said the waitress, "my name's Lauren. Do you want anything else?"

"Like Bacall, right?" asked Newby.

"Sort of," she said. "Only my last name's Kromberger." She put the check down by his plate and went away again, this time disappearing into the kitchen. Newby ate his dessert slowly, wondering if he could leave the diner and drive off without looking like a fool. He had gone through a complex set of arrangements with the girl; he would be too embarrassed now to tell her just to forget the whole thing. He sneered at his own idiocy. He would never see Lauren Kromberger again. What possible difference could it make, what she thought of him? He ought to pay his check and leave without a word. But, truthfully, he didn't feel like driving any more. He might as well wait for this Old Man Durfee. Anyway, Newby was getting curious about him.

The salesman had finished his pie and was just taking the last lukewarm gulp of coffee when the door swung open. An incredibly broken-down man came into the diner. Newby had no doubt this was Old Man Durfee, he who would be Newby's guide through the shaded, crickety roads of Gremmage to the mysterious rooming house of Aunt Rozji. If the old man were any indication, Newby thought, maybe the weary traveler would be better advised to toss a brick through a plate glass window and accept a night's lodging from the county.

Old Man Durfee was probably not all that old. To Newby, he seemed to be in his early fifties. His hair was long, hanging in greasy curls behind his ears and over his collar. The man's face was lined deeply, and the growth of stubble and the cracked, swollen lips gave him an appearance which was at the same time both repellent and pitiable. His eyes were nearly closed by the heavy pouches which limited them, and he gazed at Newby briefly through red, watery slits. He wore a faded plaid shirt and a pair of ancient corduroy trousers, which were much too short for him. He had no socks, and his sharp, filthy ankles hung between the torn cuffs of the pants and his decaying slippers. He carried a dirty blue towel. He looked at Newby again and mumbled something; then he took a seat at the counter. After a few seconds he stood and shuffled slowly to one of the booths. Newby watched him without emotion. Old Man Durfee sat in the booth, then rose one more time and moved around to the opposite seat.

"You know," said Newby, "if you sit in that other booth behind you, and I go to the counter, and you come here, we'll have mate in three moves."

"I couldn't find the right place," said Old Man Durfee.

"A lot of us have that trouble," said Newby.

"I have a regular place. I come in every night, and sit in the same place. Sometimes I forget which it is, though."

"Well, good night," said Newby, getting up to go. Just then, Lauren the waitress returned.

"Do you play chess?" she asked. "I heard you speaking just now."

"Yeah," said Newby. "I carry a little magnetic board with me when I travel. There's nothing else to do." For some reason, Lauren giggled. Newby shrugged and headed for the door. "I'd like to play," said Old Man Durfee. Newby stopped suddenly, halfway to the door. The drunk's voice had been loud, clear, and authoritative. "I used to be pretty good."

"I have to go," said Newby, not turning around.

"You had time for the pie," said Lauren. "You can stay for a game. Old Man Durfee just lives to play chess. I wish *I* knew how. Besides, he's going to take you over to Aunt Rozji's, isn't he?"

The salesman turned around and went back to his booth. "Okay," he said. "I suppose the fates are conspiring against me."

Lauren frowned slightly. "You don't have to, if you don't want to," she said. "I just think it would be nice."

"Daviolsokoff *vs.* Drean," said Old Man Durfee. "Copenhagen, 1926. Remember the second game? The Forgotten Rook. A real masterpiece."

"Were you there?" asked Newby.

Old Man Durfee stared for a moment, his red eyes narrowing even more. He coughed, and the wet, thick sound disgusted Newby. "No," said the drunk. "I read about it. I just read about it, that's all."

"What difference does it make?" asked Lauren.

"I just want to know what I'm up against," said Newby. "I've heard about chess hustlers before, you know. I know how you small-town types are always gunning for people like me."

"We don't get many people like you," said Old Man Durfee.

"This town isn't so big," said Lauren.

"No, it's not," said Newby. "I wish it was. Then we could all go bowling or something."

"They have bowling hustlers, too," said Lauren. The salesman just nodded.

"I just like to read about chess," said Old Man Durfee. "I don't get to play very often. I read, though. I've read just about every word on chess there is in town."

"It's not a very big town," said Newby sarcastically.

"No, it's not," said Lauren.

There was an uncomfortable silence. Newby toyed with the dishes and objects on the table top. He was very aware of a low mechanical humming from the kitchen, and of a flickering tube in the fluorescent lights. "Well," he thought, "I'll just get up, say goodbye, and duck out. This is infantile. It's turning into a scene from *Marty,* for Pete's sake." He didn't leave, though. A minute later, the door of the diner opened again, and an old woman came in.

"Aunt Rozji!" cried Lauren. "What an incredible coincidence!"

Newby just snorted and turned to observe the woman. She was very old. Her steps were tiny and so obviously painful that Newby wondered why she didn't spend her days on a cranked-up hospital bed. She was thin, gaunt; cracked leather shrunken on a frame of spun glass; mere purposeless tufts of white hair; erratic motions so bizarre that gestures could not be distinguished from involuntary spasms; a complex bed of wrinkles and lines that led the observer's eye away from hers—Newby knew that he might never learn the color of her irises; a black dress that drooped between knee and ankle, decorated with pink and green floral specks, and a pair of huge, square, black shoes. She moved slowly, bent over, squeezed closer to the moist earth every hour. She wouldn't die for a while, though; like a battered wreck of a car, she wouldn't be worth trading in. While she could perform the slightest function in the world, she would be kept around.

"We were just talking about you, dear," said Old Man Durfee, rising from the booth and helping her to take a seat.

"Were you?" she said. Her voice was cracked, as dry as the old drunk's was saturated. She spoke in a heavy European accent, some strange Slavic influence. "I was thinking about you, too. I came down."

"She doesn't come in very often," said Lauren to Newby. "She's a little frail to be making the walk from her house."

"I'm amazed that she came at all," said Newby.

"And surprised that she arrived just as we finished speaking of her, eh?" said Old Man Durfee. The drunk didn't wait for Newby's reaction. He turned back to Aunt Rozji. "This young man plays chess, dear."

"Chess?" said Aunt Rozji, turning to peer around the corner of her booth. "You play chess? Then you came to the right place. Young Durfee plays chess. Did he tell you?"

"Yes," said Newby, sighing, realizing that the final nail had been driven in place, the last brick cemented to wall him up for the night in Gremmage.

"He needs a place to stay tonight," said Lauren. "We've already set up a game for him with Old Man Durfee, but he has to be back on the road in the morning. I thought maybe you could rent him a guest room for the night."

"Rent?" said Aunt Rozji. "*Shueblik*, if he wants to play

Young Durfee, I won't ask him to pay."

"That's very kind," said Newby. "But I'd be happy to."

"No, no, no," said Aunt Rozji. "You give me happiness by playing Young Durfee. It has been such a long time."

"I'm glad I drove through, then," said the salesman. "It sounds like you haven't had a chess-playing stranger in quite a while."

"That's true," said Lauren. "But the other travelers find something else to do."

"Gremmage has a lot to offer," said Old Man Durfee.

"For such a small town," said Lauren.

"No," said Aunt Rozji, "it's not a very big town. But it tailors itself, you will find. It fills your needs. Tonight, it is chess. Young Lauren, find us the board."

The waitress bent down behind the counter for a few seconds. Newby sipped some of the stale water from the glass by his dishes. He heard a rattling of silverware and the heavy sliding of bottles. He wondered what sort of an opponent Old Man Durfee would be. He didn't especially care.

"I found it!" said Lauren. She waved a flimsy cardboard chessboard, with squares colored black and orange. It had been a long time since Newby had seen a chessboard with orange squares.

"The pieces?" asked Aunt Rozji.

"They're here, too," said Lauren. She held up a grease-stained paper sack.

"Fine," said Old Man Durfee.

"Fine," said Newby. "Should you go get Mrs. Perkins? Maybe she'll want to watch this battle of the century."

"No," said Lauren. "She has to get ready for breakfast in the morning. She's a busy little bee."

"I wonder what she does for fun around here," said Newby idly.

"She takes mambo lessons," said the waitress. "Over at the Y." Newby winced.

"Well, then," said Old Man Durfee, as Lauren opened the cheap board on the counter and everyone else took seats, "I think you should have white."

"Thank you," said Newby.

"Not at all," said the drunk. "I do have the home court advantage, so to speak."

"We're all rooting for Young Durfee," said Aunt Rozji.

"It's nothing against you, you understand."

"Sure," said Newby. "He's the hometown boy." Old Man Durfee snickered.

The two men wordlessly arranged their pieces. Newby just wanted to get the game over with as quickly as possible, drive Aunt Rozji back to her house, get a good night's sleep, and flee the entire town at first light. This was not his idea of the most entertaining way of spending an evening.

"Your move?" asked Old Man Durfee.

Newby exhaled heavily, reached out, and moved his pawn to Queen Four.

"Ah, the Queen's Gambit, an excellent choice," said the drunk. "A conservative opening. The king-side openings lead to more spectacular games. You've taken the opportunity of seizing the center of the board, a good strategic idea, backing up your threat with immediate protection from your queen. You are trying to tempt me into surrendering a defensive position in exchange for the pawn which you shall move to Queen's Bishop Four. Shall I take it? Let us see!" The old man moved his own pawn to Queen Four, and smiled at Newby.

"Playing with Old Man Durfee is fun," said Lauren. "He knows so much about the game. I can learn a lot just from watching."

Newby only nodded. The drunk was a little strange; the salesman wondered just how much about chess Old Man Durfee really knew. Newby decided to move off the usual opening routines. He posted his knight at King's Bishop Three.

"Wonderful, wonderful!" cried Old Man Durfee. "You see, Aunt Rozji, you see, Miss Kromberger, how his knight defends the original pawn move, while itself strains forward to the attack. A most practical move, and one I entirely expected. The pawn allurement I spoke of will no doubt have to be postponed through this development. I can find no fault with Mr. Newby's play. I shall make it myself." Old Man Durfee moved his knight to King's Bishop Three.

"An axis of symmetry forms through the middle of the board," whispered Lauren.

"Are you afraid, Young Durfee?" asked Aunt Rozji. "Is that why you mimic each of your opponent's moves? That cannot be wise. Do not forget that he has the advantage of the first play."

"Then watch," said Old Man Durfee, laughing gently.

"For Pete's sake," thought Newby. Without hesitation, he moved a pawn to King Three.

"Good God, man!" cried the drunk. "What have you done?"

"I've moved," said Newby.

"Yes," said Old Man Durfee, "but are you sure?"

"Is something wrong?" asked Lauren.

"Terribly," said the drunk. "Our friend has blundered badly. He has as good as lost the game, here on the third move."

"Perhaps you should allow him to retract his move," said Aunt Rozji mildly.

"All right, then," said Old Man Durfee.

Newby smiled. "Can I have a Coke?" he asked. Lauren nodded and went to fetch it. "My move will stand," he said. The drunk shrugged.

"I can see that Mr. Newby has bottled up one of his bishops," said Aunt Rozji. "That can't be a good idea."

"No, it isn't," said Old Man Durfee. "Besides, he has moved a pawn instead of developing a piece. That will hurt him later on." He moved his own pawn to King Three.

"Now, why in heaven's name did you do that, too?" asked Lauren.

The drunk made a funny expression. "Charity," he said. Aunt Rozji laughed.

Newby still said nothing. He was making the preparatory moves of the Colle system, and apparently the drunk didn't recognize them. Old Man Durfee would be in for a surprise. Newby quickly made his next play, bishop to Queen Three.

"All right, I suppose," said Old Man Durfee. "Now watch. I move a pawn to Queen's Bishop Four. See how it opens up my pieces? That's very important. Your men are all hemmed in."

"What did you say your name was?" asked Aunt Rozji.

"Newby," said the salesman.

"Where did you say you were from?"

"Stroudsburg." Newby moved a pawn to Queen's Bishop Three.

Old Man Durfee jumped to his feet and began wildly pacing about the diner. Newby wondered how such a dissipated, worn-out person as had entered the place could have become so animated. "I give up!" shouted the drunk. "I try to help him a little. I don't take advantage of his stupidity. But does he learn? No. Does he do anything about the idiocy of his position? No.

All right, Newby. You asked for it." Old Man Durfee sat down again. He considered the board for a minute, then made his play, the other knight to Bishop Three.

"Oho," said Lauren. "Things are beginning to pile up there in the middle."

"Ah, Young Newby," said Aunt Rozji, "that lead pawn of yours is attracting a lot of attention."

"And it's not even such a big piece," said Lauren.

"No," said Newby, "no, it's not." He took his queen's knight and put it in front of his queen, at Queen Two.

"That's stupid," said Aunt Rozji. "I hope you don't mind me speaking frankly. You are not a fit opponent."

"I won't say anything," said Old Man Durfee. Newby smiled coldly. The drunk played his bishop to King Two.

"I castle king-side," said Newby.

"It doesn't take much skill to do that," said Old Man Durfee scornfully. "Observe how easily I remove your one threatening piece." He moved his pawn at Bishop Four ahead one square, attacking Newby's bishop.

"I retreat," said Newby. He moved the bishop back a square, until it stood in front of the other, unmoved bishop.

"When is somebody going to kill another piece?" asked Lauren.

"Wait," said Aunt Rozji. "All in good time."

"Pawn to Queen's Knight Four," said the drunk. "Notice now how I open up the bishop, and threaten with an advance of my queen-side pawns."

"I see," said Newby. He moved the pawn at King Three ahead to King Four. He swung around on the stool. This was the key move in the old system he was playing. Now, at last, Old Man Durfee must be seeing the trouble he was in. All the restrained force of the white position was now set loose. It was a simple, deceptive line of play, and one very familiar to experts in the 1920s and '30s. But it had lost favor since then; Newby had guessed correctly that Old Man Durfee lacked the sophistication to understand this line of attack.

"Ah, well," said the drunk. He gazed up at Newby, his eyes suddenly bleary again, his voice thick and barely intelligible. "I don' know, now. Lemme see."

"Something wrong, Young Durfee?" asked Aunt Rozji.

"I don' know, now." The drunk shook out his filthy blue towel and folded it up again.

"You can't let that pawn move forward again," said Lauren. "It would chase your knight away, cost you a turn, and ruin your center position."

"You don't have much choice," said Aunt Rozji.

"Right, right, I know," said Old Man Durfee. "Okay, you bastard, I'll take the pawn. I still don't see what it'll get you." He took the pawn with the queen's pawn.

"Ah," said Lauren, sighing, "first blood!"

Newby recaptured the pawn with the knight from Queen Two. At once, Newby's pieces commanded the center of the board. His position, previously cramped and unpromising, was now obviously superior to black's.

"I castle," said Old Man Durfee.

"Are you worried now?" asked Lauren.

"*Everybody* castles," said the drunk with some irritation.

"Don't worry, Young Durfee, we won't abandon you," said Aunt Rozji.

"Queen to King Two," said Newby.

"Don't rush," said Old Man Durfee. "We have all night." The drunk studied the board. "All right, now. Cautiously. You have me, if I let you get away with it. I see your plan. Is it not as follows: Your knight takes mine, I take back with my bishop, then you move your queen forward to King Four? You'll checkmate me on the next move, taking my rook pawn with your queen. If I rush to do something about that threat, you win the isolated knight on the other side of the board. That's what you're after, isn't it? I protect that knight, ruining your scheme. I move bishop to Knight Two."

"Well done, Young Durfee!"

"We're with you," said Lauren.

"A partisan crowd," said Newby.

"We have to be," said Aunt Rozji.

"There's little enough else to do," said Lauren.

"All right," said Newby, "the knight at Bishop Three up to Knight Five."

"I have to save the pawn," said Old Man Durfee, looking around helplessly. He moved the threatened pawn forward to King's Rook Three.

"We understand," said Aunt Rozji.

"It's a cardinal rule, never to move those protective pawns in front of your king, unless you have to," said Lauren. "But, as you say, you'll lose it otherwise: knight takes knight, check.

Bishop takes knight. Knight takes pawn. And you're also attacking that offensive knight, so I suppose it's the only move you have."

"How have you allowed yourself to get into this untenable defensive position?" asked Aunt Rozji.

"Knight takes knight," said Newby. "Check."

"He proceeds anyway," said Lauren, astounded.

"As do I," said Old Man Durfee. "Bishop takes knight."

"Queen to King Four," said Newby.

"It's as you foresaw," said Lauren. "If he slides his queen down, he'll have you mated on the next move. You saw it coming. Why didn't you plan a better defense?"

"My hands were tied," said Old Man Durfee. "I can only create an escape route." He moved the knight pawn to Knight Three.

"You're stalling," said Lauren.

"I think that's enough for tonight, don't you?" asked Aunt Rozji. Newby realized that, for some time, her words had been spoken without a trace of accent. Now, though, she sounded like a recent immigrant from Czechoslovakia.

"If you say so," said Old Man Durfee.

"Why don't we play on?" asked Newby. "The end can't be too far away."

Lauren looked irritated. "I think we need an official referee here," she said. "How about Aunt Rozji?"

"She's not the most impartial judge I could ask for," said Newby.

"It's okay with me," said Old Man Durfee.

"I'll bet," said Newby. "All right. Aunt Rozji, you can be referee."

The old woman smiled, a narrow, quivering expression. "Good, good. We stop, then. Tomorrow morning, we finish."

"We finish fast," said Newby. "I have to be on the road early."

"Nine o'clock, here?" said Aunt Rozji. Lauren, Newby, and Old Man Durfee nodded.

"Can I drive you anywhere?" asked Newby.

"No," said Lauren. "My daddy comes to meet me."

"I'll find my own way," said Old Man Durfee. "Do you have maybe a quarter, though? I need another quarter for a pint of Thunderbird."

"Here," said Newby, giving the old drunk the money. Newby

shook his head as Old Man Durfee shuffled out of the diner. The salesman took Aunt Rozji's arm and led her out to his car. The old woman said little as they drove to her house. The narrow, red brick-paved streets were dark; slender wells of light beamed down from streetlamps, but otherwise there was only the occasional floating yellow from a porch light or a distant pair of rat-eyes on the back end of a car. Trees grew dense and tall. The air was warm and moist, and pleasant smelling. Newby enjoyed the low thrumming sound of the tires on the street.

"Pull up here," said Aunt Rozji at last. "I suppose you'll want to get right to sleep."

"Yes, I guess so. I have a little work to do first, but I can look forward to another day of driving tomorrow."

"After your tournament is completed, of course."

Newby pulled out the ignition key and shrugged. "Oh, yeah. Sure," he said. They went slowly up the flagstone walk to the huge, dim house. The front door was open. They went inside; the salesman was given an impression of old furnishings, polished dark wood paneling, hundreds of china figurines, fat chairs and sofas, final boredom. He carried his suitcase up the stairway, at the top of which Aunt Rozji said he'd find his room and the bathroom. She was too old to climb the steps herself, and she apologized. Newby called down that the room was fine, said good night, and stretched out on the bed for a few minutes' rest. He was asleep instantly.

Newby dozed fitfully; he had planned to sort out the brightly colored cloth samples in his case before he went to sleep. The case rested at the foot of the bed. The salesman's legs were bent to avoid the samples which were stacked on the folded comforter, with the suitcase tight behind his knees. He was cramped and uncomfortable, but he had not meant to fall asleep. He had only removed his shirt and tie; he had not even slipped out of his shoes.

After a few minutes he began to dream. They were strange visions, dreams of a kind he had never had before. He was used to sleeping in a different bed every night, awakening in odd, unknown towns that he might never see again. It wasn't that he was isolated and alone that caused his dreams. It was something else.

For a time he dreamed of shapes, just meaningless shapes. Great, looming blocks, towering cylinders, stacks of rectangular solids in unattractive olive greens and dark browns. Then the shapes began to be *located,* to find a setting. Spaces formed among them and remained constant. The shapes were on a large plain. The shapes became buildings, trees, parked automobiles. It was still dark, midnight, no light but the dream light of Newby's tired imagination.

Newby became part of his dream. Before, he had only viewed the nightmarish setting. Now he himself walked through it. The ominous shapes-become-buildings were vast, ancient houses, lined one after the other along a narrow, brick-paved street. Each house was set well back from the sidewalk. The front doors sparkled with crystal, rainbow flickers, gleams reflected from an unreal source. The windows on the first floor was invariably dark, shaded, inviolable. Windows on the second story were drawn up tight, also, but lamps were lit behind the drapes. Shadows whipped along the vertical folds of the curtains, as furtive strangers rushed about the interior rooms on secret errands. Newby walked past each house, examining every one as he strolled, feeling a peculiar sense of uneasiness. The insects chorused like massed rattlesnakes. A pair of night hawks swooped the star-glittered sky. Newby was frightened by the moon.

"Hi." Immediately, with a shock of dream intensity, the scene became particular, real, a little more tangible and a little less lonely. The salesman looked down. He saw a young girl, perhaps ten or eleven years old. She was wearing a white blouse, a plaid blazer from a parochial school, and a gray felt skirt with rustling crinolines beneath. There was a pink poodle cut out and fixed to the skirt. "Hi," she said again.

"Hello," said Newby.

"You know why I'm out so late?" she asked.

"No. Of course not."

"My name is Theresa Muldower."

"Why are you out so late?" asked Newby.

"Because of the Russians." She looked up at Newby with a curious expression. "I hate the Russians, don't you?"

"Sure," said Newby.

"I hate the Russians so much, the only thing in the whole world I hate more is polio."

"Me, too."

"My daddy's finishing up the fallout shelter tonight. We're going to have a party in it. Only he thought he'd have it done by now. I'm usually sent to bed at nine or ten. Ten on Fridays and Saturdays. But we're all waiting for him to finish the fallout shelter. Mom says she can just see how the Russians are going to H-bomb us all tonight, and we won't get to have our party. Daddy says it's okay with him, as long as the fallout shelter's finished. Do you have a fallout shelter?"

"Not yet," said Newby.

"You don't have much time," said Theresa. "You ought to get one. Before the Russians H-bomb us."

"If I built a fallout shelter," said Newby, "and if the Russians H-bombed us, I'd be all alone in there and I'd get polio."

"From a rusty nail."

"Yes," said Newby. "From a rusty nail."

They walked past some more houses. After a while a voice somewhere ahead of them called Theresa's name. "I have to go," she said.

"Is that your parents?"

"No," she said. "I don't know who it is." Newby watched her uninterestedly, as she skipped away ahead of him. Somewhere down the block, in a black tangle of shadows, he saw someone gesture to her. He stopped on the sidewalk and watched. The person held out his hand; Theresa took it. The street was lit by fire. Orange sparks first, then ribbons of flame spat outward from the girl's body. Newby didn't want to move, but in the dream he was suddenly right there, beside her, watching, saying nothing, doing nothing, watching Aunt Rozji and Old Man Durfee. The fiery light made gruesome, disgusting masks of their faces. They nodded silent greeting to him. Theresa looked wildly around her. She strained her arms toward Newby. The salesman could only observe. Fire spurted from her eyes and ears. Trickles of flame dribbled from her nostrils. She rolled on the ground in the pain of nightmares. When she tried to scream, only a fine gray ash came out of her mouth. She writhed. The flames from her eyes grew smaller. Her motions became convulsive, slowed, then stopped. Aunt Rozji and old Man Durfee each took one of Newby's hands. The three stepped over the unmarked corpse of Theresa Muldower and walked along the cavernous street, beneath the arching trees, past the ramparts of houses.

"And you have come from the east?" said Aunt Rozji, in a hollow, distant voice.

"Yes," said Newby.

"Knowledge in the east," said Old Man Durfee.

"And you travel into the west?" said Aunt Rozji.

"Yes," said Newby.

"Death in the west," said Old Man Durfee.

"And you bring with you?" asked Aunt Rozji.

"Fear," said Old Man Durfee. "Pain. Desire for cleansing."

"Expiation," said Newby.

"There is no expiation short of death," said Old Man Durfee.

"And there is no death," said Aunt Rozji. "No death, no death, three times, as the figures of art, as the candles, the scepters, the chalked arribles, the incense, the passes of hand, the laden words, as all these are used up, death is forgotten. Without death, there is no redemption."

"Without redemption," said Old Man Durfee, "there is fear."

"There is pain," said Aunt Rozji.

The two old people still held Newby's hands; with their free hands they touched his head. Throbbing agony grew in his temples. He could not breathe. His body began to sweat and shake. His chest was crippled with stabbing pains. His legs would not hold him. He fell. He awoke.

The suitcase had fallen on the floor; perhaps it was that noise that had roused Newby. Whatever it had been, he was grateful. He still felt his heart beating rapidly. His hands were moist with the dampness of terror. That child! He was afraid and repulsed to think that his own mind could invent such a hideous thing. He scooped up the cloth samples, intending to arrange them in their proper groups; instead, he quickly grew bored and shoved them all into the case. He undressed slowly, trying not to think about his nightmare. He went to the bathroom and brushed his teeth with the chlorophyll toothpaste his wife had bought. He remembered how much he hated to bring it with him. Everything in the world was being colored, scented, or flavored with chlorophyll these days. He didn't notice any difference. It was only an advertising fad. He hated to be conned by advertising. After his brief toilet, he returned to his room, pulled back the bedspread, and went back to sleep. He had no more unusual dreams that night.

In the morning he was awakened by Aunt Rozji, calling up the stairs to him. "Good day, Young Newby," she said. "It is morning. Have you rested?"

"Yes," he said, rubbing his eyes regretfully. "More or less."

"Good, then," she said. "It is time to renew your combat."

"Oh, yes. I was trying to forget."

"That is very gracious of you," she said. "But do not worry about besting our local champion. We are good sportsmen in Gremmage."

Newby dressed quickly and came downstairs with his suit-case. Aunt Rozji was ready to go. She told the salesman that breakfast could be taken at the diner. Together they went out to his car.

It wasn't there. From Aunt Rozji's porch, Newby could see the place along the tree lawn where he had left it. An empty space, now, between a black Studebaker and a red and white Dodge. He felt an anger growing, an ugly feeling, a sickness in his stomach. "My car's gone," he said through clenched teeth.

"Your car?" asked Aunt Rozji.

"It's gone, damn it."

"Are you sure you left it here?"

"You know damn well where I left it," he said. "You were with me."

"Perhaps someone took it by mistake," she said. Newby didn't answer. "Well, I suppose you ought to tell the police."

"You have police in this idiotic town?" he asked.

"Yes," she said. "Even towns as small as this sometimes have crime."

"So what do I do now?"

"You must walk with me to the diner. The police department won't be open for another forty-five minutes. We can have breakfast first. Perhaps the others will have something to suggest."

"What happens if you have an emergency after the police go home for the night?" asked Newby.

Aunt Rozji looked at him in surprise. "Why, we all chip in," she said. "We all work together. That is how we shall find your car." A while later they arrived at the diner on Ridge Street. Newby was out of breath, but the old woman seemed in good shape.

"Good morning," said Lauren cheerfully.

"Young Newby's car has been stolen," said Aunt Rozji.

"Stolen?" said Old Man Durfee, already studying the final position of the chess game from the day before.

"You know," said Newby. "Unauthorized theft or something."

"I don't think I'm in as much difficulty as we believed last evening," said Old Man Durfee.

"That's certainly good news," said Lauren.

"I don't give a damn about that," said Newby. "I have work to do. I want my car."

"Sit down," said the waitress. "Have some coffee. Do you want a muffin? French toast?"

"Don't you have to go to school?" asked Newby.

"No," she said. "This isn't such a big town."

"It really isn't," said Old Man Durfee.

"Whose move is it?" asked Aunt Rozji. "I forget."

"Mine," said Old Man Durfee.

"No," said Newby, "I think it's mine. You moved that pawn to Knight Three."

"Yes," said Old Man Durfee, "you're right. I'm sorry. What's your move?"

"It's obvious," said Newby. "I'm going to call the cops and see if they've recovered my car. Then I'm going to go leave this nuthouse as fast as I can."

"Can I move for you?" asked Lauren.

"You don't know how to play, remember?" said Newby. "Here. I'll take your king pawn with the knight. Now I'm attacking both your queen and the rook guarding your king."

"That's very true," said Old Man Durfee slowly.

"'Don't be cruel, to a heart that's true'," sang Lauren.

"Will you be quiet?" asked the drunk.

"'Don't be cruel'," she sang.

"All right," said Old Man Durfee, "before I take your knight, I wonder if you'd do something for me. I had these made up last night. Would you go through these two pages? It's sort of a little quiz. It won't take you very long. I think the results may surprise you. Maybe you ought to do it before you try talking with the police." The old man handed Newby two pages, covered with questions in blurry mimeograph ink.

"What is this?" asked the salesman.

"Here," said Lauren, "you can use my ballpoint."

Newby read the first multiple-choice question: *What is today's date?* The answers were *a) March 8, 1956; b) September 12, 1954; c) June 26, 1959; d) August 30, 1957*. Newby had some difficulty deciding which answer was appropriate. The trouble bothered him. He hesitated a few seconds, then checked *a*. The second question was: *What was yesterday's date?* The possibilities were *a) May 21, 1955; b) January 2, 1951; c) November 15, 1957; d) April 28, 1958.* More confused, he checked *c*. There were a few more questions in a similar mode, requiring him to decide what the date of a week from Friday would be, and so on. He did the best he could.

The second page asked questions of a more concrete nature. *Where are you? a) in a town in Colorado; b) in a suburb of Dallas; c) in a European nation that has not existed since the end of the First World War; d) in the garment district.* Newby checked *b*, hoping that it was the closest to the truth. He really wasn't certain. The next question asked him the same thing, and presented him with even more baffling choices. By the time he completed the two pages, he was very uncomfortable. He was beginning to feel a little unreal, a bit lightheaded, dreamlike.

"Do you feel like you've been pushed into a different world?" asked Lauren.

"Sort of," said Newby sadly. "What's going on?"

"You see," said Old Man Durfee with a kindly smile, "you really can't trust yourself any longer. You've lost a little of the real you. It's nothing important, but we thought you ought to know."

"It happens sometimes," said Aunt Rozji.

"You have to learn to relax," said Lauren. "Things that are important in a big town like Stroudsburg, just don't seem so vital here."

"This isn't such a big town," said Old Man Durfee.

"No," said Newby, "no, it's not."

"Now," said the drunk, "I suppose I have to take your other knight with the bishop pawn. I do so."

Newby glanced over the quiz sheets again. He wondered if he ought to change a few of the answers. *Who is President of the United States? a) Harry S. Truman; b) Everett Dirksen; c) Dwight David Eisenhower; d) John F. Kennedy.* He had originally checked Truman, but on second thought erased that and marked *c*. "I like Ike," he thought. "I really do." *Have the Russians orbited their first Sputnik yet?* That was *no*. *Have the quiz show scandals been exposed? No*, but interesting. Maybe it was *yes*, come to think about it. He decided to leave that question and come back to it. *What kind of a day was it?* Newby marked *A day like all days, filled with those events which alter and illuminate our time.*

"None of this makes any sense at all," he said.

"What difference does that make?" asked Aunt Rozji. "What has reality ever done for you?"

"Good morning, everybody," said a newcomer.

"Morning, Bob," said Lauren. The waitress turned to Newby. "This is Bob Latcher, the shoe repairman. Bob, this is Mr. Newby, a visitor to our town."

"Morning, Mr. Newby," said Latcher. "Sad to have you here today, of all days. Have you heard the news?"

"About Mr. Newby's car?" asked Old Man Durfee.

"No," said Latcher. "About that Muldower girl." Newby started, then struggled to catch his breath.

"Theresa?" asked Lauren. "What about her?"

"They found her near her house," said Latcher. "She was done in all peculiar. She was all burnt up from the inside. She looked fine on the outside, excepting that she was dead. But when they touched her, her body all collapsed, like a puffed-up popover. Just powdered into ashes."

"That's odd," said Lauren. Newby buried his head in his hands.

"Want breakfast, Bob?" asked the waitress.

"No," said Latcher, "I just came in to see if I could find Larry Muldower. I wanted to tell him how sorry I was. About his daughter and all."

"He's probably in his new fallout shelter," said Newby in a strangled voice.

"Yeah, that's right," said Latcher. "Thanks." The man waved and left.

"Sad about the little girl, isn't it?" asked Old Man Durfee.

"It just goes to show you," said Aunt Rozji. "Some people just shouldn't go walking around late at night." She smiled at Newby.

"'Like a puffed-up popover,'" said Lauren. "What a typically rural use of simile."

"Hick," said Newby, "not rural."

"I think we ought to try to make this chess match a little more interesting," said Aunt Rozji.

"I find it fascinating," said Newby.

"A little more interesting," said Old Man Durfee.

"Will you take a check?" asked Newby.

Aunt Rozji and the drunk laughed. "No," said the old woman, "I don't mean that way. The way I see it, Young Newby has mate in no more than seven moves. Now, don't look so glum, Young Durfee. We can't always emerge victorious. But I wonder if our handsome visitor would be interested in giving you another chance in this game. A sort of handicap."

"I don't think so," said Newby. "I just want to get going."

"If it's your car that you're so worried about," said Lauren, "you might as well take it easy. I suppose the police are going to be occupied all day with old Theresa Popover."

"Don't be cruel, Young Lauren," said Aunt Rozji.

"Are you going to play, or aren't you?" asked the drunk.

"He *has* to," said the old woman. Newby nodded. "Well, then. Here is what I say, in my capacity as omnipotent referee. From now on, every time you take an opponent's piece, your own piece that did the capturing will change to the type of the captured enemy including pawns. So if you take your opponent's queen with a pawn, you'll have two queens."

"That's ridiculous," said Newby. "You just can't change the rules of chess like that."

"*She* can," said Lauren. "You agreed to abide by her decisions."

"She's like the inscrutable forces of nature," said Old Man Durfee, evidently enjoying Newby's uneasiness.

The salesman shook his head, but said nothing more. He looked at the position of the chess pieces. Aunt Rozji was correct; as things stood, he could finish off Old Man Durfee in just a few more moves. But now the situation had been changed. In a legitimate game, the thing for him to do would be queen takes knight pawn, check. Newby chewed his lip. If he were to do that, under Aunt Rozji's arbitrary rule change, he would capture the pawn, but his queen would be demoted to that level. He would lose his most potent weapon. The entire strategy of his game would have to be altered. The thing to do, apparently, was work with the pawns, promoting them by successfully capturing higher-ranking enemy pieces. The more he looked at the board, the more confused he became. "All right," he said at last. "I don't even care any more."

"You ought to," said Lauren. "This is an important game."

"How is it important?" asked Newby.

"It's very symbolic," said Aunt Rozji.

"It's the forces of simple life here in rural America against the snares and wiles of corporate industry," said Old Man Durfee.

Newby stared at them. They smiled back. "Do I look like a shifty-eyed con man?"

"You *are* a salesman," said Aunt Rozji.

"You *are* from Stroudsburg," said Lauren.

"The big time," said Old Man Durfee.

Newby sighed. They were really out to get him. He laughed bitterly, and moved his queen bishop from its original square down to King's Rook Six, capturing the old drunk's pawn there.

"Why did you do that?" asked Lauren. "You lost your bishop, you know. It turned into a pawn, now."

"I know," said Newby. "Sometimes a pawn can be more useful than a piece. I'm going to beat you at your own game."

Aunt Rozji made a cackling sound. "I ought to warn you," she said, "I haven't decided yet whether I'll change the rule about normal pawn promotion. If you move that pawn ahead two squares, you may or may not get the queen you're after."

"I'll chance it," said Newby.

Old Man Durfee picked up the rook which guarded his castled king. "Here," he said. "This rook will stop you." He moved it forward a square, so that Newby's pawn couldn't advance without inviting capture.

Newby didn't hesitate. "I wasn't planning that at all," he said. He swept his queen down and captured the knight pawn. He turned the queen upside-down to indicate that it was now a pawn, standing on the square next to the bishop-turned-pawn of the previous move. Together the two pawns stared straight at the drunk's suddenly vulnerable king.

"The position isn't as bad as it looks," said Old Man Durfee.

"That's good," said Lauren. "It certainly looks bad."

"I've got this bishop tying him up," said the drunk.

Aunt Rozji stood up from her stool. "I think it's time we recessed for lunch."

"Lunch?" asked Newby. "It isn't even ten o'clock yet."

"Lunch," said the old woman. "I think young Durfee could use the opportunity to study the game, and you might find it comforting to report the theft of your car. Perhaps the police have solved the untidy mystery of little Miss Popover's death. I think that I am in need of a nap, in any event. Young Lauren will stay here, guarding the game and making certain that no pieces are inadvertently moved."

"I surely will, Aunt Rozji," said the waitress.

Newby realized that argument was futile. He shrugged and

stood up. "What time should I come back?" he asked.

"Oh," said the old woman lazily, "perhaps three o'clock."

"She does like her naps," said Old Man Durfee.

The day was sunny and warm. Newby felt a shock of heat as he left the diner; rippling waves floated in the air above the black asphalt of Ridge Street. The temperature would get even higher by afternoon. Newby had no idea what to do for the next five hours. He supposed that he ought to walk into the center of town to the police department. After that, he could kill time browsing through the poor collection of stores. Get a haircut. Sit on the square and read magazines. Find the library. Maybe just get on a bus and leave.

The town was much like many others he had seen in the last four years, during which he had been a salesman for the Jennings Fabric Corporation. He knew without looking what sort of things would be in the windows of each shop: the faded cardboard signs of beautiful women with bright yellow poodle cuts in the beauty parlor, the brassy saxophones on stands in the display of the music store, the barbecue sets and the taped-up sign—*Tulip Sundae 35¢*—in the five and dime. It made him feel better, somehow. The odd assortment of people in the diner didn't seem to be typical. The impulse to run away grew; he could easily give up his car as lost, take the insurance money, buy another. The company would give him a week off without pay. His suitcase was in the diner, now, but he could tell them the samples had been in the trunk of the Packard. He might even be reimbursed for his personal things. "No," he thought, "I'm letting that dream spook me. I won't let myself be manipulated like this. I just have to settle down."

He strolled past the store windows, bored, still a little sleepy. He came to the police department, the last building before the square. He went up the granite steps and opened the door. There didn't seem to be anyone inside. He sat on a bench under an old framed photograph of Eisenhower, wearing his army uniform. Newby waited. A clock on one wall moved past 10:30. Then to eleven o'clock. Finally, a police officer appeared from the back of the building. He nodded to Newby.

"I want to report a stolen car," said the salesman.

"In a minute, buddy," said the policeman. "We have a real emergency today."

"The Muldower girl?"

The policeman stared at Newby for a moment. "Yeah," he said slowly. "What do you know about it?"

"Nothing. Just what this guy Latcher told me in the diner."

The other man nodded. "All right, then. Your car's going to have to wait."

Newby stood and stretched. "Do you know how she died?" he asked.

"Yeah," said the policeman. "The coroner said it was some kind of stroke. I ain't never seen nothing like that, though."

"It was magic," said Newby.

"You're nuts," said the other man.

"What time should I come in to check on the car?"

"We'll be tied up all day," said the officer. "Come in tomorrow morning." Newby nodded, but inside he was annoyed. Another night, another day in the town. He'd have to call his wife, have her get in touch with the Jennings people, have her send him some money.

The salesman left the police station and walked into the small parklike square. Narrow gravel paths ran straight as a surveyor's transit could make them, among huge elms and oaks, diagonally from northeast to southwest, from northwest to southeast. At the center, where the paths intersected, there was the promised cannon and a pyramid of cannon balls. The end of the cannon's barrel was stuffed with paper cups and broken glass. There was a drinking fountain next to it, with a step for little children to use. A tiny trickle of water ran from the rusty fixture. No amount of handle turning could make the trickle run harder. The fountain was impossible to drink from. It made Newby very thirsty.

Old Man Durfee walked toward him along a gravel path. The drunk didn't seem to notice Newby. The old man moved in wide, sweeping curves, stumbling, talking to himself. He still carried his filthy blue towel, looped through the binder's twine that served him as a belt. Old Man Durfee passed Newby by the drinking fountain and continued across the square. The salesman watched him; several yards away, the drunk left the path and walked toward a broad, shady tree. Aunt Rozji stepped out from behind it. The two grasped hands and sat down, slowly, painfully. Newby watched them curiously. The two old people chatted. The drunk no longer seemed as inebriated, the old woman no longer as decrepit.

After a few minutes a middle-aged homemaker passed by, pulling a two-wheeled shopping cart filled with bags of groceries. Aunt Rozji raised a hand and waved to the woman. Newby moved closer.

"Hello, Aunt Rozji," said the woman pleasantly.

"Good morning, Mrs. Siebern," said the old woman. "How are you today?"

"Healthy, thank God," said Mrs. Siebern. "The last couple of days I haven't been so well."

"But today you feel fine?" asked Old Man Durfee.

Mrs. Siebern scowled at the drunk. "Yes," she said, her tone more disapproving. She turned back to Aunt Rozji. "How is your sister these days?"

"Fine," said Aunt Rozji. "She doesn't complain, the dear. Onyuish is three years younger than I, you know. But she has such troubles with her back."

"Well," said Mrs. Siebern, "have a good day. I have to get home. Eddie bought one of those power lawn mowers and he stayed home from work just to tinker with it. I want to get back before he cuts off both of his feet." The woman turned her back to the old people sitting on the ground; Aunt Rozji gestured to Newby. The salesman was surprised that the old woman had been aware of his presence. Her motions indicated that she wanted Newby to engage Mrs. Siebern in conversation. He hurried to catch up to the woman.

"Excuse me," he said nervously. "I'm just passing through this town, and it looks like I'll have to stay here the night. I was wondering if you could tell me if there are any good hotels in the area?"

Mrs. Siebern shaded her eyes and looked at him for a few seconds. "Well," she said slowly, "Aunt Rozji has some nice rooms for travelers, but she's particular about her guests. You'd have to speak to her. Here, let me—" She turned around to introduce Newby to Aunt Rozji, but the old woman and the drunk had risen and moved one to each side of Mrs. Siebern. Now they took her arms and led her from the gravel path. Old Man Durfee looked back at Newby and winked. He signalled that the salesman should follow them. Newby did.

"Here," said Aunt Rozji, "let's sit here under this mighty oak, eh?"

"I really have to get back to my Eddie," said Mrs. Siebern.

"Oh, he's old enough to handle a grasscutter, dear," said Old Man Durfee.

"It's television's fault," said Aunt Rozji. "All the husbands on those comedy shows look so stupid. All except Robert Young, and he's just fatuous. Your husband will be all right."

"Take this, Newby," said Old Man Durfee, handing the salesman an ancient, leather-bound book. "Follow along. Read the part that's underlined."

"This oak, all like oaks, oak trees blended in universal commune," chanted Aunt Rozji. "Pillar of sacred wood, leaf-secret bower, shelter us, cloak us, hide us now."

"This oak, our strength," said Old Man Durfee. "This oak, our weapon, this oak, our souls."

"This oak, its roots to the very earth's heart delving," read Newby haltingly. "Now, its limbs, our hands, delve this woman's spirit fire."

Newby glanced up. Mrs. Siebern's face bore an expression of surprise; then her features slackened, twisted again, seemed to contort with utter agony. Like Theresa Muldower, she tried to shriek, tossing her head wildly, kicking and thrashing. Her voice was stopped; from her mouth came only a blue, cold mist. Her eyes turned white, her lids drooped and were sealed shut with ice. Her blood froze where it ran down her chin. Old Man Durfee and Aunt Rozji held the woman tightly as she shook in the last stages of her ice-death. Her skin was tinged blue, her muscles chiseled in hard ridges beneath. The two old people eased the corpse gently to the ground, but even so, Mrs. Siebern's frozen right foot snapped off with a gentle tinking sound. A blue-white powder lay about the stump, dusting the rich green grass with what had been flesh, bone, blood, all living.

"Quick now, Young Newby," said Aunt Rozji. "We must finish."

The salesman looked at the book. He had the next speech, too. "Weakness, weariness, done to an end," he said. "Misery is now no longer, as acorn's shell is by the oaken shaft blasted."

As in the dream of the night before, the drunk grasped one of Newby's arms, and the old woman took the other. They walked away from the corpse quickly, back the way Newby had come. When they arrived at the police station, he stopped. "I have to go in," he said. "I have to report my car."

"You've already done that," said Old Man Durfee. But neither of the old people tried to stop him. Newby ran up the steps and into the station. He woke up on the bench. The clock said it was almost two.

"Another dream," he thought. He was too unnerved, though, to do the proper thing; he didn't have any intention of walking through the square to see whether Mrs. Siebern really rested there, cold, dead, and blue. Instead, Newby headed back toward the diner.

He met Lauren on the way. "Hello," he said. "I thought you were supposed to be guarding the chess pieces."

"Oh," she said, pouting, "I always get stuck with dumb jobs like that. Nobody would want to mess with the game, anyway. I wish one of these days they'd let me help in the bigger jobs."

"Like Theresa Muldower?" he asked. "Like Mrs. Siebern?"

"Mrs. Siebern?" said Lauren. "Well, they finally did it. I'm glad. Her husband teaches chemistry, you know. Gave me a C+ last year. You know, you look a lot like Howard Keel."

"Howard Keel?"

"He's my second-favorite actor."

Newby laughed. "I suppose I ought to be flattered. Who's first on the list?"

"James Dean, of course," she said. "I send him birthday cards and everything."

Newby took a deep breath. "He's dead, you know," he said finally.

Lauren shook her head. "I don't believe it. In New York, even Stroudsburg, you believe those things. Here you don't have to. It doesn't make any difference what happens here, and what happens out there doesn't have any effect on us. I can believe what I want. This isn't such a big town, you know."

"Yes, I know."

"'Don't be cruel,'" she sang.

"We should be getting back soon," said Newby. "It's almost three."

"You're not going to let that old nosebleed wino and Madame Ooglepuss boss you around, are you?" asked Lauren.

Newby waved a hand. "I thought you were on their side."

"That was until I realized how much you look like Howard Keel. 'To a heart that's true.'"

"I always get Howard Keel mixed up with Phil Gatelin," he said.

"They're nothing alike," she said.

"And neither am I."

"I don't know what you're talking about," said Lauren. They pushed open the door to the diner and stepped into the frigid blast of the air conditioning. Newby was stunned to see another Lauren Kromberger still sitting on one of the stools by the counter.

"What's going on?" screamed Newby.

The Lauren at the counter looked up and gasped. She went behind the counter and came back with a broken bottle, which she waved at the first Lauren menacingly. "It's just part of your dream," said the Lauren with the bottle. "Sometimes you have to shake them off like this. They're like nightmare hangovers." The armed Lauren took a few steps toward the Lauren that stood next to Newby. The salesman watched, mystified. The girl he had come into the diner with shrugged and leered at him, then began to fade and waver. In a minute she was completely gone. The waitress put down the broken bottle and sighed. "Did they get somebody else?" she asked.

"Who?"

"I don't know," she said. "You were the one out there. I've just been sitting in here the whole time."

"I mean, did *who* get somebody else."

"Aunt Rozji and Old Man Durfee, of course. Wait a minute." She picked up the bottle and started moving toward Newby. "Maybe you're part of my dream." Newby didn't fade. Lauren smiled and sat down again, patting the stool next to hers. "Come on," she said. "They'll be back any minute."

"They *got* Mrs. Siebern," he said.

"Oh, that's all right, I guess."

"What importance does this chess game have?" he asked.

"None, really," she said. "I mean, it won't go into Chess Review or anything, if that's what you're asking. I doubt if anyone else in town will even find out who won. You won't have any trouble finding other people to play you. You're really very good, you know."

"I don't want other people to play," he said impatiently. "I just want to go home already."

"You'll have to learn how to relax," she said smiling. "You

have a really neurotic thing about getting away."

"I've seen some strange things in the last day," he said.

"How do you know they're real?"

Newby was annoyed. "If they're not, then I must be pretty sick."

The waitress nodded. "That's right. But there's a good chance that what you've seen *is* real. In which case, you're certainly not reacting with the proper horror, the essential dismay."

"My emotions seem to have been blunted," said Newby. "I think it's Aunt Rozji's doing. If she can perform her hideous tricks, she can just as easily hypnotize me into not running into the street screaming. Besides, they're only dreams."

"Old Mr. Latcher didn't think Theresa Popover was a dream," said Lauren. "And wait until they find Mrs. Siebern on the square."

Newby looked at her closely. "I never told you that's where they got her."

Lauren smiled once more. "See? It may all be a dream. But if it's not, then you have to worry. Your emotional reactions have been dulled. You admitted that yourself. Psychiatrists call that 'planed-down affect,' in their peculiar jargon. That, coupled with the difficulty you had on the little quiz this morning, would indicate that you're well into advanced schizophrenia."

"Then I *am* imagining all this?" he asked, not especially concerned.

"No," she said. "You're schizophrenic only if all this is real."

"Never mind," he said. "Can I have a Coke?"

Lauren brought him the soft drink. He sipped it, trying to make sense of her words. What did he know about schizophrenia? Very little, actually. Just some things he'd picked up from watching television. *Medic*. The business about the split personality. He thought his brother-in-law might be like that. But why would Newby's symptoms wait until just now, here, in the tiny village so far from anything, before they became noticeable? If he were going insane, how could he just calmly discuss the matter with the waitress? How did she know so much about what he was feeling?

How much of what had happened *had* been only dreams? Might he still be asleep?

He swallowed some more of the Coke and picked up one of the discarded chess pieces, his demoted bishop. It felt heavy in his hand, in a way that dream objects never do. "This is one sure way to get locked up," he thought. "All I have to do is ask a doctor if I'm just dreaming. They'll never see me in Stroudsburg again."

"Is there a phone I can use?" he asked.

"Over there," she said. "By the juke box."

He went to the phone, fished some change from his pocket, and dialed the operator. He got the number of the Green & Greene Bus Company, and gave them a call.

"Good afternoon, Green and Greene," said the girl who answered. "Can we help you?"

"Yes," said Newby. "I was wondering if you could tell me if there's a bus from Gremmage to Harrisburg?"

"No, I'm afraid not," said the girl. "You'd have to get the bus to Oil City, change there for Pittsburgh, and change again for Harrisburg."

"Fine," said Newby. "When is the next Oil City bus?"

"Oh, I'm sorry," she said, her voice conveying true concern and pity. "You just missed it this morning. There won't be another one for a while. They only run once a week."

"I see," said Newby. "What do people do if they have to go somewhere?"

"They drive, mostly," said the girl. "That's why there aren't more buses. It all works out, don't you see?"

"Yeah," he said. Then he hung up. It had been a long shot, anyway. He went back to the counter.

"Do you think you can beat Old Man Durfee?" asked Lauren.

"No," said Newby. "I don't think I want to."

"That's wise," she said. "There's a lot more to him than most people would suspect."

"Is he, uh, going steady with Aunt Rozji?"

Lauren giggled. "No," she said, "they're just good friends."

"She'd make 'December Bride' look like cradle-robbing."

"They do some of that, too," said Lauren. "Only in the wintertime, though. Propitiating the frost nixies, and all that."

"Hello, hello!" cried Old Man Durfee. Newby turned around to see the drunk holding the door open for Aunt Rozji.

"Hello," said Newby.

"Talking about us, were you?" asked the old woman, as she hobbled across the floor to the counter.

"More or less," said Lauren.

"I don't know anyone else in town to talk about," said Newby.

"Small men talk about people," said Old Man Durfee. "Medium men talk about things. Big men talk about *ideas*."

"Well, we were discussing some ideas, too," said Lauren.

"That's all right, child," said Aunt Rozji. "Don't let that old wetbrain bother you. He doesn't talk about *anything*."

Old Man Durfee took his place on the stool. "Well," he said, "might as well get going with this again. Whose move was it? Mine?"

"Yes," said Newby, "it's yours. Fire away."

"That was last night," said Aunt Rozji. "Today is a day for ice." Newby only nodded.

"'The old hooty owl hooty-hoots to the dove,'" sang Lauren.

"Owls are birds of death to some folk," said Aunt Rozji, smiling. "And doves, well, you know. The soul, in some symbologies. So you have a specter of destruction tempting the immortal soul. It happens all the time."

"'Tammy, Tammy, Tammy's in love,'" sang Lauren.

Old Man Durfee looked up. "Yes, that's the way it always starts," he said.

"Are you ready to move yet?" asked Newby.

"'Hooty-hoot,'" said Lauren. "That's dumb."

"Hey, everybody," called a stranger.

"Hey, Ronnie," said Lauren. "That's Ronnie Glanowsky. He has a Shell station out on Logan Road."

"Hey," said Glanowsky, "have you heard about poor old Mrs. Siebern?"

"Aw, she wasn't so old," said Newby.

Glanowsky studied the salesman's face for a few seconds. "I don't believe we've met," he said.

"My name's Newby," said the salesman. "I'm just passing through."

"You know Mrs. Siebern?" asked Glanowsky.

"No," said Newby cautiously. "I was just being gallant."

Glanowsky shrugged. "Anyway, they found her lying in the square. She's dead. Just keeled right over." At the word "keel," Lauren jabbed Newby's arm; he looked at her, and she made a kissing sound. He blushed and turned away.

"What happened to her?" asked the drunk.

"They figure she had some kind of attack," said Glanowsky.

"Well, goodbye," said Aunt Rozji.

"Goodbye," said Glanowsky. He hurried out.

"Did he come in here just to tell us that?" asked Newby.

"Probably," said Old Man Durfee. "He does that a lot. Anyway, he knows we like to keep informed."

Newby shook his head. "I really thought it was all a dream."

"It was," said Aunt Rozji. "But that's no reason that it can't be real, too."

"Watch this," said Old Man Durfee. He removed Newby's queen pawn on the fourth rank and set down his knight. Then, according to Aunt Rozji's rule, he took the knight off the board and replaced it with a pawn.

"I don't understand," said Lauren.

"Well," said Old Man Durfee jovially, "I certainly won't explain it now."

"Another rule change!" cried Aunt Rozji. "Another rule change! This ought to liven up the match."

"I can hardly wait to hear," said the drunk.

"From now on," said the old man slowly, "whenever you move a rook, the next piece on the rank or file along which the rook traveled will be 'destroyed.' That goes whether the victim piece is friend or foe. So be careful."

"How about kings?" asked Newby.

"Hmm," muttered Aunt Rozji. "You're right. Kings will be immune, but if there's a piece *beyond* the king, it will be taken off the board instead."

"Terrific," said Newby.

"It's your move," said the drunk.

"I move the rook pawn to Rook Seven," said Newby. "Check."

"I take the pawn with my rook," said Old Man Durfee.

"The rook becomes a pawn," said Lauren.

"That's right," said Newby. "What about the rook, though? Does it destroy anything on the line it just moved?"

"No, I don't think so,' said Aunt Rozji. "That power stops at the end of the board. If this were a cylindrical board you were playing on, the ray would go all the way around and catch the other rook pawn."

"All right," said Newby. He was getting more and more annoyed; neither the game itself nor his opponent seemed to have much grounding in rationality. The referee served no purpose at all; other than to try to aid the drunken old man.

The waitress winked at Newby every time he glanced at her. Now the pieces in the game were adopting odd powers. And every minute he felt more trapped.

"Why don't you just try to get away?" asked Lauren.

"I don't know," said Newby. "I honestly admit that I don't know."

"That's a sure sign of something," said Old Man Durfee. "You ought to be running scared by now. Maybe we're having more of an effect on you than you think."

"Maybe he has a crush on Young Lauren," said Aunt Rozji.

"It could be a real Liz-Eddy-Debby case," said the waitress. "You could leave your plain but nice wife to have a mad affair with me. What does your wife do?"

Newby scowled. "She's what we call in Stroudsburg a 'homemaker.'"

"See?" said Lauren.

"No," said Newby.

"All right," said the girl. "I was only kidding, anyway. I don't have any interest in you at all. You don't even look like Howard Keel."

"What was all the flirting for, then?" he asked.

"Part of the scheme," she said. "To make you stay here. We needed someone to—"

"Easy, there, youngster," said Old Man Durfee. "You'd better watch your tongue, or you'll end up looking like a pail full of rising dough."

"I want to know what she means," said Newby.

"I guess it's all right to tell him," said Aunt Rozji. "We needed someone in town to look suspicious for us. We have dark deeds planned."

"More?" asked the salesman.

"What do you mean, 'more'?" asked Old Man Durfee. "We haven't done anything."

"Except the eleven-year-old popover and the middle-aged wifecicle," said Newby.

"We didn't have anything to do with them," said the old woman. "We've been too busy planning our job. We're going to knock over the Shell station. Ronnie Glanowsky's in on it, too. It's his station."

"All the rest has been my imagination?" asked Newby.

"Sure," said the drunk.

"But now we can't use you," said Aunt Rozji. "Now that

your car's been stolen, and you'll be around for a while. You'll be too well-known. We wanted a stranger to pin the rap on. We like you too much for that."

"I'm glad," said Newby. "Can we knock off this game, then?"

"For now, I suppose," said Old Man Durfee. "We can finish it in the morning."

"Yeah," said Newby. "Sure."

Old Man Durfee waved to Newby; Aunt Rozji smiled, and wiggled her fingers to indicate that the salesman should run along. He did so gratefully. The chess game, for all intents and purposes, was over. That marked some kind of turning point in the day's events. It meant that, for good or evil, the old people had taken their fill of him. Was he now expendable, in a way Theresa Muldower and Mrs. Siebern had been? Could he expect to find an unnatural death, now that they had moved on to other projects?

"That's not true, what they said about the gas station," said Lauren. She startled Newby. He had thought that he was walking alone, down Ridge Street toward Aunt Rozji's house.

"I'm glad to hear it," he said. "Two falling-apart people like them are in no condition to heist a gas station."

"They know it, too," said Lauren. "That's why they had Ronnie Glanowsky in on it. But he wanted too big of a cut, for one thing. And, besides, they couldn't get together on where they'd run for their getaway. The old man wanted Jamaica, and Aunt Rozji wanted swinging Acapulco."

"There's a basic difference in attitudes, there," said Newby.

"I suppose." They walked along a little more, neither having much to say. They turned down Aunt Rozji's street. "Why are you going back?" she asked.

"I don't know," said Newby. "I don't have anywhere else to go. I'll call the police in the morning. If they don't have my car, I'll try hitching out of town."

"Oh. Be careful."

"I'm usually careful," he said.

"You came into the diner, didn't you?"

"Yeah. That was a mistake. Look, do you think I'm in any danger from them? Now that my part is over with?"

Lauren grabbed his arm; they stopped beneath a peeling sycamore, and she looked up frightened. "Don't think your part is over," she whispered.

"What?" he said. She had spoken too low for him to understand.

"I said, you're still in it. In fact, your big moment is still coming up." She saw his anxious expression and smiled. "Don't be too worried, though. *You* won't be hurt." She waved and started walking back in the direction they had come.

"That sounded more like the dream Lauren," he thought. "The one the real Lauren chased away with the broken bottle. I like the dream better, I think." He went up the stairs to Aunt Rozji's front door. It wasn't locked, and he went inside.

"Hello," said a man in a dark suit. "You must be Mr. Newby."

"That's right," said the salesman warily.

"Well," said the man, "my name is Greg Rembrick. I'm a Young Christians' Outdoor Health leader here in town. Me and the YCOH teens were hoping that you'd play an active part in our monthly group session this afternoon. Aunt Rozji told me that she thought you'd be happy to oblige, but I can understand that this comes at awfully short notice. So if you'd like to back out, we can just get on with the meeting."

"You're holding a meeting here, now?" asked Newby.

"Yes," said Rembrick, smiling. "Aunt Rozji has been so kind to us, ever since our community social center teen canteen burnt to the ground last year. A strange fire it was, too."

"The others?"

"Oh, they're all out now, gathering different sorts of local leaves for our scrapbook. They'll be back in, uh," he glanced at his watch, "about ten minutes."

"What sort of thing will I have to do?" asked Newby.

Rembrick indicated that they should sit. The salesman took a place on one of the old woman's sofas, facing the youth leader. "Nothing difficult," said Rembrick. "We just need to have an outside adult read a short speech during our devotional fellowship non-denominational brotherhood council prayer-circle union of love."

"I see," said Newby. "I guess that would be all right."

"Fine," said Rembrick, smiling and nodding eagerly. "Fine. Thank you very much. The teens will be so happy." The two men chatted briefly, and after a couple of minutes, the younger members of the group began joining them. Not long afterward, Mr. Rembrick announced that everyone was present. He had them all stand in a circle with himself in the center. They joined hands and sang a hymn, then closed their eyes and bowed their heads, while he recited a short invocation.

"Just read those words now, if you please, Mr. Newby," said Rembrick.

"Those words?" asked the salesman. Newby saw the words written in the air in terrifying green flames. He heard no reply from the other man. Newby stood and walked slowly toward the fiery letters. He stopped a few feet from them, and began reading slowly. "As earth the father water holds," he said in a low voice, "so air may fire in its cool embrace retain. Here the yearning mind of man entails the pinnacle of knowledge, the pit of wisdom's horror." With a sudden flicker, the words changed. Newby glanced at Rembrick and the youth group; they had all fallen to their knees, their faces contorted in strange ecstasy. He continued. "Let the vast wheeling of the universe transform their knotted bowels. Let the great sky drama of blazing suns blast their hearts, shrivel lungs and steal breath, poach brains in boiling blood. Let heaven's yawning emptiness draw up their sensibilities, let the pendant mass of all the spheres and orbs crush their bones to sacrificial powder." Newby read the last of the flickering words, and they disappeared. Rembrick and his young charges were quite still upon the carpet of the parlor, their faces stretched in the extremities of suffering. As he walked, they screamed soundlessly. A blackness escaped their mouths and cloaked their heads, a dark fog in which Newby thought he could see the stark, unwinking stars of night. The blackness quickly vanished, and the salesman knew they were all grotesquely dead.

Chimes rang. There was someone at Aunt Rozji's door. Newby panicked for a moment, then fought for control. He knew that the authorities had not been able to find any element of criminal activity in the deaths of the Muldower girl or Mrs. Siebern. What could anyone say about the corpses of Aunt Rozji's floor? It could only be some kind of poisoning. Perhaps it was something they had eaten together. Newby took a deep breath, then went to answer the door.

"Hi," said Lauren. "Are you done yet?"

Newby nodded. "Just finished up a few seconds before you rang. Now what?"

"What do you mean?" she said, walking past him into the parlor.

"Well, what do we do with the bodies?"

"*We.*"

"What do *I* do with the bodies?"

Lauren shook her head sadly. "Don't you learn *anything?* What happened to Miss Popover? What did they do with Mrs. Siebern? They just left them there. We'll just leave these here for the police to find."

"I don't know what I'd do without you," said Newby scornfully.

"Look, fella," she said angrily, "I'm really glad this thing is wrapping up to a close. It hasn't been so much fun, you know. You're not the neatest guy around. I did it because I have to. I can think of better ways of spending a lifetime."

"Like what?"

"Like bombing around," she said. "Trying on gloves at Sears. Anything."

"You don't have any junior murderers' league or something?"

"The sarc remark," she said. "The emblem of the stunted intellect."

"I'm doing my best," said Newby.

"How do you feel that you've changed?" asked Lauren. "You are no longer able to state with any assurance what the correct date is. You are frequently unable to recall where you are, geographically speaking. Your emotions are not appropriate to the situation. You are rapidly exhibiting signs of sociopathic behavior. Have you detected any further deviation in your outlook since this afternoon?"

"I don't know," he said.

"Well, I think you may soon discover that you are no longer able to discern right from wrong. How do you feel about what you just did to Mr. Rembrick and the kids?"

"Nothing," said Newby. "I don't feel anything at all."

"Do you think you would have felt nothing, say, a week ago?"

"I can't say," he muttered. He stared at the misshapen bodies. He still did't feel anything.

"With Miss Popover, you were merely a witness. With Mrs. Siebern, you helped out. Here, you were on your own. Aunt Rozji and Old Man Durfee have managed to destroy the very last shred of your old self, without your even guessing what was happening. You don't know when you are, where you are, now you don't even know what or who you are. You've become a complete non-being, a blank, ready to be stamped with the first identity that is chosen for you."

"That's ridiculous," said Newby.

Lauren smiled; the expression frightened the salesman. "Do you know what?" she asked. "If Old Man Durfee gave you his quiz again, right now, you wouldn't even know how to hold the pencil."

"Sure, I would."

"You show typical ambivalent notions, common in even mild cases of schizophrenia. Sometimes you want to run away, but you never do. Sometimes you defend those two old monsters, but you know you hate them."

"What about you?" asked Newby.

"Do you mean, how do I feel about them?" she said. "Or how do you feel about me?"

"I don't know."

"Of course, you don't. You're not supposed to. That's the whole point. You've been worn down."

Newby collapsed on a sofa. He rubbed his eyes. He felt nothing. He was not afraid. He was not disgusted. He was not at all anxious to leave. He knew that it would be a tremendous effort to plan anything. "What happens now?" he asked.

"More of the same, I'm afraid," said Old Man Durfee. Newby looked up; the drunk and the old woman had come in.

"Why do you always seem to appear while I'm sitting with my eyes closed?" he asked.

"Why do you always seem to have your eyes closed when we arrive?" asked Aunt Rozji, busily examining the bodies on her floor. "Young Lauren, would you be so kind as to call the police?" Newby laughed.

"Are you amused, Newby?" asked Old Man Durfee.

"No," said the salesman. "It just seems like you're going to try to use me as a scapegoat now."

"That's an idea," said Aunt Rozji, raising an eyebrow.

"'Hooty-hoot,'" said Lauren. "'The old owl of doom hooty-hoots to the dove.'" She dialed the phone and spoke to the police officer who answered.

"Ask them about my car," said Newby.

"I have some interesting statistics," said Old Man Durfee. "I took the trouble of digging these up this afternoon. It seems that for every hundred thousand person in the United States, there are some two hundred ninety people with schizophrenia of one form or another. Of course, 'schizophrenia' takes in a large number of different disorders. But of those nearly three hundred suffering souls, only half are being treated. That leaves another hundred fifty maniacs per hundred thousand running around loose."

"Should I turn myself in?" asked Newby skeptically.

"You already have," said Aunt Rozji. "We'll take care of you."

"You already have," said Newby to himself.

"If you went into a hospital," said Lauren, hanging up the telephone, "you'd probably be locked up for quite a while."

"Thirteen years is the average," said the drunk.

"Thirteen years," said Aunt Rozji gently. "Just think of it."

"Some murderers get out in less time," said Newby.

"We don't like to talk about that," said the old man.

Aunt Rozji sat down next to Newby, and took his hands in hers. Her old skin was rough, with sharp, hard points of callus that stabbed Newby's fingers. He felt a general anxiety, without specific cause. He wanted to stay and find a secure home, or go and discover his lost identity, or something; he wasn't sure. It was the uncertainty, rather than the unusual events and the piling up of dead persons that upset him. "You may well be the victim of simple schizophrenia," said the old woman. "It has taken these somewhat bizarre happenings to point it out to you. You thought you were well-adjusted and normal. It must be quite a blow to your stability to find out that you're not."

"What happened to your accent?" he asked. "What happened to Old Man Durfee's drunken wino ways?"

"Most simple schizophrenics never realize they're ill," said Aunt Rozji. "They seem to be merely a bit antisocial. They become vagrants, like Young Durfee, although his case is quite a bit different. Perhaps your brain will turn even stranger, leading to hebephrenia, characterized by inappropriate foolishness and giggling, or, at other times, unexplained weeping. What about hallucinations? Have you been troubled by them?"

"So far, they've been rather nice," said Newby. "I haven't actually been convinced that I've *had* hallucinations, you see. I'm more or less taking the word of Lauren for that."

"She ought to know," said Old Man Durfee. "She's been a hallucination often enough herself."

"Thank God you're not paranoid," said the old woman. "You're not catatonic, either. You've a lot to be thankful for."

"I am," said Newby.

The chimes rang again. Lauren answered the door; it was the police. They came in and stood around the corpses on the carpet. Newby was surprised by their reaction. Many of the police officers gasped in horror, or ran back outside, sickened. The salesman had thought that a policeman would see many such sights in the course of his career. He was amazed that they would be so affected.

"Who found these individuals?" asked a sergeant.

"He did," said Old Man Durfee, pointing to Newby.

The sergeant nodded. "I suppose they couldn't go undiscovered for very long," he said. "This isn't such a big town."

"No, it isn't," said Old Man Durfee.

"There doesn't seem to be any indication of foul play," said the sergeant. "I won't have to question you, in that case. But the final word will have to come from the coroner."

"In just a few seconds," said a small, gray man who was busily prodding the dead bodies. "Ah. Their bones are shattered from within, as though they fell from an enormous height. But there are no outward signs at all. A most curious case."

"There have been a number of them of late," said the sergeant with a rueful smile.

"I judge that they all died from some manner of apoplexy," said the coroner.

"All?" asked Aunt Rozji. "At the same time? What a strange coincidence."

"There have been quite a few of those, too," said Old Man Durfee.

"Well," said the sergeant, "I want to thank you people for your help. We'll have somebody come by in the morning to collect these jokers. I'll just ask that you not move any of the individuals here in the meantime. We'll want to get plaster molds and things like that. Clues. You understand."

"Certainly," said Old Man Durfee. The sergeant waved and followed the coroner to the door. After the police had gone, Lauren turned to Aunt Rozji.

"Why do they need clues, if they all died of apoplexy?" she asked.

"To help find a cure for apoplexy, I guess," said Aunt Rozji. "The police department has become much more scientifically minded since I was a girl."

"Now we can relax," said the old drunk.

There was an immediate hush in the dim house. In the sudden silence, Newby wondered what he had been listening to in the minutes previously: clocks in the parlor ticking, electric hum of kitchen appliances, wood creaking in the humid heat, restless tapping of fingers and shoes, noise from the street, neighbors mowing lawns, airplanes, all these sounds died together. It was perfectly still, a waiting moment, an interval, a preparation.

"Ah," said Aunt Rozji, "you will be happy to learn that everything that concerns you is now in its absolute final stage."

"That cheers me up considerably," said Newby.

"I took the liberty of ending our little contest," said Old Man Durfee. "With Aunt Rozji's help, of course." The drunk smiled roguishly at her, and the old woman laughed.

"May I enquire as to the results?" asked Newby.

"I won," said Old Man Durfee. "The enmity between us is ended. Aunt Rozji took over your moves and, with the aid of a few more spontaneous alterations of the rules, I was able to checkmate your harried king in splendid style."

"Well," said Newby, somewhat bored, "let me congratulate you. How was this marvelous stratagem wrought?"

"First of all," said Aunt Rozji, "I added a condition that no piece could be moved unless the nearest pawn of the same color could make a congruent move at the same time, legally. So each player would then be moving two pieces per turn, his desired piece, plus the nearest pawn."

"As you can imagine," said Old Man Durfee, "this cuts down somewhat on the number of available moves each player has to choose from. As it developed, I was better able to visualize the situation."

"Better than Aunt Rozji, at least," said Newby.

"Well, we all agreed to bow to her judgments. Then, finally, I was given the weapon to break your position. Aunt Rozji declared that the queen was to be given a new power. She called it the 'H-bomb capability.'"

Lauren laughed. "For an immigrant, she certainly has a way with words," she said.

Old Man Durfee gave the girl a disapproving look. "In any event," he said, "at any one time during the game, the queen could be placed on *any* vacant square on the board. All pieces, friend and foe alike, on the eight adjacent squares are considered 'destroyed,' and removed from the game, except the kings.

You can see what terrible havoc this piece and wreak on any well-defended position. And, you may recall, you no longer had your queen. Well, given this instrument, it was no great trouble to bring your tattered army to its knees."

"It doesn't sound like you have much to be proud of," said Newby. "It didn't end up to be much like chess."

"The rules are always arbitrary," said Aunt Rozji. "It's just that you're used to them being arbitrary the same way each time."

"I'm sorry," said Newby.

"That's all right," said Old Man Durfee.

"Well," said Aunt Rozji, standing and stretching her thin, spotted arms, "let's get going, Young Newby. Your epiphany awaits."

"What?" said Newby. "I thought it was all over. You said yourself that I was pretty much depersonalized. How can a diluted being like me have an epiphany?"

"You'll see," said Lauren, tugging at Newby's hand. "Come on." The four people walked to the door and out onto the porch. It was getting cooler outside, although the humidity was still uncomfortable. A fresh breeze brushed through the dense leaves around Aunt Rozji's house.

"Where are we going?" asked Newby. "Back to the diner?"

"You'll see," said Lauren.

"The diner's played its part," said Old Man Durfee. "It doesn't make any real difference *where* we go now. Just start walking."

Aunt Rozji took the salesman's arm. With a shock, Newby waited for Old Man Durfee to take the other; that was how it began, both for Theresa Popover and Mrs. Siebern. Greg Rembrick and the YCOH teens had all joined hands before Newby had killed them. He was relieved to see that the old drunk had fallen back to speak softly with Lauren. He turned his attention to the doddering woman at his side.

"I wonder if you've noticed this interesting fact," she said. "After each of the introductory interludes, you seemed to awaken as from a nap. The episodes seemed to you like dreams. To a large extent they were. To that same extent, you are now."

"This is a dream?" asked Newby, not sure what she meant.

"Well, partly so," she said. "Can you think of any difference between the affair of the Young Christians' Outdoor Health group and the earlier encounters?"

"Well," said Newby slowly, "I was on my own with the last one. I didn't see you or Old Man Durfee until the whole thing was over. In fact, I saw Lauren before you came in."

"That's true. And you ought to be congratulated. You handled the matter with precision, taste, and dispatch. But now you're such a formless person. It is indeed a great waste. You have little effect on the world, you know."

Newby laughed sadly. "When have I ever had any effect?"

"That's just it," said Aunt Rozji. "We're trying to change that for you."

"I appreciate it."

"Now, think again," she said. "What other differences can you find?"

"I give up," said Newby.

"Well, you've never roused from the Young Christians' Outdoor Health dream. Everything's continued in an unbroken line since then."

"Yes," cried Newby, "that's true! I knew there was something wrong."

Aunt Rozji stopped on the sidewalk and stroked the salesman's arm. "Because we love you, Young Newby," she said, "and because Young Durfee conquered you at chess, we're going to help you. It is in our power to leave you as you are, a breathing cipher. We have done it before. But we have taken a special interest in you. We will push you that final step."

It was very dark. Newby couldn't decide whether night had swiftly fallen, or if the blackness were some artificial trick of his dream. A round yellow moon hung in the sky, huge, far too big, as if it were resting on the horizon instead of staring down from the summit of the sky. Newby glanced at the moon and felt an unpleasant chill. The cold yellow light seeped through his eyes into his veins. He had to look away.

He heard the ragged scraws of the evening's birds, as they fought over insects. He heard the cicadas shrilling at him. There was no way that he could interpret their warning. He walked on. Aunt Rozji and Old Man Durfee were silent. Lauren was humming "Volare." Newby walked past the sealed houses, each flashing tiny lights from the crystal faces mounted in windows and doors. The houses presented no threat tonight, though. Newby could sense that they were merely curious observers. The solitary figures that glided within them were almost as powerless as he. They watched, but they could be of no help,

either. The great buildings seemed to roll past, one by one.
Newby was aware that he was walking down a steep, shaded
hill. The street was no longer paved with red brick, but instead
was covered with a black material imbedded with diamond
points of light. The minute beams from the blacktop tried to
communicate, but he would not understand.

He looked back at the houses, his only and impotent allies.
They were gone. They had become massive abstract shapes,
black solids blocking sharp-edged swaths of the night sky. He
walked past towering cubes and rectangular pyramids. The
moon's light colored them unpleasant shades of dark yellow-
green. The trees were gone, too. The insects and birds were
gone. All sound was gone. Lauren and the old people were
gone.

Newby moved through a flat landscape; the ground was
hard beneath his feet, level, without rock or curb or root. The
vast shapes dwindled in number as he passed, until at last he
could see only one, far ahead of him on the moonlit plain. He
hurried toward it. It was the only clue to where he was, how
he might get out, who he might be. He ran, and he seemed to
run for hours, but the black bulk in the distance did not come
closer. After a time, the moon settled below the horizon, leaving Newby to the pale light of the stars. The monstrous shape
became a black patch on the black shade of night. He ran, and
he was amazed that he did not grow tired.

When at last he reached the gigantic green-black thing, he
saw that it was not a smooth facade, as the other shapes had
been. Bits of starlight caught in grooves and pits on the object's
face. Although the block rose hundreds of feet above his head,
all the peculiar hollows were within each reach. Newby stretched
his hand out and felt one of the markings; his fingers traced a
letter A. He explored further; all of the carvings proved to be
letters. He could not read the entire inscription at once. He had
to search out its meaning, letter by letter, word by word. He
raised himself up and deciphered the first word. "This," he
said aloud. The next word. "World," he said. He was able to
read them more quickly. "This world," he said, "this island of
stone. This trimmed and dressed block of marbled mud. This
hanging ball in space, this single monument to me. I am alone.
I, this block of stone. I, this captive world. I read these words.
I become these words. I become this mighty pedestal of stone,
whose function is to give form to these words. I become this

reckless celestial sphere, whose function alone is to support this might pedestal of stone. I am here, alone, and my function is to read these words." Newby paused, his voice becoming hoarse. He looked back at the letters he had already traced. Their indentations into the rock had filled with a spectal lumination. He could easily read them, now; the words yet ahead, though, were still hidden in the darkness.

He continued. "If any doubt my existence, let him doubt himself. If any question my purpose, let him question himself." Newby felt suddenly afraid. His throat felt dry, his blood rushed, roaring, in his ears. He could not stop. "As the words, the rock, the world career through the empty night, let him who reads these words shake within himself, like a long-dead leaf rattles withered in the winter storm." Newby felt his mind coming loose, his personality falling from its anchored place in the intangible secret place of his soul. There were no more words. Newby stepped back and stared at the steady radiation that outlined the letters. He took a few more paces away from the immense stone thing; he turned and saw himself still standing by the rock face, his hands plunged to the wrists in the cold white flames.

"Hey!" cried Newby. He wanted to run. He wanted to escape, back across the plain, through the jumbled mountains of stone, until they became houses again; he wanted to run toward the single mighty tower and his silent image. He did neither. He stood and watched, as the other Newby fell to his knees and began to pray. The other Newby worshiped the terrible pillar of stone, and the glowing letters carved in its side. The other Newby shrieked incoherent words; he waved his arms slowly above his head, then folded his hands in a submissive attitude of adoration. "Don't put your hands together!" shouted Newby, horrified. It was too late. The other Newby jerked violently, as though he were pulled about by invisible wires. The man's skin seemed to shatter and flake away. Newby stared as his doubt began to crumble, bits of formerly vibrant flesh falling to the ground and degenerating to powder. A gust of wind puffed the dust, all that remained of the other Newby, away in a misty cloud of gray.

"Good God, what's going on?" said Newby, his eyes filling with tears.

"You've molted yourself," said the voice of Aunt Rozji.

"You've left your dream self, like an insect abandons its dead, husky skin."

Newby turned to find her. The empty plain was gone. The towers of stone were gone. He was back in Aunt Rozji's parlor. "I don't understand," he said.

"That's a very good sign," said Old Man Durfee. "If you *did* understand, we'd have more of a job to do. You're one of us, now, in a way. You're a real Gremmager. You're ready to find a job here, find a place to live, a new wife, perhaps. You're ready to help us whenever another stranger comes to visit."

"We'll let you know if we ever need you," said Aunt Rozji.

"You're not schizo, anymore," said Lauren, walking over to hug him. "You're just, well, *plain*. You don't have to worry about anything ever again."

"Good," he said.

"It's not everyone that can kill his own dream self," said Old Man Durfee. "Some of us don't even have one."

"Don't be pompous, Young Durfee," said the old woman. She turned again to Newby. "You're completely assimilated now. You're very lucky. This town is very selective about whom it chooses."

"It can afford to be," said Old Man Durfee.

"Because it's not such a big town," said Lauren.

"Hooty-hoot," said Newby. "Hooty-hoot."